dark future

JADE DRAGON

THE WORLD, TOMORROW. Laced with paranoia, dominated by the entertainment industry and ruled by the corporations. A future where the ordinary man is an enslaved underclass and politics is just a branch of showbiz. This is the Dark Future.

Black Flame continues its awesome series, which explores a twisted vision of the future. Now the action turns to the Far East after Frankie Lam inherits his deceased brother's job in the Hong Kong office of a shadowy multi-national corporation. Spirit-ancestors, organised crime, religious cults and disposable pop stars all feature in James Swallow's latest addition to this acclaimed series.

More action from the Dark Future

THE DEMON DOWNLOAD CYCLE

DEMON DOWNLOAD
ROUTE 666
Jack Yeovil

THE EDDIE KALISH SERIES

GOLGOTHA RUN
Dave Stone

THE AMERICAN MEAT SERIES

AMERICAN MEAT
Stuart Moore

dark future

JADE DRAGON

james swallow

BLACK FLAME

For the punks, the edgerunners and the xiong can sha shou.
You know who you are.

A Black Flame Publication
www.blackflame.com

First published in Great Britain in 2006 by BL Publishing, Games Workshop Ltd., Willow Road, Nottingham NG7 2WS, UK.

Distributed in the US by Simon & Schuster, 1230 Avenue of the Americas, New York, NY 10020, USA.

10 9 8 7 6 5 4 3 2 1

Cover illustration by Jaime Jones.

Copyright © Games Workshop Limited, 2006. All rights reserved.

Black Flame, the Black Flame logo, BL Publishing, the BL Publishing logo, Dark Future, the Dark Future logo and all associated marks, names, characters, illustrations and images from the Dark Future universe are either ®, TM and/or © Games Workshop Ltd 1988–2006, variably registered in the UK and other countries around the world. All rights reserved.

ISBN 13: 978 1 84416 378 6
ISBN 10: 1 84416 378 4

A CIP record for this book is available from the British Library.

Printed in the UK by Bookmarque, Surrey, UK.

No part of this publication may be reproduced, stored in a retrieval system, or transmitted in any form or by any means, electronic, mechanical, photocopying, recording or otherwise, without the prior permission of the publishers.

Publisher's note: This is a work of fiction, detailing an alternative and decidedly imaginary future. All the characters, actions and events portrayed in this book are not real, and are not based on real events or actions.

AMERICA, TOMORROW

My fellow Americans —

I am speaking to you today from the Oval Office, to bring you hope and cheer in these troubling times. The succession of catastrophes that have assailed our once-great nation continue to threaten us, but we are resolute.

The negative fertility zone that is the desolation of the mid-west divides east from west, but life is returning. The plucky pioneers of the new Church of Joseph are reclaiming Salt Lake City from the poisonous deserts just as their forefathers once did, and our prayers are with them. And New Orleans may be under eight feet of water, but they don't call it New Venice for nothing.

Here at the heart of government, we continue to work closely with the MegaCorps who made this country the economic miracle it is today, to bring prosperity and opportunity to all who will join us. All those unfortunate or unwilling citizens who exercise their democratic right to live how they will, no matter how far away from the comfort and security of the corporate cities, may once more rest easy in their shacks knowing that the new swathes of Sanctioned Operatives work tirelessly to protect them from the biker gangs and NoGo hoodlums.

The succession of apparently inexplicable or occult manifestations and events we have recently witnessed have unnerved many of us, it is true. Even our own Government scientists are unable to account for much of what is happening. Our church leaders tell us they are holding at bay the unknown entities which have infested the datanets in the guise of viruses.

A concerned citizen asked me the other day whether I thought we were entering the Last Times, when Our Lord God will return to us and visit His Rapture upon us, or whether we were just being tested as He once tested his own son. My friends, I cannot answer that. But I am resolute that with God's help, we shall work, as ever, to create a glorious future in this most beautiful land.

Thank you, and God Bless America.

President Estevez

Brought to you in conjunction with the GenTech Corporation.

Serving America right.

[Script for proposed Presidential address, July 3rd 2021. Never transmitted.]

Ladies and Gentlemen, at this time Virgin SubOrbital would like to announce that our flight is entering the descent phase toward the Hong Kong Free Economic Enterprise Quadrant and our arrival at Chek Lap Kok SkyHarbour is on schedule for seven forty-five pee-em, local time. Your cabin staff wish to remind you that there is still time to make any purchases of perfume, smoking materials, caffeinated products, cyberware or pharmaceuticals from our in-flight duty free catalogue; simply press the blue dot on the datascreen installed in your seat arm. Passengers are free to move about the cabin and take drinks at the upper deck bar or use one of our recreation pods in the discreet cabin. However, we would ask all clients to note that once the seat belt sign has been illuminated, all passengers must return to and remain in their seats as the aircraft makes its final approach to Chek Lap Kok. For your comfort and safety, neural induction coils mounted in the headrest of your seats will automatically engage to help minimize any discomfort due to pressure changes in the cabin. In the event of an emergency landing, these coils will also lull you into a dreamless, peaceful sleep while the cabin is flooded with ShokFoam™. Should you have any questions about today's flight, please feel free to discuss them with one of our polylingual flight attendants. We know you have a choice when selecting the carrier for your company's international transit needs, and we thank you for choosing Virgin SubOrbital today.

1. once upon a time in china

FRANKIE WORKED HIS jaw and frowned, shifting slightly in the depths of the padded acceleration couch. The conformal cushion gave a sensual sigh and moved to accommodate him, but he fidgeted again. The book he'd loaded into his palmtop remained unread, his attention unable to hold past page six of *What Gangcults Can Teach Us About Management*. Stuffing the computer into his carry-on bag, his eyes returned to wandering over and around the smooth lines of the airliner cabin. On some level he felt like he was failing to project the right image. The other men and women in their seats, each an arm's length away from the other and surrounded by an expensive halo of legroom, all seemed so at ease in here as to be profoundly bored with it all. Moving so she wouldn't know where he was looking, Frankie observed the lady in pinstripes with the Eidolon cheek-tatt. She was still having the same conversation she'd started as they came out of boost phase from LA-Double-X, in poppy little spits of subvocalisation that weren't real words, talking to a dermal mike in her larynx. A privacy masking field made it impossible for him to figure out what she was so animated about, but by the way she kept miming a gun – forefinger extended, thumb a falling hammer – it was clear somebody back in NorCalifornia was getting reamed. Next to her was a large man who looked like a sumotori, forced into a black Ozwald Boateng suit that might have made an elegant pup tent in another life. The big fellow was engrossed in the screen he gripped with fat sausage fingers; the sound was on direct beam, but Frankie could see the tanned face of ZeeBeeCee's Tammy Popeldouris engaged in serious conversation with Juno Qwan, while the idol singer's new vid played picture-in-picture.

A gentle swell of turbulence rocked the liner, reminding him where they were. He sniffed the air; the same canned, conditioned taste that the atmosphere in the office had, that the airport lounge had too. The cabin was seamless in muted reds and pale cream, matching almost perfectly to the décor of the executive embarkation area at LAXX, and no doubt to the egress lounge at SkyHarbour and any one of a hundred other airports around the world. Usually that sort of thing made Frankie feel safe, the idea that the corps were helping to maintain a homogenous profile across the world, so that anyone could find a Buckstars or a MacDee no matter if you were in Manchester or Mumbai... But all of a sudden it seemed too plastic to him, just a veneer over a dangerous, unfamiliar place. He looked away, forcing down the little flutter of butterfly nerves rolling around in his gut. He was supposed to be a professional; this sort of giddy rush was the kind of thing a single-term window gazer would experience, not an echelon executive like him.

I should be making the most of this, he thought. It wasn't every day he got to fly transcontinental; what with the shifts in the fuel markets and the rise of franchise terrorism post Y2K, aviation had moved back to the rarefied state it was in at the dawn of commercial flight – when only the military and the very rich could afford it.

Frankie let out a controlled breath and, for what must have been the hundredth time during the flight, he unfolded the photo.

There they were, the two of them with big, goofy grins on their faces on the upper deck of the Star Ferry, the lights of the city a rainbow blur behind them. He tried to remember who had taken the picture – one of the other grads, maybe that thin girl from Foshan who got posted to orbit? They both looked so happy there, fuelled by too many bottles of Tsingtao and the elation at making the cut at the corporate academy. That was before the company had parted them, sent him to the other side of the world while his brother got to stay home and rise like a rocket through the ranks of the head office. Frankie felt the bite of resentment and instantly flattened it. No. Alan deserves his success. *Deserved* it. He was always the more diligent of them, and Frankie knew it. While Frankie had toiled to make any kind of advancement at the Los Angeles division, Alan Lam had caught the eye of the upper tiers and skipped entire grades on his way to the top floors.

Not that any of those things mattered now, a morose inner voice reminded him. When the summons from Yuk Lung Heavy Industry's headquarters had pinged into life on the LA branch office d-screen, there was a moment when Frankie's supervisor had automatically assumed it was for him. Burt Tiplady, all one metre sixty of his arrogant, noisy self, had swaggered over to take the comm, oozing smarm. Burt had been waiting for four years to get cherry-picked by Hong Kong. The look on his face when he realised the message was for Frankie, not him, was worth every day that Lam had weathered his bellicose presence; but try as he might, Frankie couldn't rekindle that feeling right now. The cold hollow that formed as Burt passed him the screen to read had overwritten that one moment of elation.

Alan was dead; the company expressed its deepest sympathies, and requested the presence of his brother in the Hong Kong office on the next available stratojet.

That was two days ago. Time had passed in a whirl. The forms authorising his transfer were attached with the comm, and he'd gone back to his dormplex in Santa Monica to find his gear already stowed for transit. YLHI wanted him to come home, and so he did, propelled on a cushion of numbness and faint guilt. Frankie had not spoken to Alan in a year, and even then it had only been a cursory hello-goodbye, something to do with that GenTech problem in Texas. Once, they had been inseparable.

Now, the company that had parted them was all that connected them.

Frankie sighed and it came with a shudder. He felt isolated, impossibly disconnected from the young guy in the picture, his hand around his brother's shoulder, laughing and carefree.

"Going home?"

Frankie looked up with a start and blinked. The flight attendant had materialized from out of thin air, a tray of data needles in the crook of one arm. She had ice blue eyes that matched the sliver-grey glolights in her blonde hair. The smile on her lips was utterly perfect. "I'm s-sorry?" he managed.

"Are you going home? To Hong Kong?" She indicated the picture with a gentle incline of her head. "Meeting family?"

"Yes." His throat went tight. "Can I, um, have a drink, please?"

"Of course. Glen Fujiyama on the rocks, wasn't it?" She produced the tumbler of whiskey from a trolley at her side.

Frankie took a deep sip, feeling stupid for asking for it like a child begging for sweets. He was in the rare air of the high corporates now, and no one who travelled here had to ask for anything. They were entitled to it.

As if she saw it in his mind, the attendant asked, "Is this the first time you've flown with us?" She smiled again. "Congratulations on your promotion."

"Yes," he repeated. "Thank you."

She indicated the tray of software, the varicoloured pins like a spread of fly-fishing lures. "Can I interest you in an entertainment programme? Something from the cinema of the Ukraine, perhaps?"

Frankie shook his head.

"We have sensual recreation automata on board, if you'd prefer. They support a wide range of romantic configurations."

Another sip. "I'm fine." This time he said it with the right tone of dismissal and the attendant melted away with a final, perfectly sculpted smile. He nursed the drink as a low rumble worked its way through the liner's airframe. Through the half-open window blind, he could see distant hazy blobs that represented the coastal city sprawls of Vietnam. With every passing second the stratojet brought Frankie closer to the point of no return, the moment looming up in front of him where finally, irrevocably, he would have to face the hard reality that his brother was gone. But as much as he tried to convince himself that the churn of emotions in his gut was some ridiculous hope that this all might be some huge mistake, he knew in his marrow that Alan had perished. There was nothing arcane about it, no ephemeral spiritual bond between siblings. He just knew it; it seemed right somehow, correct in the order of things.

No, the sick dread that gathered at the corners of his thoughts had a different source. His transfer had come directly from the office of the chief executive officer of Yuk Lung Heavy Industry, from the man who ruled the corporation like a feudal warlord. Mr Tze. If he had a first name, no one spoke it. In an age when the corporate hierarchy was the new royalty of the Twenties, the master of YLHI was a reclusive, shady figure. He never left Hong Kong, rarely even ventured from the towering citadel headquarters of the company, and only then to the fortress compound he maintained along the Pearl River. The man wore his command of the corporation like a suit of ancient armour and he was as ruthless as the Mongols that some said he descended from. The mere idea of being in this man's physical presence threatened to overwhelm Frankie if he dwelled on it too long. See, there were *stories* about Mr Tze. The kind that only ever appeared on viral samizdata netcasts in the instants before Datapol shut them down. To even admit to having watched such seditious material would warrant instant termination of contract for Frankie. He drained the last of the drink and lost himself in the motion of the ice cubes in the tumbler, moving over one another as the aircraft's nose dipped toward China.

Distantly, Frankie Lam heard a soft chime and the ends of his seatbelt snaked across his waist, their steel heads meeting with a decisive click, locking him in place.

"THERE WAS THIS time," began Lau Feng, fingering the unkempt stubble on his chin, "I think we were near Guilin, when this girl came up to us on the path."

"Mmm." Ko gave one of those nothing replies, just a noise at the front of his lips to indicate that he was hearing Feng without actually listening to him. The youth squatted in the lee of the concrete stanchion and threw a quick left-right glance about the underground car park. He knew the security drone sweep patterns better than the guys on the monitor desk.

"She had the nicest eyes. Green. Or something." Feng's hand drummed on the breastplate of his armour, and wandered like a bored spider down past his belly and across the threadbare strips of boiled leather that made up his battle skirt. "Anyway, she wanted to come with us. She'd stolen her father's sword. Very emotional about it all."

Ko peered closely at the sensor plate on the car locking mechanism. It was a retrofit, reasonable quality European manufacture, probably a Moulinex or a Krupp. He reached for the bright pink disposable cellphone that he'd picked from the pocket of a small boy in the departure terminal and levered off the back with his balisong knife. "You've told me this story before," complained Ko, although not with any real strength behind it.

"So the captain, he laughs at her, because she was just a girl. And she took his head off with the blade. Just like that." Feng mimed the motion across his neck. "Like that," he repeated. His stray hand settled on the hilt of the lionhead sword at his hip. "I admired her for it, you know? But in the end we had to hurt her to get the weapon away."

Ko actually bothered to give him a look. "Will you shut up? Can't you see that I'm trying to concentrate?" To punctuate his statement, Ko tugged on the front of his jacket and pulled the kevleather tight. He had the guts of the cellphone in one hand, the microtransmitter inside it making distressed squawking sounds as it fired off spasms of misfired signals. Lights blinked on the lock once or twice, which meant Ko was close to getting the door to open.

Feng sniffed and cocked his head. "Soldiers are coming. You won't get that done in time."

"Liar." Ko glanced at the cellphone. It was overloading, getting hot in his hand. Trying to crack a microwave lock like this was always a roll of the dice; sometimes the phones would blanket the locks with enough conflicting signals that they'd run home to mama, snap back to their default settings and pop open; other times it would fry them solid. Ko was sanguine, though. It wasn't as if the G-Mek Vista GL he was crouched by was his, after all.

"Bet you a smoke," said Feng.

"Stop distracting–" Ko's retort was cut short as something came alive inside the sports car. The vehicle's lights snapped on all at once, full beam and glaring. From a speaker in the grille a synthetic voice barked at him. "Attention! This vehicle is undergoing a theft! Alert! Alert! Contact authorities immediately!"

Ko swore under his breath; suddenly Feng was nowhere to be seen and sure enough, there were two men in APRC fatigues jogging across the car park toward him.

"Phase two alert!" shouted the Vista GL. "Lethal deterrent charging! This is your legal warning!"

The youth turned and ran as the electro-zappers on the bodywork whined up to full capacity. He'd picked this part of the car park because it was close to the maintenance access wells. Ko forced his way through the gap between two chained gates and sprinted up three flights of concrete stairs. He forced himself to a slow, casual walk as he emerged into the evening, around the blunt concrete architecture of the airport's vast parking field. Faintly, he heard the deep buzz-crackle of the stunner going off below.

Feng sat cross-legged on a wall. "I warned you."

"Shut up, dead man."

The swordsman hopped down and trailed after him. Ko paused to throw the ruined cellphone in a waste drum, and Feng pointed at the vending machine next to it. "You owe me a smoke."

"Fine." Ko slammed his debit card into the machine's slot and the vendor disgorged a packet of Peacefuls cigarettes. Feng licked his lips as the youth removed the plastic wrapper and carefully set the packet on fire with a disposable lighter. The box combusted quickly and Ko let it drop to the ground. Feng stooped to follow it, watching it crumble into a mound of grey ash.

The machine had a mirrorscreen facia, and despite the gang tag scrawls across its surface, Ko could still get a good look at himself. The screen showed him on a tropical beach, cartoon cans in white and blue dancing about him with wild abandon. "Enjoy the Great Taste of Lan Ri!" said the screen. "The Flavour is Now!" Ko used the screen to check himself over; his face was a little flushed with effort, but his spikey black hair-do was still intact and the hachimaki band across his forehead hadn't slipped. He flicked minuscule dots of dust from his jacket and straightened it a little.

"You preen too much. Like a dandy." Feng had a cigarette in his hand now and he took a drag on it in the way a starving man would eat a meal.

Ko gave the pile of ashes a desultory kick; an identical and intact packet of Peacefuls went into the drawstring pouch hanging on Feng's belt. "Those things will kill you."

The joke was old, but it still raised a smirk from both of them. "The only vice I can have," said the soldier. "If you can find me another one..."

Ko nodded at the gathering of cars and bikes in the middle of the open concrete plaza. "Come on. Perhaps my luck will change."

PASSPORT CONTROL CONSISTED of a walk through a deep penetration scanner tunnel and an impressively large security automaton modelled on Kuan Ti, the God of War. The machine licked the thick black ident card in his hand with a thread-thin green laser, and took a moment to examine his HIV Negative warrant before intoning a welcome in elaborate Mandarin. Frankie walked through the lounge without stopping; the urge to get free of the identical spaces inside the plane and the airports propelled him into the arrivals area. He slowed, crossing the marble floors, looking up to take in the arching steel framework of the terminal's roof.

"Hello, Francis." The voice was soft and melodic.

"Uh. Hello." A thin Japanese woman extended a hand to him and he took it. She had warm skin, dry and soft. At her shoulders were two very different figures. The first, a younger man, pinched and a little bored-looking. This one took his bags without comment and resumed walking. The other was tall, broad about the chest and he moved in the way that only trained men did. Frankie knew the type instantly; corporate security. All three of them wore suits of a similar cut, the discreet YLHI pennant there on their lapel like his, but Frankie had to wrench his gaze away from the security agent with an almost physical effort. The tall man's face was concealed beneath a porcelain opera mask of the Monkey King, a swirl of black, yellow and white.

"My name is Alice," said the woman, "Mr Tze sends his apologies that he could not attend to greet you in person. I'm sure you understand."

Frankie nodded. She was very pale, he noticed, her skin the colour of milk.

"I would also like to extend to you my personal sympathies on the matter of Alan's passing." She gave a little sigh. "I was honoured to work with him."

A confusion of questions forced their way to the front of Frankie's mind as he understood in that moment how little he knew about Alan's life, but they defied any attempt to articulate them. In the end he managed a clumsy "Thank you."

"Transport has been arranged," said Alice. "This way."

SOME QUIRK OF legalese meant the car park outside Chek Lap Kok SkyHarbour was still classed as a public area, and so as long as they did nothing too reckless, there was little the greenjackets of the APRC could do with the go-ganger crews and wayward teens but move them on or throw in the occasional rousting when they got too rowdy. Ko privately believed that the soldiers from the mainland liked the corporates as little as he and his street racer friends did, and that they let the gangers hang out here just because it pissed off the suits. As long as they kept the level of fatalities down to an acceptable level, they would be allowed to loiter.

Ko drew closer to the gathering and his heart sank. On his face the emotion showed up as a tight curl at the corner of his mouth. There was the metallic green Kondobishi Kaze he hated, with its ostentatious gold rims and that dumbass hemi blower poking through the bonnet like a little beehive.

"Makes a change for you to see it from the front, eh Chen? Bet you forgot what it looks like, you see the tailgate so much!"

A ripple of brusque laughter followed the insult out toward him.

He returned Second Lei a level, icy stare – the same kind that Hazzard Wu gave the Master of Glocks at the climax of *Gunfighter Orphanage*'s final reel. "I let you win, Second, because you cry like a girl when you lose." Ko held his hand waist-high. "Like a *little* girl."

Lei's crude sneer froze on his face, the humour fading like vapour. "Watch your mouth, punk. You're asphalt to me, understand? I wouldn't even race you for pinks."

Ko resisted the urge to say what he really thought – that Second was a braggart and a fool, who only kept his green monster on the road because he funded it with cash skimmed from back-alley drug pushing that even the triads wouldn't touch. Instead he just looked away. Sometimes it was easier to let the fool have his way than start a fresh fight every time they crossed paths. Give the baby the teat.

But Lei had other ideas. "You know who this is?" He put the question to the assembled gangers, who quieted, sensing violence brewing. "This is Chen Wah Ko, spooky Chen, no-hope loser with his imaginary friend!" Second advanced toward him. "Where's your pal, Ko? Is he here?" Lei cast around, made a show of looking high and low. He pantomimed a shiver. "Whoo-hoo-hoo! Ko sees dead people!"

"Tell him I said he has a face like a baboon's ass-crack." Feng was there on the hood of the green car. He stubbed out one Peaceful on the windscreen and lit another.

Second looked right through the swordsman. "No? Not here? What a shame." He stepped up and prodded Ko in the chest. "You've been a freak since we were kids, Chen. I only keep you around for laughs." Second snapped his fingers and the nondescript dolly with him handed over a pop-pack of clear capsules. He took a couple and tossed them into his open mouth like candy drops. Ko's antipathy showed; drug-takers disgusted him.

"Zen, zen..." sang the girl. "I'm the quiet mind inside, pretty voice..."

"I see your grandmother..." Ko began, and Second wheeled around to face him, his eyes alight with sudden fury. "Your grandmother is very disappointed in you. She says you're too fat and you lay with unclean women."

Second's fist was cocked and in that second Ko thought the other man would knock him to the ground – he was bigger and it would have hurt a lot – but at the last moment he spat and pushed Ko away. "You're so smart, Chen, how about you walk home tonight, huh?" Lei snapped out an order and no one argued. "Nobody gives Ko a lift, understand? He don't deserve to roll with us!"

"I got a car." The lie came from nowhere.

"Oh?" Second faced him again. "Your sister has that crackerbox Ranger of yours, I saw it down in Central! Where are these new wheels, then?"

A glimmer of movement caught Ko's eye. A formation of three gunmetal Mercedes Vectors were pulling into the corporate waiting area near the airport terminal. "There it is," he replied. "I'll just go get it."

Second mumbled something under his breath about "idiot" but Ko was already walking away.

Feng jogged after him. "What are you going to do, boy?"

"A daring and stupid thing."

FRANKIE WATCHED ALICE'S man jog away with his carry-on in his hand, toward the stand of silver cars waiting on the slip road outside the terminal. She gave him a small, controlled smile. "If you prefer to drive yourself in the city, I can have my department arrange something suitable for you. For the moment, though, I would recommend you opt for a pool car and driver. Hong Kong has changed a lot since you left."

"It, uh, always does." He glanced at the masked man again.

"Mr Tze takes the security of his personnel most seriously," said the woman, answering the question before he spoke it.

Frankie frowned. The night air was cloying and strange somehow.

"Is something amiss?" asked the woman.

"It's nothing," he replied after a moment. "Just... I was born here. But now... Now I'm home and it feels... *Foreign*."

"THE THING ABOUT the Euros is," began Ko, "they got what you call an 'engineer mindset'."

The man came up from the back seat with a start, dropping Frankie's bag and slamming the door. Where the hell had this punk come from? "This is a restricted area—"

Ko was still speaking. "See, they look at fine ride like this and can't think past the test track and the wheel lab. They forget that cars drive on the Street." He pointed at the dashboard. "And the Street's got a manner of finding its way around things."

"You can't be here," said the driver, shooting a quick glance to where his passengers were waiting. "I'm calling security—"

"You know about the design fault, though, huh? Otherwise you wouldn't be driving one of them, right?" Ko pointed again. "One in every six... That's a pretty serious risk, neh?"

"What risk—" The driver turned his head to look where Ko was directing his attention and in the next second the armoured glass window was rising up to slam him in the face, the ganger's hand on the back of his head. He reeled with the unexpected impact and Ko propelled the man away on to the pavement, deftly removing the ignition tag wristlet from him as he fell. The dazed suit dropped to his knees and emitted a moan.

"Sucker." Ko slid into the driver's seat and felt it go firm around his waist. From the corner of his eye there was the firefly glow of a cigarette tip and there was Feng, ill at ease on the passenger's side. He didn't like cars very much.

The soldier gave him a look, using the cigarette to indicate the sprawled man outside. "That one, he's going to get whipped because you stole this carriage."

Ko ignored the phantom smell of tobacco smoke and shifted the car into drive; the fool had left the motor running. "What, I should shed tears for him? He shouldn't have become a corp, shouldn't have signed his life away to some rich old breadhead." Reaching under the dash, he found the cut-off remote and tore it out. With relish, Ko slammed the gears and spun the Merc from the kerb, launching out into the night past the shouting faces of the men in the waiting area. He sounded the horn – *Ba! Ba! Ba!* – as he blazed past Second and the rest, grinning.

Feng shook his head. "When are you going to learn, boy? Everyone serves a warlord, even those who think they don't."

The Merc threw Ko right and left against the restraints as he slalomed past the security gate and on to the airport highway. "Not me," he insisted, "not ever."

On the back seat, Frankie Lam's carry-on bag rolled over and spilt its contents.

The Osprey 990. Man, that's a cherry cyke, y'know? Fast like a bat outta hell, got those pannier-mounted rear smokers and a cyclops gun in the nose…. Badda-bing, can come on you like death hisself if you ain't, whatchacall, alert.

On the highway I seen one duel wit' a couple NRG-500s and clean up the blacktop like they was pushbikes. That's why the cops in the Denver Death Zone use them for race-and-chase. Fine choice. Fine, fine choice.

The point? Oh yeah. Well, last thing I reckoned I'd see was one of them fine machines flyin' through the air like it ain't no thing, straight through the window and blazin' alight. Came through the glass — crash — and straight across the floor. What? A warehouse. That was where we were. A warehouse. Can I tell it my way, or d'you wanna read it off the cop's books? No? All right then.

So. Gabby, she takes the Osprey in the face and she dead right there. Landed on her, burnt her up. All hell's breaking loose, Walt's scramblin' for his pistols and that little Poindexter, whatever he call himself Doctor Bloom, he's screamin' and shoutin' at me like it's my gorram fault. And the pigs. The pigs is making this noise like all get out.

But that's not the thing of it. In through the bust glass comes some tear gas shells, but that's nothing on a big ship for me, 'cos I sprung for nasal filter implants last year, after I got a capsicum load from the Coast Guard bulls offa Kennebunkport. I got me a Mossbach Tactical Autoloader. Y'know, the kind wit' the snail drum mag? Yeah? I'm packing double-ought gauge shells in there, 'cos we're fixing not to mix it up with no one but maybe local five-oh. Shit, we were, whatchacall, wrong about that.

Roscoe and Dooley, they're fast lads and they got them carbines. I don't see what they're shooting at, but like this (snaps fingers) Roscoe has a hole in hisself's chest like the size o' my fist and he falls all the way down from the gantry up high and lands — crunch — in the pigs. I reckoned them stories 'bout pigs eatin' man meat was hooey but no, they start in on him. Still squealing. Guess it was no surprise, though, considering. Roscoe was always gettin' into arguments with Doc Bloom when he kept hurtin' the little porkers for shits and grins. The Doc, he got mighty angry 'bout it. See, he got them pig's brains wired up like into one big 'puter, making them all think alike, or somethin'. He was usin' them to play the ponies, screw wit' the lottery, whatever. Turned the little bacon-balls into a big pink, whatchacall, processor. Illegal as all get-out, so I reckon, but no one gives a rat's ass about pigs, so who's gonna stop him?

Well, shit, we found out who.

There's this pop and the roof grows a new skylight, just like that. Down comes this dark fella – yeah, that's him – and he sends Dooley straight to hell. Bam-bam-bam, never laid a shot on this guy. He had this sword, see. Blade so sharp you could cut the virtue from an angel. Dooley's carbine, he slices that sucker in two, takes the boy's hands off into the bargain. Walt... Well, by now he's got his irons... What? Oh, they were some nickel-plated sissy guns. Anyhoo. Walt shoots at him, the dark fella, he does a gorram back flip and nails Walt with a crossbow. A crossbow! Like what they used in olden times, for Kylie's sake!

Well sir, by this here time I'm filling the air wit' lead and can I hit this boy? Can I hell! He's on me like white on rice, breaks this arm and shoots me in the leg. Takes the Mossbach just as polite as you like, puts me on the dirt. Now, I'm thinkin' that this is the end for ol' Billy, but your man just reaches in a pocket and gives me a card. Like offa poker deck, 'cept it's got a pitcher on it. A pitcher of a dancin' loon and the guy smiles at me, he says: "The Fool. This is your lucky day, William." And he lets me live.

Off he goes. He caps Bloom... He seemed real angry about the way the Doc was treatin' the pigs. Leaves me for the marshals with this here card. Lookit. Y'see? It's what them there boys call tarrow. Tarrow cards or somethin'. One o' the marshals tole me that these things got, whatchacall, mojo on 'em, black magic. Well, shit. I unloaded a hunnerd rounds at that boy and never nicked him one time. If that ain't black magic, then I dunno what is.

William "Big" Buettner, arrest suspect #6575FG, Fresno State Militia Service. Subject brought to book by Sanctioned Operative Joshua Fixx (independent), serial number 1800979.

For more information on any of the weapons systems mentioned during this transcript, Touch Here for Hyperlinx. This RealTime Interrogation is a WKIL-TV program, sponsored by Turner, Harvest and Ramirez.

2. Full throttle

THE VECTOR HELD to the road like it was in love with it. This being a weeknight and the hour somewhat late, the Northern Lantau Expressway was sparse with traffic. Ko pressed the accelerator hard to the floor and let the gunmetal sedan eat up the asphalt. Angry hoots from the drivers he slipstreamed fell away in strangled chugs of Doppler-shifted noise, the Mercedes sliding effortlessly around the other road users as if they were static islands in a shimmering river of mercury. The speed limit signs blurred past him. Each used a laser ranger to bounce off oncoming vehicles and flash up their kilometres-per-hour on the big holograph displays that floated over the highway. If you kept to the limit or below it, it beamed out a cartoon smiley face. If you overshot, you were given a grimacing scowl. Ko's speed was so high that the signs were throwing up skulls and crossbones.

"This is unnatural," said Feng, jamming a cigarette in his mouth. The guardsman held himself tight, arms braced about the cuirass on his chest. Ko threw him a look and Feng stabbed a finger at the road. "Don't turn away! You'll crash this thing into someone and kill them, and I don't want any company!"

"Yeah, if I die, who'd you haunt then?" The driver chuckled.

"You don't need to be here," said Ko. "Do your thing, go away and come back later."

"I can't always do it. Not just like that, not on demand."

"Oh." Ko grinned. "Pity. For you, I mean."

The next holosign he passed had a string of text on it: "Authorities Informed. Speed Reduction Measures Initiated."

"Uh-oh."

"What?" demanded Feng.

"Tanglers."

FIVE KILOMETRES FURTHER up the expressway, a crack opened in the surface of the road, the polymerised blacktop peeling back like a lipless mouth. Two prongs, blinking with warning strobes, extended upward and grew spines of impact-resistant piezoplastic. At their tips were pressure-jet web guns, needle-fine nozzles that could fling a polymer spray into the air. Like spider's thread, the polymer hardened on contact with the air, turning thick and gluey. It was water soluble, and it lasted for less than five minutes before it dissolved, but that was typically more than enough time to coat the wheels of a speeder and force them to slow. Ko had caught a grille full of the stuff once, back when a race against some Wanchai show-off had sent him down the wrong road. It was like driving through treacle.

The trick to beating the tanglers was to drive in a way the designers thought only an idiot would.

KO SHIFTED AROUND the neon-lit bulk of bleating robohauler and aimed the bonnet of the Vector directly at the closest pylon. He saw the thin streams of fluid hissing into the night air, crossing away and to the right, converging on the place where the traffic control computer estimated he was *supposed* to be.

"The pole with the lanterns..." Feng said. "You're going to hit it!"

"Yes." Ko ran the sedan right into the plastic upright and heard it clatter and scrape against the underside of the Mercedes as it folded beneath it. The car listed sharply as some of the tangler fluid spat over the rear tyres, but he was ready for it and there was hardly enough to cause him trouble. In the rear-view, he spotted the hauler going headlong into a puddle of the stuff and the vehicle skidded hard. The robot truck's simplistic road-brain lacked the finesse to manage such a sudden change in highway conditions and the hauler spun out, throwing up a fountain of sparks as it scraped the barrier on the median strip.

The Vector made some complaining noises and shuddered. A clatter of noise from the back seat drew Ko's attention. "What the hell is that? A bag?"

"The speed traps were ineffective." The masked man spoke for the first time, never once turning his head from the driver's seat. His voice was neutral in a way that seemed too precise to be fully human.

Frankie watched the distance markers blinking past the window as the remaining cars in the YLHI convoy followed the expressway back toward the city. He felt an odd sense of amusement at the thief's boldness, taking one of the Vectors from right under the nose of his escorts. He let his gaze wander to Alice. Her annoyance was palpable there in the back of the sedan, coming off her chilly expression in ice-cold waves. The car felt cramped, the air inside uncomfortable.

Alice paused only to listen to the report from the man in the Monkey King mask and then returned to the conversation she was having in hissy Japanese with her vu-phone. A hand-held cellular model, the compact wedge of electronics was standard-issue equipment to every Yuk Lung executive above grade three. She gave Frankie a contrite but irritated look. "I am so very sorry you had to witness that, Francis. You are barely home for ten minutes and you are forced to watch a crime unfold in front of you. Rest assured, the thief will be caught and punished." She turned back to the phone and barked out something angry.

"Damn kids," said Ping, the guy who'd taken his bag at arrivals. Coiled in the front passenger seat, he sported the beginnings of a nasty bruise on his cheek. "Oughta ban the lot of them from the 'port. Only go there to race up and down the highway." He started to say something else, but Alice gave him a sharp glare; it was Ping's fault the car had been taken, and so he had forfeited the right to speak because of his laxity.

"Highway patrol enforcers are inbound," reported the Monkey King. "He'll be at the bridge before they get here."

Frankie wondered where the agent was getting this data from. There had to be an audio-video link inside the mask, or else some cyberware implant looping a feed from the police band. He heard the masked man make a tutting sound under his breath as he guided the Mercedes around a stalled robohauler and through the thick slurry of spent tangler foam. The other car in the group was quite a way behind them.

Alice looked up and met the driver's eyes in the rear-view. Frankie saw something unspoken pass between them.

"He's going to go for the WarPark off-ramp. I can catch him. With your permission?"

She nodded, and with a grunt of power from the engine, the driver threw the Vector into top gear.

Alice punched in a different number. "Traffic control, this is YLHI mobile 41312, enacting clause six of the Corporate Self-Defence Act. Advise all enforcement agents that this is a duly noted and legal exercise of our company rights." She hung up without waiting for a reply and snapped the cellphone closed.

A thought formed in Frankie's mind. "My bag... Where's my carry-on bag from the plane?"

Ping looked at the floor. "In, uh, in the car." He pointed in the general direction of the road.

"Don't worry," said Alice. "The moment the vehicle was stolen, the contents of your personal computer were flashloaded to our central server and then the machine was wiped. Your company phone was also automatically severed from our internal network."

"That's not what I was thinking." He extended his hand to her. "May I?"

The woman gave him a dubious look, but passed him the vu-phone all the same. Without really being sure of what motivated him, Frankie hesitated with his finger over the keypad, trying to remember his own number.

* * *

With one hand on the wheel, Ko rooted through the contents of the carry-on bag on his lap. In-flight toiletries kit. A dead d-screen. Half a bottle of Copperhead mineral water. Some entertainment softs still in the wrapper. And...

"Eyes on the road!" said Feng.

The Vector drifted hard, missing a slow-moving drop-top by less than an inch. "I can do two things at once," Ko held up the last object in front of him. A corporate cellular telephone. "Crap." These things were worth a lot to the right people, and Ko knew half a dozen hackers who would part with a lot of yuan for an intact celly with all the hardwired comms protocols inside; but there was also the fact that these phones were wired with satellite locator chips that could light him up like a homing beacon. Ko tossed the bag into the back seat again and slammed the phone on the dashboard three times in rapid succession, splintering the case. A glimpse of wires and circuits peered out at him from a break in the plastic. "Ah, why risk it?" Ko reached forward to open the window. "Best to toss it, just in case—"

It rang with the gentle chirp of a nightingale.

"HELLO?" THE VOICE on the other end of the line was young and wary. "Who the hell is this?"

Alice was watching Frankie very carefully. "Stealing cars is not a good way to win friends and influence people, kid." He kept his voice level. "You should stop this before you get hurt."

The reaction he got was exactly the one that he would have given in the same place. "Screw you, wageslave! Go polish your shoes or something."

"What are you trying to accomplish?" whispered Alice.

Frankie waved her into silence. "That was pretty slick what you did back there. With the tanglers. That took balls. You gotta be good behind the wheel to pull off something like that."

"Don't flatter me, pal."

He kept speaking, ignoring the interruption. "Or of course, it could just be that you're lucky. Are you the lucky type? All balls no brains, gonna wrap yourself around a lamp-post one day?" The words bubbled up from inside Frankie, spooling out of some place locked in his past. It was strange to hear Alan's words coming out of his mouth, but there it was. Suddenly he was inside that stupid kid's head, thinking what he was thinking, going where he was going.

"Eat my dust, suit. This ride is too fine for cashwhores like you."

Frankie nodded. "Heh. Yeah, Mercedes Vector. Smooth, isn't it? Like driving on silk."

THERE WAS SOMETHING in the man's voice that made Ko stop with his thumb hovering over the disconnect key. It wasn't anything he could quantify... Just that ghost of a wish denied, the deep need, the thrill that came from the drive. Ko could hear the faraway longing in the corp's voice, the mirror of it in his own. A memory of something his sister had once said floated to the surface. *Octane in your blood. You need wheels like other people need air.*

"I did what you did," the man was saying. "What are you, eighteen? Nineteen? Blazing around Castle Peak Road and the turns over Tai Mo Shan in some hyped up two-door, I bet. One step ahead of the greenjackets. Making yuan off races and taking pinks where you can."

"You don't know me." Ko looked around and saw that Feng was gone. The denial sounded feeble in his ears.

"Yes I do. I used to be you. What, you think stealing cars and road racing was invented by you and your buddies?"

Ko saw the honey-coloured glow of the WarPark emerge as he passed Discovery Bay; they were doing one of the regular *Apocalypse Then!* promotions to bring in the punters, and the air over the theme park's dome was lit with tracer fire and controlled napalm bursts. All at once, Ko understood what this creep was up to. "Weak, chummer, real weak. You think you can play me, distract me so you can get up close?" He made a spitting sound. "Let me tell you who I am, mister corporate man, mister I-used-to-be-you. I'm not some highway punk you can step on. I got connections, see, I'm *known*."

The voice came back, quick and sarcastic. "Who you with? The 14K or the Wo Shing Wo? Pinching cars for them so they can ship them off to the mainland? I bet you get a lot of yuan for that."

The WarPark exit was coming up fast, and Ko eyed it. If he went in there, it would be easy to ditch the Vector, slip away, maybe fence the d-screen and the phone for some pocket change. But this presumptuous suit was starting to piss him off. If he could get the Merc back across the bridge, he could get it to the docks in Tsing Yi and sell it. Yeah. Plenty of yuan for that.

"Hey, corp, listen." He leaned in to whisper into the cellphone. "Maybe you're not lying to me. Maybe you used to be a fast-mover back in the day. But that was then. You sold out, chummer, pissed away your freedom for a nice suit and an office cube. Now all you're fit for is sucking my fumes!" Ko slammed the phone hard against the dash and stamped on the accelerator again. He cut across the lanes and surged into the feed towards the city.

Frankie looked at the phone. "He... Cut me off."

"I see the vehicle," said the Monkey King. "He's going for the bridge."

"Deal with him." Alice took back the phone and frowned. "This has gone on for too long already."

Acceleration pushed Frankie back into the seat and the passive restraint around his belly went taut, the memory plastic reacting to the velocity change. He tried to peer over the shoulder of the driver, but the masked man filled the seat, and he could only manage glimpses of the road ahead and the ghostly digits of the head-up display painted on the inside of the windscreen. The towers of the Tsing Ma Bridge were growing before them, blinking with cherry red strobes at their tips.

Monkey King touched a panel on the dash, revealing an array of flip-switches for the Vector's weapons systems. "I would like permission to employ lethal force."

Alice gave Frankie the smallest of looks and shook her head. "No. Secure the vehicle and criminal intact, please."

He didn't bother to say what all of them knew; that the security agent was probably good enough to take out the kid with only minimal damage to the other Merc. Alice was trying to present a non-threatening face. Frankie suspected that if he had not been in the car, the answer would have been very different.

The driver tapped a control and from the front bumper came a clack-hiss of oiled components. Along the Vector's prow, the polycarbonate impact buffer parted to allow a series of hydraulic ram plates to emerge. Each had a saw tooth look to them, patterned with square spikes like the face of a tenderising hammer. Volters whined up to capacity, contact triggers released and ready for an impact.

"There," said the Monkey King with a slight incline of his head. Frankie caught sight of the rear of a silver sedan as it passed around a shuttlebus and crossed the first archway of the bridge.

He became aware of Alice watching him. "Was that true?" she asked, with a very faint hint of distaste. "The things you said to the thief, that you were once in a gangcult?"

"It wasn't a gangcult," he said automatically. "Not like the Americans have. Just stupid kids and fast cars."

"And yet you made something of yourself." The words were so bland and neutral, Frankie could not be sure if she were complimenting or insulting him.

KO SAW THE second Vector coming when the backwash from the bridge spotlights caught the gunmetal shape in their glow, a silver shark on dark asphalt. Then he was rumbling over the causeway and on to the bridge proper. The two kilometre stretch of flyover arced from Ma Wan to Tsing Yi island over the Lamma Channel, and below Ko could make out the boxy shapes of cargo submersibles, nosing through the sluggish water toward the floodlit freight terminal. All he had to do was get down there, and he'd be golden.

Feng was standing on the lip of the bridge and pointing into the sky. Ko sped past him, almost too quick to register the guardsman there with one hand pressing a smoke to his lips and the other stabbing at the northwest. Ko looked where he pointed and saw flickers of light moving toward the bridge, the glint of reflection from the spinning rotors. Police helo-drones, fast little ducted-rotor aircraft bristling with gun pods.

The other Vector was coming up fast. Ko swerved to avoid another slow mover and boldly cut across the path of the pursuing car. The corp driver gunned his engine and followed him across the lanes, never once losing a moment of concentration. The second Merc surged forward and slammed into the rear of Ko's car. He heard the rear bumper crack under the impact, the deep hum of electric discharge.

Ko had the weapon pallet open already. He didn't really like dropped munitions – they always seemed a little unsporting to him – but this wasn't a situation he could be friendly about. Ignoring the fans of lasers sweeping down the bridge toward him from the drones, he tap-tapped the drop switch and let a cluster of poppers tumble from the rear compartment as he pulled away. The size of tennis balls, the small spheres bounced once-twice-three times to arm and then detonated in loud, bright explosions. More a disorienting, less a destructive weapon, poppers were designed to baffle a tailgater rather than kill them.

The second Vector skidded a little as one of the front tyres deflated; but in the next moment the wheel was refilling itself and the Mercedes made up the distance again. Ko swore under his breath. The driver of the other car was now visible in the wing mirror. Was that guy wearing an opera mask?

The Vector rammed him again and broke off the rest of the bumper and number plate, grinding them to shards beneath the Merc's wheels. Ko flicked a glance up at the drones. The robot flyers were deploying taser catapults, ready to fire electro-harpoons into the car's hood to shock the computer-controlled engine to death. One hit would turn the Vector into an expensive roller skate and Ko would coast to a halt, sealed inside a steel coffin until the APRC came to arrest him.

"I don't think so." Ko thumbed another switch and ignited the one-use smokescreen canister in the boot. Instantly, a thick cloud of inky blue haze coughed from the back of the Vector, fogging the highway.

THE MONKEY KING made the little tutting noise again as the smoke enveloped the car, and he tapped a control on the steering wheel. A glimmer of light washed over the windscreen and suddenly the highway ahead was rendered in computer-generated gridform, data feeding from the hood's radar sensors to the head-up display. He turned the Vector into the fugitive car and rammed him a third time, pressing the arcing electric probes into the exposed innards of the vehicle. The thief swerved again and slammed on the brakes, dropping away past the driver's side.

In the back seat Frankie saw a blur of silver vanish behind them; then they emerged from the smoke cloud and into a glitter of red targeting lasers.

THE POLICE DRONES lost the stolen vehicle just for a moment in the swath of blue mist, the metallic particulates in the discharge baffling their sensors. But traffic control had given them a target sillhoutte to look for, and, when the shape of a sliver Mercedes Vector flying YLHI colours presented itself, both the robots fired without hesitation. The first harpoon went wide, clattering uselessly against the crash barrier; the second struck the bonnet and locked, a combination of molecular glue and magnetic coils holding it fast. The dense capacitor in the harpoon's head released a massive bolt of power into the engine and killed it instantly. The Vector turned into an uncontrolled skid that rammed it into a bridge stanchion. The car described a seven hundred and twenty degree spin before coming to a shuddering halt in the nearside lane.

The drones started to bark pre-recorded phrases, ordering the people inside to remain where they were and not attempt to leave their vehicle. Neither unit spent any time scanning the other silver Mercedes Vector that raced away past the stalled vehicle, the horn sounding three times in a rude salute.

In the back seat of the dead car, Frankie Lam watched the other Vector vanish toward the city and fought down the urge to laugh.

RIKIO HAD AN Ushanti sub-machinegun in his hand as Ko stepped out of the sedan. "What the hell is this?" he demanded, waving the weapon around, taking in the whole of the dockside warehouse around them with an exasperated gesture.

"Reckon you might like it." Ko showed teeth, keeping his tone fast and light. He knew better than to underplay it when dealing with triads, even low-level Red Poles like Rikio. "Mostly intact, bit of bumper damage..."

"I'll say," said the gunman, craning his neck to look at the wounded rear end. "Why'd you bring this trash here?"

"Trash?" Ko spat. "How many of these you get to see, Rik? It's hot off the highway, man. Hell, even if you chop-shop it, this sweet ride will make you your bonus for the month–"

"Hot is right," said the other man, letting his free hand wander through his five-toned punch-perm. "Get this outta here. I don't know you. I ain't seen you."

All at once, Ko's studied cool disintegrated in a jolt of anger. "The fuck? What did you say to me?" He grabbed a handful of Rikio's green silk shirt and snarled at him, oblivious to the machinegun. "You just cut me off 'cos you're too chickenshit to take this?" In a flash, the adrenaline rush and the latent anger he'd been nursing all day came together in a single outburst. "We came up together, man! Now you act like you don't know me?"

"Back off." Rikio pushed him away with the muzzle of the Ushanti. "You're not 14K, Ko. You could be, but you're not. You're a loner. That means I don't have to do you any favours–"

"What's going on here?" The voice halted both of them. Ko's anger froze solid. The man approaching them was a small, wizened figure. In his youth, the elderly fellow had probably been a big guy, heavy but dangerous with it. What he had lost to age, he'd replaced with presence. Rikio's manner was instantly obeisant.

"Sifu Hung. Sorry, sorry, sir. Just a small disagreement. Nothing important."

Big Hung. Ko's blood ran cold. This old man was the senior boss of the entire 14K triad, half of Hong Kong's criminal enterprises firmly in the pocket of this dumpy doughball ex-contender. The youth marvelled at the idea of it; the stories he had heard about Big Hung's ruthless nature, of the fear he instilled in other men – and now to look at him, the mobster looked like nothing more than a fat old geezer in an expensive suit. The elderly guy leaned closer. Ko smelled cologne and the faint aroma of tiger balm.

Hung gave Ko a measuring stare, and he made it clear he didn't like what he saw. "You don't belong here, boy. Stop bothering my lads and get lost." More men were approaching now, Hung's personal guard. All of them held shiny handguns in deceptively casual stances.

"Ko brought a car…" began Rikio, in an attempt to justify himself.

Hung turned his puppy-like brown eyes on the Vector and sniffed like he smelt something bad. "Corp wheels? Is this boy a fool?" he asked Rikio, "He won't earn our graces by doing a stupid thing like this." He gave the car a dismissive wave. "Burn it."

"What?" Ko blurted. "But—"

Hung eyed Rikio, ignoring Ko so completely that it silenced him. "Torch it," he repeated. "And then make the idiot go away."

FOR OLD TIME'S sake, Rikio let Ko take the bag from the back seat and leave with just a few bruises and a split lip. By the time he was at the highway, the night had closed in and unleashed the rain. Feng was waiting there for him.

"You lie with pigs, you become dirty," said the swordsman.

Ko made a spitting noise and kept walking.

We are not so blind that we cannot see. Do you understand what will happen when the sky cuts like SILK and the BEAST pours in?

Do not accept the way of no mind and the CALMNESS of the false Zen — this is a lie made to entrap you, a coil cast down from the dragons in the towers! Turn your face from false IDOLS. Find truth in your HEART.

The poison of dead emperors taints the Fragrant Harbour! Touch life and live! Go on and LIVE!

>   Excerpt from a tract distributed in Temple Street Market.
>   Origin and author unknown.

3. happy together

HE TRIED THE Banana Dog and the Rama-Rama, Club 19Nine-Tee7 and the House o' Boots before he found his Toyomazda Ranger wedged poorly between two light buses in a side street off Waterloo Road. A few doors down, a shiny chrome elevator led to the Lucky Dot Bar. So, then. His sister was back there, making a fool of herself, braying that mock nasal laugh she put on when she faked amusement at the off-colour jokes of rich guys.

Ko approached the car and his face fell. She'd left it unlocked – *again*. The old familiar bite of that special anger and frustration he kept for his sibling rose and fell in his chest. He slid into the front seat and made quick and angry work of gathering up MacDee wrappers and dozens of tiny vodka bottles, the kind that crowded hotel minibars. He threw them into a public flashburner and stomped back to the Ranger, the rain drumming off the awning of the store next to the parked car, clattering off the sunroof. He sat and watched the silver doorway. Every so often, two light strips either side of the elevator would illuminate and people would blunder out, cursing the acrid rain and unfolding their umbrellas. Mostly they were identikit corps, men and women with little or no difference to them. Some were fatter than others, some had better suits, but they all stumbled around the street like they owned it, pushing people out of their way or kicking at the slow-moving bots that wandered past them, projecting holo-adverts.

The evening moved on in slow, unpleasant surges, and Ko took the time to tape the cuts on his face with a spool of DermFix from the glove compartment. From behind the steering wheel, in the morose damp, he glared at the corporates and the gaudy hangers-on who trailed them in and out of the Lucky Dot. Ko's fingers dug into the plastic of the wheel with such powerful, impotent fierceness, it made his eyes tight in his head. A knot of them slipped and giggled as they moved toward the main road, at their head a raucous woman in the scarlet kimono of a senior Paradise executive, dragging a boywhore behind her. Under a thermoplastic parasol, she led her gaggle of suits right in front of the Ranger and for a moment Ko imagined the look on her face if he were to stamp on the gas and ram the lot of them against the flank of the minibus. He saw it unfold in his head as a colourless manga strip: cut frames and jagged edges spattered with pools of black ink blood, wheels spinning on corpses. Screaming. Terrible laughter.

"That hatred will burn you alive one day." Feng shifted in the back seat.

Ko didn't bother to look at him. "You have a bloody proverb for every day of the week, don't you?"

"I'm just making an observation."

He closed his eyes, and when he opened them he was alone again.

The night drew in and the transit company programmer came to load the routes for the light buses. He gave Ko a sideways look from under the hood of his acid-resistant rain slicker and did his work. The two buses came to life in blinks of neon running lights and rumbled away to service the shift workers massing at the Metro stations. Tubed in from the outlying shanties across the border wall in Shenzhen, Hong Kong's population would swell by a third once the day ended as cooks, cleaners and prostitutes came in to fill the low-rent gaps in the city's service infrastructure. By dawn they would all be gone again, pockets lined with a few more yuan, the messes made by the suits cleaned up so the rich could do it again the next night. The migrant workforce was visible at the edges of every street, edited out of the world that people like the kimono woman moved through.

The digits on the dashboard display moved with glacier-like slowness toward closing time, and the higher they climbed the more suits ejected themselves from the Lucky Dot. In big, splashy steps, a skinny man in a laser-cut Mirany original lurched over to the Ranger and collided with it. Ko jerked awake from a clammy doze and cupped his balisong knife in his hand.

"C'mon! C'mon!" the drunk called to a group of similarly dressed men. "I gotta car! Let's play go-gangers!" He tugged at the door handle, but Ko locked it. The man frowned, his beer-fogged brain slow on the uptake. "Hey." He banged on the window. "Geddout. I want this car. I'm driving."

"Fuck off," Ko replied, and showed him the length of the blade.

The guy frowned, unperturbed by the implied threat, and then dug out a roll of yuan. He waved them around. Paper money was a novelty for a lot of corporate types who had been raised inside walled executive enclaves, where wealth only existed as ones and zeros. Hong Kong's night economy was still traditional at heart, though, and cash remained a quaint throwback in many quarters. The suit peeled off hundred-yuan bills and threw them at the Ranger, one after another. "Gimme the car, street boy. I can buy you. I can buy anything! I wanna play!" He yelled at his friends. "I want to be Hazzard Wu!" He slapped the window with the flat of his hand. "*I promise not to kill you...*" he chortled, repeating Wu's signature line from last year's big hit, the action racer flick, *Spider*.

From the back of the group came a man who was decidedly not a drunk. He reeked of corp security. With gentle force, he guided the other man away, pausing only to gather up the wet banknotes and throw Ko a slight shake of the head. "This way, sir," he heard him say. "There's a limo waiting."

"A limo!" shouted the drunken man, and his gaggle of friends repeated him with noisy, idiotic gusto.

The lights around the door blinked on again as the lift dropped from the Lucky Dot on the fourteenth floor. Nikita came out and she listed like a galleon in high seas, her face puffy and red with drink, screwing up in irritation at the rain. Another girl came with her – a bottle-ginger Korean dressed in retro kogal style – and trailing behind a bald fellow with a simpering, pleading look on his face.

Ko was out of the car in one swift motion, the balisong still concealed in the curve of his fist. "Niki!" he shouted, and beckoned her toward him.

Nikita threw Ko a look and then smiled back at the Korean and the man. "Are we going to have a party, then?"

The faux-ginger girl gave Nikita a sharp prod that was not the friendly jab she pretended it was. "I'll take it from here."

"He wanted to go with me—"

"Girls, I like you both..." said the bald guy.

"With *me*," snapped the Korean and this time she gave Ko's sister a shove.

Nikita brought up her hand to slap the ginger girl, but Ko was there. He grabbed her wrist and turned it. Her slow-burning ire instantly turned on him and she bit Ko where his forearm was bare.

The Korean was already melting away. Ko ignored the pain and dragged his sister, screeching and complaining, back to the car. He forced her into the passenger seat and they set off.

NIKITA SPAT AND hissed at him on the way back to the apartment. Now and then she would look directly at him and he could see the dull, doll-like cast in her eyes that told him she was stoned. She alternated between ranting and babbling, the coherence of her speech ebbing and flowing. Ko just concentrated on the driving and tried not to think about it too much. Every time he did, every time he thought honestly about his dissolute sister's self-destructive life, it made his gut tighten and his temper flare. She worked at places like the Lucky Dot ostensibly as a hostess, which in real terms meant she was paid to look pretty, and ply the corp clients who frequented the bar with overpriced drinks while they pawed at her. It was just slightly less sordid than being a sexworker. Nikita wasn't like the girls in the Mongkok sinplexes – although Ko often said she was to get a rise out of her – in some ways, she was worse. It made his blood boil to think that the highlight of her day would be some suited creep, like baldy back, there making eyes at her.

"Least I got a job," she slurred.

Ko realised too late he'd spoken his thoughts aloud.

"Not like you," Nikita went on. "What do you do, little brother? Play with your stupid cars–" she smacked the dashboard. "Run stuff for the triads 'cross the border, *steal*? I'm trying to make something of myself."

"How? By playing corp wannabe, by sucking up to every suit that comes through the door? What, you think one of them is going to fall for you and make you his mistress, shower you with diamonds and credits? One day, one of those scumbags is going to take you for games back at his place and you'll end up spent and dead!"

"Don't judge me!" she shot back. "You're just like Dad–"

Ko stamped on the brakes and the Ranger screeched to a halt in the middle of Kwun Tong Road. In a low voice, without looking at her, he said, "Don't talk about him."

Nikita fell silent and after a moment they drove on.

EVENTUALLY, FRANKIE HAD to use the Penfield beside the bed just to get some sleep. Half-considered thoughts and strange, ghostly dream fragments hovered at the edges of his weary mind. Exhaustion and jetlag struck hard the moment he laid eyes on the bed, the inviting spread of cream and chocolate-coloured silk sheets open to him in the middle of the suite. Alice talked about the meeting, but he wasn't really listening. He remembered falling asleep in his suit.

Once or twice he awoke with that peculiar kind of disassociated fear that comes from finding yourself in a strange bedroom. The subtle electromagnetic aura of the Penfield generator eventually sent him into deep REM and finally Frankie relaxed. He thought, just once, that he had seen the Monkey King in the room with him; but that blurred like rainwater on glass and faded.

A service bot woke him by singing a traditional folk aria. It was a silver ball balanced on two convex wheels that emerged from its flanks. A rotating head presented a pair of cute eyes and a sine wave mouth. It giggled like a child as it did its chores, making him coffee and tuning the shower. The device offered him a trio of vitamin and nanobooster tablets as he got dressed, gravely informing him of the dangers of dehydration on the international traveller. Frankie didn't argue; his face felt like old paper. When he was done, the metal ball rolled away along the corridor and used arrows projected from laser slits to direct him to the hotel's rooftop heliport. Alice was waiting for him in an idling spidercopter, with Monkey King in the cockpit.

"Where's Ping?" The question popped out of his mouth as he strapped himself into a seat.

"Occupied," Alice replied, as the rotodyne drifted off toward the towers of Central.

Frankie watched the world go by, the glass and steel skyscrapers passing beneath him, the near-distant glitter of Kowloon across the bottle green waters of the bay. There was no need to provide a spidercopter to take him to Yuk Lung's headquarters — a car would have got him there almost as quickly — but the gesture was obviously important. Everything about Francis Lam's return to Hong Kong was being choreographed with infinite care and precision. For his part, Frankie could not be sure if it were to make him feel special or just inferior.

Monkey King flew them around the dagger-like shape of the China Bank building, giving the sheath of protected airspace around the fluted NeoGen pyramid nearby a wide berth. The rotorplane turned and made an orbit of the YLHI tower. The company headquarters resembled a column of creamy green jade rising like a pillar of heaven; bright ribs of lunar steel studded the sheer walls, and at the level of the ninetieth floor the ultramodern lines of the tower suddenly stopped. Capping the building was a reproduction of a Qin Dynasty castle, deposited there like something from an ancient legend. Only the discreet clusters of satcomm dishes and ku-band antennae seemed out of place. As the flyer approached, a helipad unfolded from a hidden balcony to accept them, a bee settling into an open flower.

Alice read a message from her watch and beckoned Frankie. "Mr Tze will receive you in the library."

They were met by one of Monkey King's counterparts. This one had a mask of green with red and white detail, a little trim of gold here and there. Frankie searched his mind and came up with a name: Deer Child, a mountain guardian from an opera that he couldn't recall the title of. Deer Child was shorter and stockier than Monkey King, but they were cut from the same cloth. The masked man had the same smooth gait and effortless sense of menace about him.

Frankie followed Alice into the castle and Hong Kong vanished behind him. Inside, the building was warm and close, full of the natural noise of feet on stone floors and creaking wooden doors. Tapestries and art hung on the walls, and there were suits of armour at each intersection of corridor. Frankie wondered if they were more than they seemed; if an alarm sounded, would they suddenly leave their plinths and stand to the defence of the castle's master?

He glimpsed other rooms as people passed them along the way, doors opening and closing with flashes of glass and steel, banks of holographic monitors and server farms. Behind others came the snapping of wooden practice swords and the patterns of voices from sparring fighters. They emerged in the library and Frankie wandered to the centre of the room to get the measure of the place. Books lined every inch of vertical space, rising far out of reach to the ceiling. Trios of full-size terracotta soldiers, some holding weapons, guarded discreet lamps in the corners of the room, looking on across the centuries with blank stone faces. Frankie hesitated by the low table in the middle of the library and something made his eyes fall to the oak platform. A box made of brushed aluminium sat there, shiny and out of place.

From behind him there came the thud of a heavy door and an intake of breath that was deep and sonorous.

"Francis," said Mr Tze. "Welcome home. I am so sorry we were required to meet under these terrible circumstances."

THE RADIATOR COMPLAINED as Ko turned the temperature up a notch or two, the elderly pipes rumbling and knocking. He padded through the apartment in his socks, the quiet routine of breakfast so as not to disturb his sister ingrained in him. He microwaved a couple of meatpockets and made strong tea. The atmosphere inside the apartment was patchy; where the kitchen and the closet-sized bathroom lay against the outer wall, it was chilly and damp from the rain; the two bedrooms and the living room – the patch of space Nikita laughingly called "the lounge" – were warmer, closer to the central courtyard in the middle of the block where caged heat from the lower floors wafted upwards. The apartment felt gloomy and confined, as if the resonance from their argument on the way home had followed them in and leached into the walls. The sullen ambience in the room was infectious.

Through the walls he could hear the woolly sounds of the Yip family next door, the strident noise of the mother ordering the kids out to school and the usual arguments in return. One of Ko's other neighbours had told him the Yip boys both had ADHD, but Ko was less inclined to be so generous. The kids were just noisy, unruly and argumentative, and the Yips and the Chens had come to loggerheads over it on many occasions. Nikita didn't help, with frequent bouts of playing her musichip collection at ear-stunning volume. Plenty of times Ko had come home to hear the strains of some Petya Tcherkassoff ballad reaching down the stairwell from the eleventh floor. He hated that whiney sovpop. Ko's musical tastes ran to rapcore and PacRim turbine bands like Nine Milly Meeta, 100 Yen or the Kanno Krew.

He glanced over his shoulder as Nikita's door opened and she clattered into the bathroom. Ko tried to think of more pleasant things as she went through her regular purge ritual in there. Watery morning sunshine filtered in through the peeling UV sheets on the window, casting a faint cage of shadows across the floor where the safety bars crisscrossed outside. Ko wandered over, nibbling at his food, letting the hot tea warm his chilled fingers. In the dull glass he saw a frowning reflection, and peered past it, scanning the street below. The wan daylight revealed skinny tower blocks looking like something from the building set of a patient but unimaginative child, tall rods of polymerised stone growing out of the face of the Kowloon hillside, their footprints barely enough to cover the acreage of a conventional two-tier home like the ones in the walled enclaves. Through the gaps between the other towers, Ko could spy parts of the city beneath its constant cowl of yellow-grey smog. Soon that view would be gone forever. Another new housing project was already sprouting on the hill, a series of con-apts that would rise to twice the height of Ko's block. Right now, they were just greenish humps in the middle distance, fuzzy shapes like desert cacti from the vat-grown bamboo scaffolds that concealed them. In a few months they would be finished, and a hundred thousand new citizens would feed into Hong Kong from across the border. The city had slowly been advancing out from the bay for centuries, gradually consuming every bit of spare land from the outlying New Territories. There would come a time when the Hong Kong Free Economic Enterprise Quadrant would collide with the ferrocrete wall that marked the edge of True China. Ko did not want to be here when that happened; for a moment his brain flashed on that idea, of he and Nikita as wizened little eldos, still here, still fighting, but too old to go anywhere else.

He forced the thought away with a shudder and did the three-click finger snap that made the television switch on. Ko paged through the channels with the sound on mute, passing the multiple ZeeBeeCee feeds, PandaVision and NBO. Most of the stations were carrying clips from the new Juno Qwan album and Ko chewed his lip. The singer had a weird attract-repel quality to her, with the way she would yo-yo between hi-fashion pop diva one day to gothic lolita the next. Ko would never admit it, but he actually liked some of her stuff. She did this song – it was a b-side, maybe? – called "Doppler Highway" that had just the right kind of lonely in it, conjuring up the same melancholy freedom that Ko got from a night ride through the hills. He hesitated, watching the silent vid. Juno was wrapped in a holodress, the outfit morphing and changing as she walked along a sun-dappled beach, planes of light shifting to reveal just enough flesh that you knew she was naked underneath. She moved over sand raked into geometric shapes and water-smoothed stones. There were trains of letters and numbers on her clothes, moving and warping. Cool, perfect blue waves lapped at her bare feet and overhead was a cloudless cerulean sky. Juno's smile was relaxed and calm, but her eyes were a little sad, as if she felt sorry that you were not there on that idyllic beach with her.

"I'm the perfect smile. Touch my thoughts and flow, there's no world we can't know." Nikita walked into the room, singing along with the silent starlet. "I love her stuff. She's so deep. Didn't think she was your type."

"She's not," Ko changed the channel and found a weather report.

Nikita made a face and gathered her jacket off the threadbare sofa where she had deposited it the night before. She produced a fold of crisp yuan and held it out to him. "Rent money," she explained. "There's extra in there, too."

Ko made no move to take it. "Where'd you get that?"

She blew out a breath. "I don't want to do this, Ko. Just take the damn cash."

He wanted to; part of him really wanted to say no more and let it go. But that wasn't how it was going to play out. Before he was even fully aware of what he was doing, Ko's mouth was running away and they were sliding straight back into the same patterns they had followed since they were children. "Let me guess, you were exceptionally good at selling drinks in the Dot? Or perhaps you gave that bald loser a blowjob—"

The slap came from nowhere and stung him with its ferocity; but the anger in the swipe wasn't reflected in his sister's eyes. All he saw there was fatigue. "You don't have the right to lecture me on what I do, Ko. You're a thief, little brother, and you're not a very good one at that. If you grow the hell up, you might just understand enough to have an opinion, but until then, shut up and *pay the rent*!"

He pointed at his chest. "Thief? What does that make you, Niki? You want me to say it?"

"Don't you dare…"

"You want me to call you what you are?" His voice was rising, and so was the fury, coming on hot and strong. "I'm not the one behaving like a child! Which of us is the one living in a fairy tale, sis? Who is the one looking for a prince charming in a laser-cut suit?" He waved a hand in front of her face. "I live in the real world, not the stupid plastic dreamland those corp bastards do!"

"Wake up!" Nikita snapped. "Look around, Ko, the corps *are* the real world! They *run* the real world! You're not part of that machine, you get hammered down!"

"I'd rather be poor and free than in their pockets!" he replied.

"And it shows! Look at you! You watch those stupid movies and you play like you're some hustler ronin, but you're going nowhere! I'm making something of myself, Ko." She advanced and prodded him in the chest. "I'm ready to do whatever I have to. You? You've got nothing but a bunch of half-assed principles and a downward spiral."

He tried to frame a reply but nothing came.

"I'm not ending up like…" Nikita stumbled over the words. "I'm not going to stay here for the rest of my life. I've got *goals*." She threw the money at him and he caught it.

"You lie with pigs, you become dirty," Ko said in a low voice. "Your boyfriends at the Dot, it's their kind that is screwing us all, not just you and me, the whole damn planet! You want to be part of that?"

She snatched up her bag and drew a silver card from within. "I *am* part of it, Ko. I'm connected."

"What the hell is that?"

Nikita waved the smartcard in the air. Ko recognised the design as a single use corporate security pass. When he was younger, he'd often picked them from the pockets of drunk salarymen in the bar district. "I wasn't going to tell you because I know you'd blow your stack, but what the hell, you'd find out eventually." She leaned in. "I'm moving up, Ko. I've got a patron."

He swore explosively and grabbed at her, snatching the strap on her bag. Nikita kept hold of the other end and an angry tug-of-war ensued. "I'm not letting you go uptown! I forbid it!"

"You what?" she sneered. "You can't order me around, Ko. I'm the eldest, I do what I want to!"

"You stupid bitch—" The bag strap tore and the contents scattered on the floor.

Nikita dropped to her knees, gathering up the stuff. Something plastic flashed in her grip, a disc of bubble-packed capsules. Ko's hand shot out and he grabbed her wrist. He had height and weight over his sister, and she squealed as he turned her arm the wrong way. "Stop it!"

Ko tore the packet from her hand. There were nine bubbles, three of which had been emptied. The other six contained ice-blue pills made of clear gelatine. They glistened in the sunlight, and the letters Z3N were clearly visible on them. The packet bore no manufacturer's markings.

"Give those back!"

Ko crushed the pack in his fist and turned a furious glare on his sister. "You stupid, stupid bitch! Did he give them to you? That bald bastard, was it him?"

"No—"

"I'll fucking kill him. I'll find that wageslave and run the fucker down."

"Those are mine." Nikita shouted at him, and the words hit like a shock of cold water.

"What?" Ko's rage disintegrated.

"They're mine, you idiot!" His sister pushed away from him; anger and despair, frustration and regret framed her pretty face. "You are so naïve, Ko."

The blue fluid seeped around his fingers from the cracked capsules. Where it touched his skin, it tingled. Ko threw the packet into the burner and ran his hands under the sink in the bathroom.

While he was there, he heard the front door slam, loud like a gunshot.

Tze advanced across the room and enveloped Frankie's hand in his. Rough skin, hard like old leather crossed the younger man's pale office-worker fingers. Tze leaned into him, and Frankie felt profoundly naked beneath the man's flinty gaze. The

CEO of Yuk Lung had hard amber eyes set deep in a face tanned by exposure. Tze wasn't as tall as Frankie had been expecting, but the man was thickset and broad across the chest. He looked more like a wrestler than a corporate executive, and it wasn't hard to imagine him as the Mongol warrior some compared him too. Frankie imagined Tze in horsehide and armour and knew he'd be as comfortable with it as he was here and now in his spidersilk Tommy Nutter original.

"Alan was a good man," he rumbled. "He had vision and character. He will be missed."

Frankie swallowed. "I... Please, sir, I haven't yet been given the details of what happened..."

Tze threw Alice a look and she gave a shallow nod. "A bad business, Francis. I hesitate to speak of it here." He looked away. "Be assured that the company is expending every effort in the matter. Your brother has been granted full honours."

"Thank you," said Frankie. "But if I may ask how—?"

"Alice will brief you this afternoon," Tze said, with a finality that ended the line of conversation like an axe-blow. "But before then we must address a matter that concerns *you*, and you alone."

"I don't understand."

Tze gestured to a portly woman hovering near the door, and on cue she came closer. Her face was a little too perfect for the body it was on. "Francis, this is Phoebe Hi. She is a cousin of our corporate clan, from the RedWhiteBlue group."

Frankie gave her a weak smile. RedWhiteBlue Inc. was YLHI's entertainment division, a hit factory churning out music, vids and home vircade games across half of the Pacific Rim. Hi gave him a plastic blink of seamless teeth. "I worked closely with your brother," she said. "I hope to do the same with you."

Tze gave her the slightest of nods and Hi retreated a couple of steps. "Yes, my boy. I've brought you here because I hope you will accept a gift from us."

"Gift?" repeated Frankie, his head spinning.

The other man rubbed at his tightly trimmed beard. "I know that nothing can replace your brother, but it is my hope that you will allow me to demonstrate the regard in which he was held by Yuk Lung." He placed a fatherly hand on Frankie's shoulder, the other reaching for the metal box on the table. "I want you to take Alan's place here in Hong Kong. I want you to assume his duties and position within our clan, with all the responsibilities and rewards that entails. Will you join us, Francis?"

As if there was any other answer to give. "Of... Of course, sir. But I..."

Tze put a finger to his lips. "Ssh. No doubts, lad. We have none of that here."

Frankie nodded. "I, uh, accept, sir. It's an honour."

"We are a traditional corporation, Francis," Tze continued, opening the box. "In this day and age, to some that makes Yuk Lung seem... peculiar in its practices." His fist came up and in it was an ornate four-fold brass dagger. "This is a ghost knife. It is more than two thousand years old." He offered it, blade-first.

Gingerly, Frankie took it, feeling the razor sharp edges pulling at the skin of his palm. Tze smiled a little and cupped Frankie's hand in his, pressing the younger man's flesh into the blades. Where it cut him, it felt icy cold.

"It is important," Tze said, tightening his grip, "for men to understand that the wheel turns only when the axle is oiled by blood."

Session #542, resuming at 3.38pm.

DR YEOH: *Are you ready, Sally?*

SALLY: *Okay. Can I get a smoke?*

DR YEOH: *I'm afraid not. We've talked about that before. You can't smoke in the clinic.*

SALLY: *Oh yeah. Right.*

DR YEOH: *So. Let's continue. We were talking about your friend, Cynda.*

SALLY: *Not my friend any more.*

DR YEOH: *Why is that?*

SALLY: *I told you. I saw what she had in there.*

DR YEOH: *In where?*

SALLY: *Inside her head.*

DR YEOH: *What did she have in her head, Sally?*

SALLY: Worms. Black worms and snakes.

DR YEOH: How did that make you feel?

SALLY: Sick. I thought she was my friend, but she…

DR YEOH: Take your time.

SALLY: All these years and she had worms in her head. I shared a flat with her, a bathroom. We drank from the same cups. I never would have if I had known.

DR YEOH: How did you find out about the worms?

SALLY: Yonni brought these geltabs around. New things, never tried them before. We had some drinks and we dropped a few.

DR YEOH: And then you saw…

SALLY: Worms. Coming out of her eyes and nose. She was screaming at me, she said I was going to kill her.

DR YEOH: Perhaps you only thought you were seeing worms. Perhaps it was the tablets, did that occur to you?

SALLY: No. I've tripped before. I know the difference. This was real. As real as you are in the room with me right now. Do you think I would have? Do you think I would have if I hadn't known they were real? That would have been crazy.

DR YEOH: What did you do next?

SALLY: She had a big plaster cat on the mantle. I never liked it. I beat her skull in with it and killed the worms. I know it worked because they were all gone after that.

DR YEOH: How did that make you feel?

SALLY: Better.

Session #542 ends.

4. the game of death

Fixx saw the taxi-sampan come around the corner on to Decatur Street and stepped lightly from the balcony and on to the prow of the chugging boat. The aged fellow at the helm peered up at him from under a woollen cap, his sunken brown face giving Fixx a sour look in return.

"Give a man a ride?" he asked, as the sampan bobbed in the wake of an airboat.

The sulky driver jerked his thumb at the people in the passenger compartment and set off again. Fixx swung himself over the windscreen and joined the surprised family of tourists in the back. Father, mother, two boys. Dad was already fumbling for a Day-Glo taser on his belt, Mom shocked by the sudden arrival of a large black man in a ballistic kevleather long coat. The boys watched, wide-eyed.

He took off his espex and gave the lady a winning smile. "Joshua Fixx, ma'am. My most profuse apologies for taking advantage of your boat." He kissed the back of her hand with gentle reverence.

Dad had the taser in his fist now. "Just a darn minute, pal! This is our taxi!"

A SoCal accent. Fixx had the measure of these folks in a heartbeat; some midlevel whitebread splashing out on a transcontinental vacation to shut up his bored wife and whiny kids, venturing out from the west coast with little or no idea how the rest of the You Ess of Ay actually worked beyond the walls of their gated community in the burbs.

"How are you liking Newer Orleans?" He said the name of the city like *N'Arlens*, because that was how the touristas expected it. "She's a peach, ain't she?" He took in the riverine streets with a casual gesture, removing a twig from his sleeve. In the distance, a French horn was razzing the sky at a rooftop café deep in the Vieux Carré.

Dad brandished the taser like it was a holy cross against a vampire. "Don't make me use this!"

"Ah, hush yourself now." Fixx snapped the twig right under Dad's nose and the man went slack, head lolling forward. A line of drool emerged from his lips along with a low snore. Fixx gave Mom an apologetic look and threw the taser into the water as the taxi turned on to Canal Street. She clucked and flailed over her husband, unable to wake him.

"Hey mister," said one of the boys, the elder of the two. "Did you kill my dad?" He wore a *Subburb Sux* screen-T with Mallratz gangcult colours.

The other boy elbowed his brother in the ribs. "Doofus! He's put him out, is all." The younger one had a sunscreen jumpsuit and ghille hat.

Fixx smiled thinly. "Sorry about that. He'll come around soon."

"How'd you do that with a piece of wood?"

"Ask a favour of nature, boy. Sometimes she'll help you."

The eldest folded his arms. "I know what it is. It's that voo-doo. He's a voo-doo man. He's got what they call them loo-ahs, or something."

"Loas," said Fixx absently.

"Naw," said the younger, and pointed at Fixx's chest. "He's an op. I seen his guns when he got on." The kid shuffled forward in a conspiratorial manner. "You got a pair of SunKing 10-mil longslides in a cross belt, there."

"Good eye."

A smug grin. "I wanna be a sanctioned operative one day. Like that Timberlake guy on ZeeBeeCee."

"He's not a real op." said the other boy, "He just plays one on TV."

"Don't care." The kid gave Fixx a long look. "You do interdicts? Takedowns? Highway work?"

"I go where fate sends me."

The elder sneered. "I don't like it here. I wanna go back to Oxnard."

Fixx studied the younger kid. "How about you?"

The boy shrugged. "S'okay, I guess. Sometimes it smells funny. And the music don't stop."

The sampan rode the swell as a cigarette boat rumbled past, a languid drag queen draped over the twin fifty-cals on the prow. Fixx showed the tungsten caps in his teeth as he gave them a genuine smile, amused at the boy's description. "That's Mardi Gras for you. These days, carnival never ends. Was a time when you could walk these streets afoot," he said, sniffing the air. The ever-present tang of faint rot, azaleas and curdled petrochem presented itself; but there were alien scents too, ash and old blood out of place on the breeze. He tapped the driver on the shoulder and indicated where he should turn toward the Place Benville. "Back before the Cat Fives and the Big Tides, though, before you were born. Now there's no place that don't live off second floor or higher. The Venice of the South…" He leaned closer to the younger lad. "Parts of the city, she sank, you dig? Tempests and floods just kept comin'. Now the depths belong to the dead and the drowned." From a hidden pocket in the long coat, he brought a handful of bleached bones, all of them careworn and yellowed through thousands of uses. Fixx bent low and shook them in his hand like dice.

"Maitre Carrefour, are you listenin'?" he whispered. "If it would please your honourable self to visit your blessing on your worthless son Joshua, so that along my day I might be obliged to serve the good of things." He said something else that the boys could not make out and turned the bones on to the deck.

"Told you he was voo-doo," said the older kid.

Fixx frowned and fingered the bones, nudging them a little, considering the patterns. Things had not improved; if anything, the bones told him it was worse. Quickly, he scooped them up, destroying the message. Ahead of the boat, the grey arc of the Hyperdome was becoming visible behind the buildings and Fixx stood up, scanning the sides of the boulevard for a place to alight. The original stadium that stood there had collapsed years ago, brought down by the surge tides fanned by Hurricane Mandy; the replacement sat like a dark jewel in the heart of Newer Orleans, cupped in a setting of murky waters.

A hovercraft coming the other way floated closer and Fixx stepped on to the stern. He gave the boys a look over his shoulder. "I got some advice for your dad, when he wakes up. You tell him you'll have more fun over the Gulf at DisneyCity."

"You're going to kill someone?" asked the younger lad.

"Never can tell," said Fixx, and leapt to the other vessel.

THE GIRL'S FACE was reflected everywhere he looked. Holos of her dancing in the evening air over the curve of the 'dome, flyposters in fluorescent shades three or four layers thick on the walls, her eyes winking from video billboards. Then there were the people. Men and women dressed as her, hair in various imitations of her auburn topknot, the faux-Egyptian eye make-up from her first album or the gothcore look she sported for the second disc. The crowds were a funhouse mirror for the girl, a thousand copies of her tall and short, fat and thin, dark and light. It was like a net had been cast through the universe, pulling together every alternate version that could, did or might have existed, gathering them here to coalesce at the feet of the one true original. The actual, the real, the genuine article.

At first, the girl seemed to be a hazy idea at the edge of his mind, the vague concept of a person distant and removed, thin as smoke, fading whenever he tried to concentrate on her. But as time passed, she filled in. The sketch of her grew depth and presence, moving slowly from his deep dreams to moments awake when his mind wandered. She was coming closer, he realised, and with her she dragged a bleak thread of something that his conscious mind shied away from. The girl was connected in a way that she did not comprehend, and Joshua slowly began to understand that it was his purpose to show her how. He had jobs to do – real jobs, paying cases and ongoing investigations – but none of those kept him awake at night, cold and sweating. This was an affair of an entirely different sort.

Fixx made no eye contact with any of the copies. He found them distracting, and this matter was of enough seriousness to him that he wanted nothing to cloud his path. He took a ticket from the pocket of a person deep in argument with a T-shirt vendor, and pressed on to the Hyperdome's entrance.

Over the doors in red neon letters eight metres tall, Juno Qwan told the world that she was in Newer Orleans for one night only.

THE DULL REPORTS of the support group's climactic number built and built, reaching down through the backstage spaces in hollow, confused echoes. On the wall inside the wings, the countdown clock to the main event was inching ever closer to zero, and the tech crew were scrambling over the last few mike checks and hook-ups. There had already been six fatalities among the staff on the tour and they were itchy with short-timer's fever. Newer Orleans was the last stop, and after they were done here tonight they would leave America behind.

Heywood Ropé tasted the vibe in the air, the adrenaline scent messages from the roadies thick about him. They parted before the slim man, desperate to be seen to be busy, not one of them caught at rest. Good. These weeks on the road together had bred only more fear of him, and that was exactly how he wanted it to be. He reached the platform behind the stage where the band were shaking themselves down, thumbing a couple of capsules or applying derms inside their sleeves as need be. The forever-placid cast of his face tightened a little, revealing the hard lines of the skull beneath.

"Where is she?"

None of them answered. They all just looked in the direction of the dressing room, some sighing, others frowning.

For one blinding instant, Ropé wanted to reach out and break someone's neck; anyone, he didn't care whose. A bullet of hot anger smashed into him, smouldering. His hands clenched into fists. He was so sick and tired of ministering to these pathetic children, with their paltry and ridiculous addictions, their idiotic fears and emotional fragility. In that second, he longed to stride back to the tour bus and remove the Glock subgun secreted in his luggage and start culling them. Gentiles, he thought. I loathe you all.

Instead, he slammed an iron shutter over those feelings and produced a thin smile that never went beyond his lips. "Fine," he said aloud. Ropé knocked once on Juno's door and entered, locking it behind him.

There was little light inside. Most of the bulbs around the make-up table were inert, shattered and sparking. The mirrors were all gone, reduced to jagged shards. Juno looked up at him as he came closer, just for a moment, and then returned to her task at hand. She was using part of a chair leg to grind the broken bits of mirror into smaller and smaller pieces. Juno had already worked a lot of the glass into powdery fines that glittered all over the red carpet floor.

"Don't worry," she said, in a matter-of-fact voice. "I'll be out when I'm finished. I just have to break all the mirrors in the world first."

A sigh escaped him. Apart from that incident in the limo on the way to the studios in Chicago, there had been no sign of anything approaching this level of instability. Ropé realised reluctantly that she must have been storing it up, getting away with small, concealable things like bouts of self-harm.

"Juno," he said. "You're on, darling. Everyone is waiting." As if on cue, the crowd out in the dome roared as the pre-show video started up. He offered her his hand.

Her perfect face watched him, clouded with animal fear. She was wearing the schoolgirl outfit from the "Locker Room Heart" video: the exaggerated pigtails, the microskirt and bobbysox had scored huge numbers with the lolita-complex fans. "They love me. They'll understand."

"Understand what, sweetie?"

"I saw it." She tapped her temple, and Ropé noticed that her fingers were bleeding. "The sky tearing open. All these things flying out." She made fluttery gestures with her hands. "A big mouth full of screaming teeth. It wants to eat the world. Darkness. All the worms and the people tearing up–"

"Juno." Ropé reached into his pocket and removed a leather case. "Perhaps we could talk about this another time." The case opened like a book, with a puff of cold vapour. Inside there was a device that resembled the grip and trigger of a pistol, but instead of a breech and barrel there was a glass tube ending in a micropore mesh. The case had a small nest of ampoules next to the device, and Ropé loaded one into the tube.

She came to her feet in a rush, the chair leg shivering in her hands. "I don't need that."

"Juno, love." He concentrated on the words to make them utterly kind, totally without any accusation or venom. "I don't want you to be upset. I care about you too much for that. It makes me sad to see you like this."

"Heywood, you do believe me, don't you?" The chair leg drooped. "I can see these things, sometimes in the day now, not just in dreams." Her eyes unfocussed. She was exploring the thought. "Mirrors. I'm going to be killed by mirrors."

"Juno, you're a star, and stars are immortal. They can't be killed by anything."

She looked at him again, this time clear-eyed. "Okay. Put that away and I'll come out."

He smiled, guiding the device back to his pocket. "Look, I'm putting it away."

Juno dropped the chair leg and came to him for a hug. "I'm sorry. I don't mean to be any trouble–"

"I know," he said in a fatherly voice. When she had both hands around him, Ropé grabbed her pigtails and wrenched her head backward. She started to scream, but the noise died in her throat as the injector device chugged where it touched her jugular. A shot of electric blue fluid vanished into her bloodstream and Juno staggered back a step, her eyes hazing.

Ropé spat and put the device away. "The show must go on," he told her.

"Yes," she said thickly, her doll-like face brightening. "Oh. Yes."

* * *

Inside the Hyperdome it was blood-warm and moist with the exhalations of a capacity crowd. Juno Qwan's star was still climbing and with a string of international hits and another album on the way, the petite Chinese singer had all the hallmarks of becoming a cross-genre smash. The music wasn't Fixx's cup of tea, though. It lacked soul by his lights, it seemed bereft of meaning; but he was clearly in the minority tonight. The sanctioned operative moved through the outer edges of the crowd as "Locker Room Heart" belted out across the stadium. The lights went down and came back again in flashes of colour, spinning strobe wheels and trailer spots sweeping the crowd like searchlights over a writhing human sea. From above, concealed in the steel rafters of the 'dome, misting nozzles cast a fine, cool haze over the throng. The towering holos of Juno glittered in the vapour, the giant doppelgangers following her every move.

Fixx saw her up on the stage, strutting and moving with her dancers, faking sexual positions with the backing vocalists. The band segued into "Bitch Queen" and "The Future is Now" before she threw off the schoolgirl outfit and changed tack. The atmosphere became sultry and intimate with a cover of "When the Night Comes", calming the crowd. Fixx moved slowly and carefully through the ranks of Juno's fans, letting the Brownian motion of their enrapt swaying push him ever closer to the rails of the mojo barrier surrounding the stage.

He crossed into the main mass of people and without warning his path was blocked by a hooded guy with a sleeper wand and a meshweave shirt that said *Venue Security*. The man rose from the waves of fans, one hand pressed to an ear bead, the other pointing the wand. The guard spoke but the music was too loud to hear a word of it. The letters on his top changed into a tickertape marquee.

*Where the **** are you going?* scrolled across the shirt, an automatic censor routine kicking in. Many of Juno's fans were pre-teens.

Fixx pointed toward the stage as she started to sing the love song "Paper Sunday".

Let bee sea your ticket, sun.

The audio pickup on the guard's throat wasn't doing the job properly. Fixx produced the pass he'd stolen and handed it over. When the man's eyes dropped, he pushed forward.

What the duck? The guard went to grab him and jab with the arcing tip of the sleeper wand; Fixx turned his wrist and disarmed the man. With a knuckle, the operative struck a nerve point near the security guard's clavicle and the man dropped to the floor. *Uиииииииии.*

Next came "Halo Kisses" and then Juno did a piece off the unreleased album called "Apple/Eye". Fixx reached the edge of the general admission crowd and pressed into the thick of the hardcore fans, a hundred bodies deep in the mosh pit. Juno's spotlight died and everything went dark.

"Zen, zen," sang the girl. "I'm the quiet mind inside, pretty voice." The crowd erupted into a storm of cheers and Fixx blinked as he felt a light rain on his face. "Touch" was the song that had made her career, the hit that had stayed at number one on the Billboard chart like it had been nailed there. "I'm the perfect smile," Juno crooned, the Hyperdome singing with her. "Touch my thoughts and flow, there's no world we can't know."

As the bassline kicked in, the stage went supernova white. Lasers fanned across the arena, cutting shapes, numbers and letters into the misty air. The holograms of Juno morphed and changed, flickering between her different outfits. Her face came forward off the holotank podium and wove patterns of fire above them. People cried out in surprise and tried to touch them. Angels. Fixx could see angels up there, made from glass and light.

The skin across his face was tingling and Fixx shook his head, hard. When he ran his fingers through his close-cropped step-cut they came back wet. The artificial rain was warm, speckling the shoulders of his coat. He could see some people tipping their heads back and welcoming it with outspread arms.

"Sea of stones, sand waves," Juno's voice echoed in his skull. "Harmony, come with me."

"This is wrong," he said aloud, but his voice vanished into the roar of the crowds.

"Taste the blue," sang the girl, each word a shock to his heart.

The glass angels in the rafters fell toward the crowds and as they came they changed; bright wings became masses of writhing serpents and faces fell apart into knots of maggoty flesh. Fixx struggled to find his guns but the press of people about him was so great he could barely move. Juno was still singing, and in the spaces between the words a woman in lolicon gingham shouted "Isn't she great?" into his ear, wild with the thrill of it all. "My eyes are golden!"

"Star at dawn, bubble in the stream. Zen, zen, I'm the quiet mind inside, pretty voice."

The laser fans turned to ropes of blue and green fire. Crossing in the air, the beams fell into the masses and laid lines of screaming, burning bodies in their wake. The smell of burnt flesh reached Fixx's nostrils and sense memory engulfed him in a flood. For one shuddering instant, he was –

– *there with Cajun Pork Cathy and her Longpig Boyz out on the rusted Gulf Coast oilrigs as they did the work of the Dark Ones, turning ferryboat passengers into chum for Deseret's blood rites. His guns hot in his hands. Cathy's head clean off at the neck. Crimson fountain. The Queen of Cups, inverted. Screaming. The meat smell.*

Fixx snapped back as the crowd picked him up. He was driftwood in the swell, the panic alive about him. The operative shouldered against the flow and slid back, standing his ground as the screaming hordes washed around him. The lasers sputtered and shrieked, darts of murderous coherent light striking like thunderbolts. The angel-things fluttered and shredded into storms of snakes, vanishing as they fell or slithering into shadows.

As "Touch" reached its crescendo and faded, the sound of sirens pealed over the crash of feet and breaking glass. Fixx shook his head, the wet fog clutching at his mind, making him feel drunk and slow. Fat droplets spattered about on the floor, sparkling in the spotlights.

More men in the talking shirts were sweeping Juno and the band off the stage. Impossibly, there were fans in the circles and the skyboxes on their feet and applauding, tears of elation streaming down their faces. Fixx threw himself at the mojo barrier and fell short, rebounding off the metal with a tingle from the stunner field.

Juno Qwan saw him. She turned and looked at him with those eyes, the porcelain face that clogged every instant of television airtime, every billboard and viddy. Fixx tried to find her name but his throat tightened. The girl looked down on him, beatific and empty.

Then the men in hoods were taking her away, and darkness settled inside the dome like the end of the world.

TZE DISCARDED THE suit like a shed skin and dressed himself once more in the kingly robes of blue and gold. The only conceit to the present day world were the handmade Italian shoes beneath the flaring curve of fabric. There were many vices that Mr Tze granted himself, but sometimes the simplest were the ones that provided the most pleasure. The shoes fitted him as perfectly as if he had been born with them, and with a sigh playing about his lips, the CEO of Yuk Lung Heavy Industries dismissed Deer Child and gathered himself.

He viewed the painting of the battle at Tsing-hsien on the far wall, cocking his head so that the clock concealed in the artwork became visible. Time, then. Time to consult once more with the players in the game.

Tze spoke a command word and the window glass went opaque, painting the room with thick pools of shadow where the light of the lanterns failed to reach. The door opened to admit the Hi woman and he gave her a cursory nod.

"Sir," she replied, her mechanical smile snapping on, then off.

Tze glanced at his hand, the one he had used to press Francis Lam's fingers into the blades of the ghost knife. "We have a moment before we begin…"

"The augurs report a perfect match, sir." She knew what questions he had before they were voiced. Tze liked that about Phoebe Hi. It was one of the reasons why she wasn't dead. "Genotype correlation is very good. Professor Tang was positively beaming when he gave me the news."

"I imagine he was," Tze noted dryly. "Where is Francis now?"

"Alice has taken him to Alan's apartment. She suggested we allow him to take the residence for himself. A good solution. Far easier than setting up another secured environment from scratch."

Tze nodded. "Commend her. Forward thinking should be rewarded." In the middle of the room was a shallow ceremonial bowl. The executive mumbled a cantrip beneath his breath and bit into his knuckle, letting a couple of drops of blood fall into the brass basin. "Link," he said to the air, and from hidden slots in the ceiling a cluster of projector heads emerged on silent spider legs.

A series of holograms blinked into life around the room, appearing in a circle around Tze and the bowl. Most of them were human, but one or two were simple black monoliths bearing the character for "silence". Hi found her place among them and bowed.

Tze gave the phoenix-eye salute. "Kindred, I have good news. Our pattern continues unaffected by the trials of recent days."

"That is gratifying to hear," said a figure in the uniform of a general in the APRC. "Contemplation of other conclusions was very nearly implemented."

Tze studied the man for a moment. Other conclusions, indeed. He knew for a fact that the general had prepared an attack by stealth bomber on this building, in case Tze did not give the answer he wanted. The executive bowed. "We move forward along the path the Dragon cuts for us. His ascendance is cemented."

A grim-faced woman in a blue Highrider jumpsuit drifted forward a little; the distance it had travelled from LaGrange orbit made her signal grainy. "What about the field test? I'm eager to hear the results."

"Your keenness is appreciated," said Tze. "Data is still in the midst of collation," he threw a look at Hi, "but early signs are good."

The Highrider nodded, her image pixellating. "Encouraging."

"But, the replacement…" said another man, a rotund Japanese in a Happi coat emblazoned with corporate logograms. "The quality is adequate, neh?"

"Very good," said Hi, unable to stop herself from blurting it out. "I would go so far as to say superior, even."

Tze silenced her with a gesture. "I have given Ms Hi my leave to ensure that the pattern continues to unfold as it must. The resources of my humble clan are at the disposal of this Cabal through myself and through her."

"And what about the Americans?" said the Chinese general. "This man Nguyen Seth in the Utah wasteland with his plans?"

"They call it Deseret now," corrected the Highrider. "It is of serious concern. Additionally, the Catholic Church is deploying more agents and there are incidents of Unknown Events in Rio Verde, Krakow and Swindon."

Tze's face turned into a sneer. "Oh, the arrogance of it. The Road to the Shining City must be marked out for the Dark Ones, yes? But marked by who?" He stabbed a finger at the air. "By them? Or by us?" He showed his teeth. "This is not the time for their empty words." Tze coiled his fingers into a ball, and where the blood still flowed from his ripped skin, it ran in red lines about his fist. "It is time for our potent deeds."

When the city-state of Hong Kong returned to Chinese sovereign control in 1997, the farewell to British Governor Timothy Brooke-Taylor was an emotional affair. Like all births, it carried pain and glory within it. That simple moment — the exchange of flags on a rainy night — was ~~the dawn of a new age~~ b3ginning 0f the end and a bold future for this cessp00l of lies ~~vibrant city~~. But that future did not come without struggle. The twin epidemics of avian flu and N-SARS they 5et it up0n us that swept the globe forced China to look outward and offer ~~hands of peace~~ bu11ets & hyp0crisy to her neighbour nations. In the first decade of the Twenty-first century, as lawlessness threatened the cherished freedoms of millions of ~~people~~ cattle worldwide, Hong Kong's unique status was endangered. China's leaders understood they w3r3 afraid that to go forward meant taking a leaf from the city's glorious past. In partnership with $ell Y0ur $oul 2 them her international corporate partners, Hong Kong was ~~reborn~~ destroyed. The creation of the Hong Kong Free Economic Enterprise Quadrant (HKFEEQ) opened the door to the c0rp0rates and l3t them turn this city in2 their private playground we ha7e lo5t 0ur tiny fr33doms and we must liv3 with @ GUN 2 our *heads where the law is as flexible as the creditchip in y0ur pock3t. Hong Kong is a city to be ~~proud~~ afraid of, and together the People's Republic of China and her m0neypimp friends will lead it to a future of death RUIN des0lation ~~greatness~~.*

Excerpt from *A Fragrant Destiny: A History of the Hong Kong Free Economic Enterprise Quadrant* by ~~Brian Hok Lik~~ a c0rp0rate lack3y and ca5hwh0re.

5. heroes shed no tears

OLD YEE SHOWED him a mouth of yellow tombstone teeth and gave Ko double the normal portion of curry noodles, taking the fold of yuan with his clawed fingers. Yee was from the mainland and refused to speak in anything but a thick dialect of Mandarin. Ko understood maybe one word in three, but he mostly got by on the fact that the old geezer liked him. He wasn't exactly sure why, but Yee made good noodles and his mobile stand always seemed to be open whenever Ko was hungry. He took a plastic bottle of Tsingtao and saluted Yee with it, then skirted the snake-buses as he crossed Hennessy Road. He made for the plaza, past the tourists being funnelled into large armoured people-carriers, great blocky things painted in gaudy tropical colour patterns that hid the snouts of stun nozzles.

The big holoscreen on the side of the CloudReach Shopplex was showing highlights from the day's endorsed track duels at Happy Valley, and Ko winced around a mouthful of noodles as it slo-moed the horrific impact kill of a G-Mek V12 Interceptor striking the barrier at three hundred kilometres per hour. The car gently disintegrated into metal shavings, and an overlaid graphic pointed out the instant when the steering column speared the driver. The betting results faded away and up came the BloodPool sweepstake. Ko fished in his pocket for his ticket and realised with a frown that he'd forgotten to get one that morning. He chugged a gulp of beer to wash down the annoyance. Around him, foot traffic slowed as other people stopped to see the lottery numbers. Ko was always fascinated by the way that people from the States or the EU went crazy with their hooting and cheering when they gambled. That kind of behaviour was alien to the Chinese mindset. Games of chance required the most serious mind, not the loutishness that the gwailos displayed, scaring off the spirits of good fortune with all their noise. The tickertape ran the numbers. Low fatalities during the race day were balanced by an industrial accident at Quarry Bay and a restaurant boat hijacking that went bad out at Aberdeen. Hong Kong's daily death toll was green for good, but without a ticket the score was meaningless to Ko. The holoscreen showed a streetcam view of the winner – a little woman in a viddysilk cheongsam – and the hesitant crowd around him broke up and melted away. Ko watched a little longer as the display went on to post scores for the state-sponsored manhunt going on over in Macao. That's how to make money here, he thought. Win it, steal it or kill for it.

He finished the cooling noodles on the way toward the Causeway Bay metro station, crossing the road through a plastic tunnel. The tube glowed as he entered it, the walls fading into a grainy CGI model of a sun-kissed beach. It was meant to seem like Ko and the other pedestrians were ambling along the edge of a tropical island but the swearwords and flyposters dotting the walls spoilt the image. Ko watched a poorly rendered copy of Juno Qwan smile at him from the tree line. She had her hands cupped and glittering indigo liquid ran over her fingers. He blinked as the sublims kicked in, making him feel twitchy, and stared at the fake sand beneath his feet until he reached the other end of the tunnel.

Ko had never seen a blue ocean. A memory popped in his head, bright and hard. The day Dad had taken them on a trip up to the Peak so they could look out beyond Hong Kong Island and out into the haze. Ko had expected blue, the azure glitter they showed on the vid; but instead it was all the same dirty bottle green that lapped at the piers on the Kowloon side.

Blue. Ko wanted a blue sea, a blue sky, an endless road. He wanted freedom, if there was such a thing, but the idea of it was so ephemeral and directionless he couldn't hold it in his mind for long. He was only sure of one thing. It would cost him money to get to the blue. He needed a big score to take him there, not the pissant pocket change he got from runs and road challenges. Ko sighed, crumpling the beer bottle in his hand. It wouldn't be enough to get there alone, though. Ko thought of Nikita and the drug packet. He had to get her away too, before the city saw her weakness and killed her with it.

He went over the road with the metallic woodpecker of the crossing indicator rattling in his ears, and just for a moment he felt his black mood lift a little. There, on the shallow concrete bank where they always gathered, he saw Gau, the Cheungs and Poon clustered around one of the public benches. As ever, a string of hyped-up subcompact cars filled the roadside parking spaces. Second's green Kaze with its black-tinted windows was there at the front of the rank, but Ko couldn't see him or hear his braying laugh.

Gau had a magazine foldout in his hands, and the rest of the gang were engrossed in it. Ko saw a wide expanse of pale female flesh.

"Not real," Little Cheung was saying. "You can see it's just a render." He pointed at one visible breast. "The tits are too good."

"Too good is never too bad," broke in Ise, tugging at his orange quiff. "I'd nail that, oh yeah."

"Can you find your dick with both hands?" Gau asked. "Naw, Little Brother is right. You can see this is a fake. They mocked it up using pictures of her from that photo shoot she did in Free Malaysia."

The image was of Juno Qwan, naked on a hardwood floor, cupping her breasts and wearing an incongruous little-girl smile. The image seemed off to Ko, too. It wasn't uncommon for the tabloid screamsheets to make digitals of the idols-of-the-moment and then put them in compromising positions, just to sell a few more issues. Big Cheung patted his belly and leered at Ise. "You wanna see them boobies for real, I gotta sense-disc of her. Load it inna skin suit and you could have her all night long…"

Ise snorted. "That's jagged, man. You keep your sick fantasies to yourself."

"Hey," said Ko as he approached them.

It was as if a switch had been flipped. The mood changed instantly, the air becoming chilly by degrees. People looked away, composing themselves.

Gau met his gaze. "Hey Ko. You drive in?" It was the standard conversation-starter in go-ganger circles, but it seemed stilted and forced.

He jerked a thumb over his shoulder. "In the shop." That was a lie; Ko's Ranger was parked in a multi-story a few blocks away, hidden behind a ferrocrete stanchion. He hadn't wanted to turn up on the street with it sporting the busted headlights that were Nikita's payback for destroying her Z3N stash.

"Huh," said Gau. "Right. Didn't think we'd see you tonight."

"Not after what happened…" added Ise, without looking him in the eye.

The air of easy banter had evaporated the moment Ko opened his mouth; now the vibe was frosty and strained. Everyone there wanted him gone.

"I'm missing something." Ko said in a low voice, the first flickers of annoyance catching inside him.

"Got that right," Poon said it so quietly he almost didn't hear her.

Ko fixed Gau with a hard look. "You want to help a guy out?"

Gau looked away. "Don't think I can, man."

Ko opened his mouth to speak, but Little Chung bounced to his feet and broke in. "Look, Ko. Out at the airport, that was off-book."

"What?" he retorted. "Like to see you jack a corp ride like that!"

"Yeah, but it was zero, chummer! You never did something so airhead!"

"Ko, man," said Gau, "Rikio was by earlier tonight. He said about what Hung did. You're giving us a bad rep. You shouldn't have popped a corp's car, that makes shit for the rest of us."

"You gutless fuckers," whispered Ko. "You're always on about a big score, but you never do anything except…" He swallowed hard as the conversation he'd had in the Vector came back to him. Making yuan off races and taking pinks where you can.

"All I'm saying is," Gau continued, ignoring the outburst, "you might want to go dark for a little while, man. Just… Stay off the scope."

"Stay away from us," added Poon, just in case the point hadn't been made strongly enough.

"Shit like racing we can get away with," said Ise, "boosting the wheels off some ubersuit gets us all ass-screwed." He finally looked at him. "You make it risky, Ko. You oughta cool."

He backed off a step and looked at the group. Poon, her face hard with dislike; Gau, morose and obdurate; the Cheung brothers indifferent to all; Ise angry with him. In that moment, Ko had never felt so disconnected from them, these people he called his friends. They were turning away from him to protect the stupid little bubble of their road-tribe.

The doors to Second Lei's Kaze gull-winged open and released a pulsing musical beat. Ko recognised the chorus to "Doppler Highway". Lei emerged from the car buttoning up his shirt, two girls in Mongkok Sabre colours following him out. Their lipstick was smeared and their eyes distant. Second spat into the gutter and rolled something small and glassy between his fingers. Even from a distance, Ko could see it was an injector syrette.

Lei threw him a snide look and grinned. "Lost your way, spooky? Want me to call you a cab?"

"You're a cab!" chorused the Sabre girls, giggling in breathy unison.

"Or maybe you'd like something else?" Lei approached him, rolling the injector over his fingers. He sniffed. "Just in. Better than gel caps. Just pop it to your neck and—"

"Ooooh." the two girls mimed the action. "I'm the pretty voice…"

"Pure," he grinned. "First one's free."

"Get lost," Ko snarled.

Lei's grin widened. "You should take a page from Niki-Niki's book, Chen. Be polite like your sister." He licked his lips. "Do me a favour? Tell her I got a new shipment, I'll give her a discount for her regular custom–"

Ko's punch landed squarely on Second's jaw and he staggered backward, bouncing off a parking meter. Ko's vision hazed red. "You give that poison to my family, you piece of shit?"

Second recovered and sneered. "Don't give it to her, spooky. She pays for it."

Ko threw himself at the bigger youth and swung out, his anger making the attack clumsy and poorly aimed. Second deflected the blow and landed a heavy fist in Ko's stomach. Ko recoiled, coughing.

"Is this guy not the dumbest fucker in the world?" Second asked the assembled gangers. "Brains of a wooden duck!"

Ko spat and hauled himself up. Second beckoned him to keep going. In the back of Ko's mind there was a voice that begged him to do what he always did whenever he ended up facing off with Second. Let it go. Walk away. If he took his licks and went home, if he stayed off the streets for a couple of weeks, they would take him back in and nothing would change. It had happened before, it could happen now. If he just walked away. If he just let Second keep his top dog place, if he just took the easy way out. He glanced at the others. They made no move to intervene, content to let the conflict play out and follow the dominant alpha.

"Be smart, spooky," said Lei, licking his lips. "Just walk away."

"I am *sick* of the easy way," said Ko, earning him a confused look from his opponent. With a jerk of his legs, Ko spun about and struck Second with a spin-kick that hit like a tornado, knocking Lei off-balance. Ko heard Gau swear under his breath.

The other ganger hit out blindly and Ko caught it, air blasting out of his lungs in a whoosh of sound. Lei's girls released a short twin scream, like the bark of a vixen. Second came up and retaliated with a showy foot-sweep that missed by inches; Lei's fighting was all style and no substance, based on the repeated viewings of a million fight films. Ko, on the other hand, had been sent to a Jeet Kune Do school by his father when Second Lei was still in shorts watching *Seizure Monster* anime. Ko's style was all about application of force, hard, direct and instant. He threw punches inside the "gate" – the zone of body mass where the nerve points congregated – and felt a satisfying crunch as a dozen expensive plastic ampoules shattered inside Second's pocket. He shouted at Ko and hit him across the cheek with a glancing, sideways blow.

Ko rocked back, stars of pain glittering in his vision. He chewed them down and sent a sharp kick at Second's shin. The bigger youth shrieked as Ko's shoe tore open the skin and fractured bone. Ko followed up with a strike that impacted Lei on the cheekbone and slammed his face into the driver's side window of his emerald Kaze. Glass shattered and the car alarm began to wail.

The sound was the cue for the gang to disperse, and suddenly Gau and Poon and the others were running for their vehicles, but Ko was ignorant of all that. He was on Second as the drug dealer tried to stagger away, hands clutched to the cuts on his sour moon face.

"No–" Second said, but Ko ignored him. Ko's mind was somewhere else now, in a place where every insult and hurt he had ever weathered was now being paid back tenfold on his tormentor.

By the time the police pulled Ko off and tasered him, Second's expensive Soloto mocksilk shirt was a blood-streaked ruin. The greenjackets threw him in the back of the drunk-tanker and the robot patrol wagon drove him into the holding cells.

Fixx got to the fence of Barksdale Field without tripping any of the Air Force surplus scent-sniffers that ringed the compound. Like almost everything within the chain link barrier, Barksdale was a junkyard of elderly and dysfunctional leftovers from the American military machine of the Nineties; barely fifty per cent of the hardware worked correctly, but the trick was knowing which half did and which didn't.

The sanctioned operative left nothing to chance. His quick communion with Papa Legba on the approach road led him off into the shallow scrub, and presently brought him to the fence at the north-west end of the airfield. Fixx removed his flexsword from its holster inside the long coat and gave the weapon an experimental twirl. It looked like a fat dagger in its collapsed state. He pushed the rocker switch in the hilt to "active" and held it horizontally in front of him. The blade warmed up and began to unfold, clicking and twitching. The memory-metal remembered the shape it had been forged in and became a long, thin streak of dull titanium alloy. It reset itself in less than ten seconds, and when Fixx was happy with that, he made two fast cuts in the fence, the blade blinking in the lacklustre starlight. No alarm bells rang; no barking e-dogs came running. He smiled and slipped into the compound, crossing the end of the runway in low, loping steps. He made a zigzag course towards the hangars, where harsh sodium floodlights bled their glare into the sultry Louisiana night.

There had been a time when a man would have been stripped and on his knees for daring to penetrate the security at Barksdale. Forty years ago, the USAF had flown fighter planes, bombers and tanker jets out of this concrete nest, going about the business of defending the United States of America. That had been before the Fuel Crash and the Food Crash and the Welfare Crash and… well, before it had all gone to shit. In a time when it was hard enough to keep Americans secure from other Americans, the military turned their power inward and left everything they couldn't afford to maintain rotting in the sun. Overnight, military bases became scrapyards as the government burned what they wouldn't recycle. It was only when the corporations stepped up to bail them out that places like Barksdale went from defending the nation to being a new piece of commercial real estate.

The energy cost meant that these days only the rich had wings; but there were still things that needed shipping transglobal, still cargo that had to get to the other side of the world and not with silk napkins, glasses of champagne and dinky little meal trays. SkyeCorp made that happen. They were the company that the companies went to when something had to make it around the globe, no questions asked, no damn passport control or t-wave cameras peering into the crates. SkyeCorp made a billion a day shipping "tractor parts" to greedy dictators or "baby milk" to covert gene labs. They owned a string of decommissioned air bases across the continental United States, and with them a fleet of ex-military transport aircraft in various states of disrepair. SkyeCorp lost one flight in every thousand; but there were plenty of mothballed planes out in the Nevada desert, their clients had insurance, and it was tough to complain when the manifest said that all that got mislaid were "machine tools".

Fixx hesitated in the lee of a rusted barn and studied the aircraft. One of them was a giant, a huge C-5 Galaxy, heavy like a pregnant albatross and low to the ground on a cluster of fat wheels. There was no cockpit to speak of, not in the sense that Fixx thought of it. Where the Galaxy had been built with a cabin for pilot and crew there was now a blank banner of plastic and steel, pockmarked with sensor pits and twitchy antennae rods. SkyeCorp didn't use human pilots for the most part. It was far more cost-effective to engineer out that whole part of the system and replace it with cheap logic circuits and bio-matter processors – that is, brain tissue harvested from high-order primates. The four-engine plane had its nose lifted so that container trucks could drive aboard and deposit their loads. He could see from his vantage point that the last items of cargo were already being secured; soon the nose cowl would drop and the Galaxy would amble out on to the runway. The jets were already spinning at idle – this flight was running late. Fixx dropped to his knee and rolled the bones on a patch of weed-cracked concrete. The pattern brought another smile to his face. Good choice. This bird would take him where he wanted to go.

There were a few men milling around the front of the hangar, some running cursory checks on the aircraft, others smoking and drumming bored fingers on the barrels of their rifles – aging Gulf-vintage Colt M-16s, as third-hand as the base and the transport jet. Fixx kept the sword close and moved in toward the hangar. He could have killed every man here with the

SunKings switched to deep reticule mode, but that would have brought the house down. No. Tonight he wanted to move in silence, leave nothing but footprints and take nothing but advantage. If he had to make a kill, it would be quiet.

The op kept to the pools of shade, shifting in and out of them under the cowl of the black long coat, a piece of the night moving here and there. He reached the back of the hangar and got in through a broken window. A hooter sounded from the front of the Galaxy, and he smothered a dart of surprise; but the alarm was only a warning as the transporter's nosecone began to droop, yellow hazard strobes flashing across the concrete. The cargo doors at the back of the plane were already shut, but a side hatch was still half-open. Fixx frowned. Shut or open, yes, but halfway? That seemed strange, but he had no time to consider the reason. The flight would go if he dallied, and there were things unfolding in distant places that needed him to be there. His free hand dipped into his pocket and worried the bones a little. Yes, he had to act, not think. Fixx sprinted from cover and launched himself at the hatch. He was in and had it shut just as the hooting siren fell silent. The jets were growling up to power and he felt a lurch as the Galaxy taxied from the hangar.

He glanced around. Cargo modules two stories tall crowded around him, and items that were loose inside made desultory clangs against the walls of pressed steel. There was an alley between them that he could make it down if he held his breath, and with the sword leading the way, Fixx got to the front of the jet. What light there was came from the dull yellow glow of biolumes on the cargo gantries and the handful of plexiglas portholes in the fuselage. The Galaxy rattled and howled as it took up a waiting position at the end of Barksdale Field's Runway Left.

Fixx glanced around for some corner where he could seat himself and that was when he noticed the door. The cargo container on the starboard side, yellow with a red pennant that said "Tao Ge Shipping", made a creaking noise. The metal doors that sealed the contents in were unlocked, and one of them hung open. Each fresh vibration of the engines made the door shift a little. Fixx considered the guns again, then ignored the thought.

A stray round might punch through the fuselage. Bringing the sword to guard, he approached. He was maybe a metre away when he saw that there was blood on the handle, and more in a spatter pattern on the deck. Fixx lashed out and yanked the door hard. It came toward him with a squeal of poorly oiled hinges, revealing a sea of dirty, terrified faces.

At the front of the women – and they were all females – there were two girls in prison-surplus jumpsuits. They looked at Fixx like secret lovers caught in a tryst, and between them they held on to a man whose throat leaked red, whose struggles were getting more and more feeble by the second. The man had his trousers and underwear halfway down his legs. One of the girls held a bent piece of metal in her fist, the end of it wet with gore.

Fixx lowered the sword. The container was full to bursting with human cargo, thin and emaciated girls, all of them oriental. Joshua would have said Korean, if he was pushed, but he was no expert. They stood there, the jet screaming around them, the unlucky guy bleeding out, watching each other. Fixx knew the look in their eyes well enough. These women had gone beyond the point of no return.

The would-be rapist burbled something and went slack. His killer went to work stripping his body for anything useful. The other girl – the intended victim, he wondered? – had a nasty wound on her arm. Fixx finally sheathed his weapon and dug out a pocket medipack from his coat. "You speak English?"

The girl shook her head and took the packet, tearing it open with her teeth. The plane shuddered and began to move, picking up speed. Fixx sniffed and sat down, bracing himself against the hatch. The women, some of them fretting, copied him. In moments, there was the gut-wrenching motion of take-off. Cold crept into the cargo bay as they ascended into the night.

Fixx had a couple of packets of Insta-Kibble (*Swells In Your Stomach! Easy On Your Wallet!*) that he'd intended to eat on the way. He tore them open, and with great care, broke them into enough pieces for everyone. The erstwhile passengers sat there in the rattling chill, chewing on morsels and regarding each other with wary eyes.

Fixx settled back and drew in his coat around him.

I will tell you, if you care to listen, something of cruelty. It is a uniquely human conceit; you will not see animals indulge in it. What of the cat, I hear you ask? The cat that torments and toys with the mouse? Ah, but Brother Cat is only training himself, using his prey to stay quick and deadly. He is no crueler than the virus that strikes down the newborn, or blinds the artist. This is simply the manner of nature. As it is the manner of man to be cruel.

And so my story. Look around in the shops selling effects of the past to visitors from over the oceans, the places that overflow with bowls in black lacquer, careworn jade and the litter of a thousand years of history. Inside one day you may see terracotta warriors, the clothes sculpted upon them the same as those worn by the swordsmen of that era. Some date back to the Qin Dynasty, when China was a feudal land and ruled by the blade and the pen.

In that time, there was a man, an Emperor, who greatly feared the world beyond death. He had killed so many of his enemies that surely they would be waiting for him when he perished, a war band of ghosts with the curse of his name as their last earthly memory. This man, this Emperor ordered an army of the red stone men made to accompany him into the other world when death came to claim its price. More than three thousand of the pottery soldiers were forged – regiments of footmen, archers, soldiers with spears or crossbows, charioteers and horses – all of them to be buried with their dead lord in a great tomb that was planted with trees and grass so it would appear to be a natural hill.

And so the man, the Emperor, died, and the army of stone was created. As this work went on, an act of cruelty came to pass.

A man, a swordsman, a simple fool with nothing of the Emperor's greatness in him, a soldier in the real army upon which the facsimile was based, earned himself the ire of a minor warlord in the late Emperor's service. It is not written nor remembered, what this simple fool's misdeed was, but it was so grave – or perhaps, the warlord was so cruel – that it earned him a living death. The soldier was beaten senseless and pushed into one of the moulds used to make the terracotta men. He suffocated in there, seared to his demise and baked into the stone, bones and flesh buried along with thousands of identical mannequins.

The warlord later perished in battle and sank to the Nine Hells, as he deserved. But his cruelty extends to this day. The simple man remains lost, his bones encased in one of thousands of stone statues. Where they are, his spirit will never know. His peace is denied to him, forever.

This, then, is man's cruelty. Better to be the cat's mouse, neh?

Chinese Legend

6. dreaming the reality

THERE WAS A crackle of static on the wall screen, and the camera remote lit red to show the broadcast was going live. The woman's face faded in. "Thank you, Shania, for that update. Now, I'm joined live by Heywood Ropé, manager and psychic nutritionist for pop sensation Juno Qwan. As our viewers will know, Juno's sold-out tour came to a alarming conclusion in the stilt-city of Newer Orleans when an apparent domestic terror incident led to the hospitalisation of several audience members. You're watching ZeeBeeCee's *Entertainment Pulse* and I'm your host, Tammy Popeldouris." The honey-blonde woman on the screen inclined her head and smiled at Ropé. "Heywood, good to have you on the show."

"Great to be here again, Tammy." He returned the smile, matching her tooth-for-tooth. "Juno wanted me to express her sadness at not being able to make the interview herself, but as you can understand, the events of the last twenty-four hours have been difficult for her." Ropé showed a mask of concern, dressed with a slight sadness.

The reporter mirrored him. "Indeed. And the question Juno's fans are asking is, how is she?"

Cue reassuring smile. "She's resting, Tammy. Even without what happened at the Hyperdome, a ten-city tour across NorthAm takes its toll! But she's fine, really. If anything, Juno is more worried about her fans, who she loves so much. After the incident, she asked me to send a generous donation to the NOLA Medicareplex, and with the help of our friends at RedWhiteBlue we're doing just that." He gave a calculated shake of the head, rueful and sad. "Those poor, poor people…"

Tammy spoke to her audience. "Juno is of course at the moment on her way back to her native Hong Kong aboard her private jet – click the green spot on your d-screens for more information or to purchase a virtual replica." Her expression became neutral. "Heywood, what's your take on this awful event? From what the local police franchises report, it seems that a group affiliated with the America Alone Alliance Army were responsible for the sabotage of lightshow display equipment at Juno's farewell concert."

A frown. "I'm no political expert, Tammy, I'm just a guy who wants to bring great music to the world. But we've all heard of the A4 and they've made no secret of their dislike of foreign entertainers on their shores… Look what happened in New York, a couple of months ago…"

Tammy nodded. "You're referring to the so-called 'Brown Noise' attack on a concert by the British opera singer Robert Williams at the Carnegie Bowl. Viewers can hyperlink to ZeeBeeCee's coverage of that incident by touching red on their d-screen."

"Frankly, I think this is a failure on the part of the American law-enforcement community to properly police their country." He leaned forward to display his seriousness. "Tammy, let me tell you that some people suggested that Juno should not come to America… But Juno did not want to disappoint the fans, whom she cares for so very much."

"And those fans wish her well, Heywood. Here at ZeeBeeCee we've been inundated with emails asking after her. But regarding the incident at the Hyperdome, how do you react to stories we've been hearing that several audience members were attacked by…" She glanced at a data-screen. "Here I'm quoting… 'an angel of death'?"

Ropé's expression remained unchanged. "People under stress see many strange things, Tammy, and while our security do the best they can to screen out any attendees under the influence of illicit substances, some do sneak through..."

A nod. "An interesting point, Heywood. Only recently, I believe that the Mothers For Meddling attempted to bring a civil suit against Juno's publisher, RedWhiteBlue, for what they alleged was 'pro-drug use' symbology in her songs."

He allowed himself a moment of irritation. "Tammy, really. Those women are a group of middle-class busybodies with too much time on their hands, looking for scapegoats to blame for their poor parenting skills." He swayed as the jet bumped an air pocket. "Let's not forget their unfounded smear campaign against Senator Michael J Fox."

She smirked, content at having been able to raise a flicker of anger from him. "Back to the fans, then. The other question on their minds — and on ours, of course — is the truth behind the rumours that Juno will headline the so-called WyldSky concert on Hong Kong's Victoria Peak. What can you tell us, Heywood? True or false?"

Ropé waited for a count of three before answering. "Tammy, Juno is a very private person, as you know, and she certainly has a lot of respect for the independent positive-future groups involved in WyldSky. But I couldn't possibly comment as to her intentions on this matter."

"Here at ZeeBeeCee we've heard that Juno's publishers are actively trying to dissuade her from having any connection to WyldSky given the markedly anti-corporate stance of the event—"

He held up a hand to interrupt. "Tammy, Juno is a strong-willed and very intelligent young woman. She isn't going to let some suits tell her where and when she can't sing."

"So you're saying she's going to be there?"

A broad smile. "I'm saying anything is possible, Tammy. That's what I love about my job... I get to see the impossible happen."

The interviewer laughed. "Cryptic as ever, Heywood. Well, that's all we have time for..." The woman turned away and the screen stuttered into blackness. The remote's red eye dimmed, and Ropé saw one of the techs make a throat-cutting gesture. He stood, resisting the urge to spit.

"Are we done?"

The tech nodded. "Good job, Mr Ropé—"

"Don't flatter me," he growled, the face he'd worn during the interview shifting into something cold and immobile. "Where's our diva?"

"Still in her cabin. Her telemetry is a little wavy but it's inside normal tolerances."

Ropé bent to take a look out of the nearest window. Through the oval he could see glimpses of a black glass ocean and the steady blink of a red running light on the tip of the jet's delta wing. He turned away and made for the compartment where his mobile office was located. "Don't disturb me for anything less than the end of the world, understand?"

THE BED ENVELOPED her with coils of warm rope, sweat-hot sheets finding places for themselves to knot about her pale skin and torso. Juno tried very hard to remember how to make herself scream, but the method of it was lost to her. In a broken, detached way she saw the component parts of her thought process fall out of her mouth in coloured blocks of sound. They broke into pieces that smelled like dark.

Eyes where her mouth should be, words for tastes and noises for colours. Everywhere there were mirrors. Talking mirrors that screamed and cried or made sounds that could have been songs. She carefully recited the lyrics to "Halo Kisses" but discovered she could only remember them backwards.

Juno dragged herself off the bed and her bare feet touched the floor. She felt the singing of the wings through the fuselage, and imagined the footless depths of sky around her. She giggled and opened her arms wide. Closed her eyes and drifted over a mirror sea. Mirror see. See mirror. Mirror. *Mirror—*

She was on the floor in the corner of the room.

Flash/blink/change.

Coiled up like a foetus, shivering and afraid. Clothes ripped. Air heavy with fear. Juno's breath came in bolts, she forced it through her throat. There were invisible hands at her neck, twisting.

The girl pulled at her own hair and felt the way the flesh on her face moved. She felt wrong in this skin, the shape too tight, hung wrongly across angular bones. Juno watched the worms gather in the shadowed corners of the room. They didn't know she could see them. In the dark places they were piecing together the mirrors she had broken, fixing them when her back was turned. They left the little pieces on the floor where she could stand on them. The fragments would slip beneath her skin, work their way to her heart.

Blood taste on her tongue. She remembered being inside the egg floating in the dark waters. She remembered the screaming people who loved her. There were the angels of pain overhead – and there was the dark-skinned man. Dark like blood. Dark like sky. She would never see him again.

She began to cry as the walls grew teeth and the worms marshalled their forces. At her feet there was the needle, shiny and long and candy-bright. It ended in a bulb of perfect blue, beckoning and glistening, calling to her. With shiver-tremble hands she probed to it and gathered it up. It almost fell into the sky, she could barely keep it in her clammy fingers. "Buh-bubble inna stream,"

Juno discharged the injector into her eye and went into quiet shock.

THE CABIN DOOR sealed behind him and in the gloom Ropé crossed to the desk and took his seat. The window blinds were open slightly, slow-lidded eyes peeking a faint sky glow into the compartment. He licked his lips and touched a hidden control in the desk; obediently, a silent panel yawned open to present him with a drawer lined in rich purple velvet. Nestled inside was a book made of rusted steel. As they always did, the edges of the pages cut him when he removed it. Ropé clasped it in both hands and felt the thin streams of his blood pooling in the pockmarks and scored channels in the tome's cover. His thumb was ripped gently as he stroked the meat of it over the spine of the book. Where the blood marked out the age-worn letters it was possible to see something of the title: *The Path of Joseph*.

Ropé very much wanted to open the book, but that would have taken more of him than he wanted to give at this moment. There would be time, later. Time enough. A device in the desk chimed, and he bared his teeth. "I said not to disturb—"

Already a screen was erecting itself out of the desk's featureless top, and blinking in the corner of the display was the oval logo of RWB. This was an incoming call, a live feed overriding all his personal lockouts. There were only a few people who could do that.

He had the book concealed and his hands knotting beneath a towel when Phoebe Hi's face blinked into life before him. Ropé always thought she resembled a misassembled Darbie doll, a perfect It-Girl head wrongly attached to a tubby little body. This he kept to himself, showing the required degree of deference to his superior.

"You spun that Popeldouris bitch well. The political opinion we could have done without, though."

He shrugged. "It seemed right for the moment. It also allows RedWhiteBlue to distance itself from me. You know, 'these views are the personal opinions of Mr Ropé and not those of RWB, et cetera, et cetera.' I'm providing plausible deniability."

Hi shook her head. "Don't build up your part, Heywood. Your job was to ensure that the consumers will accept the talent's appearance at the Victoria Peak event as spontaneous on her part, an expression of free will."

"I doubt she even understands the meaning of those words."

"We want the consumers to feel unfettered, Heywood. You understand how important that is to the work." She paused. "How have things progressed since we spoke last? Any improvement?"

Ropé gave a dry chuckle. "If anything, she's grown worse. I'd like to remind you that I was against the idea of an American excursion. Too far from safety, too many distractions, too much input too soon—"

"Those choices were not yours to make," she broke in. "You would do well to remember that."

"Of course," he allowed. "Fix the problem, not the blame, neh?"

"Exactly." Hi leaned into the screen, filling it with her face. "We have the remote feed here, Heywood, and Tang's people concur with you. The instability you brought to our attention is of great concern, and I think at this stage we cannot proceed without instigating the more serious of options."

Ropé considered this for a moment. "You're quite sure?"

"Quite," repeated Hi. "A liability is not what we look for in our talent, Heywood. Can I trust you to deal with it personally?"

"And the...?"

"Preparations are being made," she said, silencing the question before he asked it. "We've leaked the party to the press. Expect a significant presence there."

"All right."

Hi cut the link and left him in the dimness. Faint shafts of light crossed the walls as the aircraft began a languid turn toward the distant city.

Ropé studied the ruins of his hands, watching the blood clot and scab over.

AT SKYHARBOUR THERE was an advance guard of machines waiting to capture the first images of Juno Qwan's triumphant return to the city of her birth. In the car park outside Chek Lap Kok, news mobiles from a dozen different networks sat in a ring, like circled wagons from the Old West. Troopers from the APRC, reluctant to look lazy on international television, patrolled around them. The go-gangers knew better than to show up tonight.

There were few human reporters in place at the arrival gateway. Only the nets at the very lowest end of the spectrum or the stringers clinging to their hopes of an exclusive, had bothered to send flesh-and-blood representatives. Stations like Wave-Net, ZeeBeeCee, Scramble News Network and CanalEuropa had posted squads of avatar drones, a gaggle of the brightly coloured remotes floating on ducted impellers or resting inverted on the ceiling. The insectoid machines deployed probes with wideband cameras and omni-directional microphones. Behind their unblinking glass eyes there were operators half a world away running them through goggles-and-glove interfaces.

SNN's drone, fire engine red with a buzzing, counter-rotating heliblade, spotted the party first and it launched itself at them. The other remotes went after it in a string of chattering motors.

Juno was behind a pair of thick polycrys sunglasses by Minnuendo. Her hat was an Inverse Smile original, a wide-brimmed sunshade in the Loren style. She wore a Dior delta dress and her shoes were from Westlake. The clothes, the way she walked, the turn of her head — all of it was engineered to say "leave me alone". Around the globe, automatic pattern scanners were taking the measure of her attire; the same outfit would be on sale in knock-off stores within less than a day.

Ropé led the entourage, a couple of the more popular band members trailing behind and a circle of four men from RWB's Overt Security Team surrounding Juno as she entered the glare of the floating cameras. One of the security men carried a handheld microwave field generator to discourage the drones from coming too close to the group. Wave-Net's remote made the mistake of drifting near for a candid shot and it clattered out of the air, landing on its back, legs kicking feebly like a gassed cockroach.

In their respective virtual studios, anchors from the networks were matted in to the live footage, smart transfer programs making it appear to the viewers that the reporters were actually there at Chek Lap Kok with the singer. They called out questions to her, but Juno excised them from her world, never acknowledging them, never glancing their way. Her face was set and thin-lipped beneath the Minnuendo shades. Ropé threw the armada of robots a clipped wave that signalled the end of this brief photo opportunity, as the security men ushered Juno into a waiting limobus. All the networks showed the same shot of the coach pulling away from the terminal with an escort of two APRC patrol cruisers. The flanks of the double-decker were a screen, and as the vehicle moved off a vid of Juno singing a cover of "Stage Fright" from her Malaysia tour rippled across it. Each station turned back to studio-bound talking heads who picked apart the brief flash of celebrity, examining every second of the footage and speculating on the singer's mindset. Several new rumours about Juno's love life were created spontaneously in the time it took the bus to emerge from the Western Harbour Tunnel on Hong Kong Island.

If the drones at the airport had been the scouts, then the armies were waiting in the courtyard of the YLHI tower. Legions of reporters – real human ones this time – jostled one another for a glimpse of the starlet as her ride came to a stately halt outside the opulent entrance. Ropé stepped out first and took Juno's hand. The girl's foot touched the stone steps and ignited a lightstorm of flash strobes and camera floods. She hesitated and turned her head up to look at them. Somewhere along the way Juno had ditched the sunglasses. The singer threw the world her dazzling smile and with a playful flourish, she took off her hat and spun it into the crowds where her fans pressed in a hundred people deep.

"Hello Hong Kong!" she called, her voice chiming like crystal. "I love you." She blew kisses and detached herself from her manager in a jubilant pirouette. Juno skipped to the closest reporter, a local correspondent for the Chinese State Channel, and beamed at him. "I'm so glad to be home again," she said, "I've missed my city and my friends so much."

Her behaviour couldn't have been more different from the cold aspect she displayed at the airport, as unlike as night and day. The crowd roared, jarring the stunned journalist to life. "Miss Qwan, what are your plans now you're back?"

She flashed that billion-yuan smile again. "I'm going to have some fun and unwind, but you can be sure I'll be singing for you all very soon."

The elation crossed the courtyard in a wave. "Are you going to perform at WyldSky?" called the reporter as she drifted away from him.

Juno laughed and threw him a coquettish theatrical wink. The chorus of her name followed the starlet into the building like radiance from the sun.

"Here we are," said Alice, as the elevator chimed. The doors parted and a wave of laughter and music swept over Frankie. He followed her out into the atrium. They were somewhere close to the upper levels of the YLHI tower, below Tze's jade castle. A broad open space some three storeys high, the atrium was a festival under glass, a classical string quartet in one corner, a massive indoor waterfall in the other, and between them knots of people indulging themselves in whatever was on offer. Frankie spied tables laden with wines and liqueurs, others with endless swathes of food, including what had to be real meat. There were more discreet offerings too, vircade pods in the shadow of the stone pillars holding up the roof, or circumspect waitstaff with dishes of capsules and droppers. Alice handed him a flute of champagne and he sipped it gingerly.

"Make yourself comfortable," she told him. "Mingle."

"Right," he said, covering his hesitation with another sip. Over the woman's shoulder he saw Phoebe Hi and a group of ruddy-faced men. He blinked as he recognised Lasse Illstrom among them, the CEO of the Midgard Securities Group; only last month the Norwegian billionaire had been on the cover of both *Business Week* and *CORP Magazine*.

Alice glanced around. "Do you like films?"

Frankie blinked. "Uh, sure, I guess."

She nodded. "Do you know that man? He's an actor."

"Where?" Frankie turned to see Hazzard Wu in close discussion with three men who could only have been the Wachowski Triplets. He was miming the motion of cocking a handgun. "Uh… Yeah. I think so." The more attention Frankie paid them, more A-list faces came into view about him. He saw the lead drivers from the Tiger Beer highway duel team, the host of *You're Out, You Loser*, a few senior men wearing officer tabs from the Army of the Peoples Republic of China. Alice excused herself for a moment and Frankie decided to sample some vat-grown salmon.

"Try the little crab things, man, they're preem."

Frankie turned to see the lead vocalist from Charlie Fish, an indie band who were big with the ghettobomber crowd in SoCal. He blinked.

"What?" drawled the singer.

"Nothing… I'm just, well, surprised to see you here. Your music, its all that anti-corporate stuff…"

Frankie received a weak smile. "Oh yeah. Well. We all gotta change some time, right?"

The man wandered away and Frankie found himself at the window. He dropped onto a comfortable sofa, and his hand drifted to the PDA in his pocket. He popped it open and studied the files Alice had reluctantly given up when he pressed her about Alan's death. Yuk Lung had used contacts with the metropolitan police division to unlock the incident report, and here it was in brutal colour on the palm-sized screen of the handheld. The cops said Alan had been walking along a Mongkok side street when a car had hopped the curb and slammed him into a shuttered storefront. He died on impact, so the coroner's report had it. The car and driver hadn't been found, but eyewitness testimony suggested that the attack had been gang-related. The conclusion was a triad hit gone wrong, most likely a case of mistaken identity. Not that this made dealing with it any simpler. YLHI had already dealt with Alan's remains, cremating him and placing the compacted ashes in a bullet-sized capsule, to be buried in the company memorial park overlooking Clear Water Bay. Frankie paged through the data again. It was all blurring into one long string of dispassionate scrawl.

"Francis," said Mr Tze, his reflection appearing in the window like a waking phantom.

Frankie snapped the PDA shut. "Hello, uh, sir."

Tze gave him a paternal smile, and Frankie absently rubbed his hand, tracing the lines of the knife cuts. The strange little ritual had unnerved him more than he wanted to admit. Tze guided him off the sofa and back towards the party. "I want you to enjoy this evening, Francis. Put behind you the pain of things past and look ahead. Will you do that?"

He managed a nod.

"That is good," Tze took a capsule from a passing waiter and swallowed it down in one gulp. "We're on the verge of a new acquisition. Something that is going to alter the landscape we move through on every level. Yuk Lung's reach will truly be global, and we will need men like you to take us there."

"Me?" Frankie let out a laugh. "Honestly, sir, I'm flattered you think so much of me, but I'm only a minor echelon executive. I'm not sure I have the right stuff—"

"You do," said Tze firmly. "I don't want men who look good on paper. I want men who have spirit." He prodded him in the sternum. "*Courage*, Francis. You're not some milksop choirboy with an MBA. You came from the street. You have an edge that none of these men raised on the corporate teat can even grasp at. I want you to make that available to me. I want you to understand that your participation in Yuk Lung's future plans is, in a very real way, of universal importance. I know that you can fill the terrible void left by Alan's passing. I know it. He knew it too, Francis. He told me so."

"Really?" Something rang a wrong note in Frankie's mind. Not since they were teenagers had Alan been one for brotherly love.

"Oh yes. And there will be rewards the like of which you have not dreamed." He leaned closer. "Men crave power, Francis, all of us. I can give it to you, if you have the will to claim it."

Something deep inside Frankie was forcing its way up, and it manifested in a feral smile. He thought of Alan's dismissive emails, of Burt Tiplady and a hundred overlooked promotion opportunities, of a lifetime of second place. It all came together in a hot rush. "Yeah," he said quietly, "I'd like that."

Tze guided him over to the elevator stack as the doors parted, and the crowd burst into a round of rapturous applause. A cluster of men emerged and parted to let the executive make a gesture of presentation. "Francis," he smiled, "may I introduce you to Miss Juno Qwan?"

Her perfect eyes met his as she stepped from the lift and Frankie's heart skipped a beat. "Hello." He felt a spark of attraction flash between them.

"Francis," she said, smiling like a supernova, extending her hand. "Dance with me?"

TZE LEFT LAM and the singer to fall into one another and passed Hi with a curt nod. The woman had done well, once again turning a problem into an advantage. He would have to keep Hi on a tighter leash, less she begin to entertain thoughts above her station. The three girls he had chosen for his comfort tonight smiled at him from the shaded table where he had left them.

Deer Child approached. The Mask had a woman in his grip, half-guiding, half-dragging her. "Sir."

"Is there a problem?" He turned an appraising eye on the girl. She had a lean, wolfish look in her eyes, and he saw immediately that all her clothes were cheap street copies of current trendsetters. He smelt greed and fear on her, and there in her eyes was the telltale glint of blue.

Deer Child handed him a silver smartcard. "There appears to be an anomaly with this young lady's invite, sir."

Tze turned the card over in his hand. The code was well past expiry. "What is your name?" he asked the girl.

She flashed him a sultry look, cool and practised. "Nikita."

He smiled slightly. "I once knew an assassin with that name. Are you here to hurt me, Nikita?"

"Only if you want me to," she whispered.

Tze's smile broadened. The girl was putting everything she had into it. He handed the card back to the guardian. "I see no problem here. Bring the young lady a drink at my table." He offered her his arm. "Join me?"

"I'd love to," said Nikita, and followed him into the shadows.

http://junofans.rwb.vnet/r584923921/chatroom_enable
Halo_kisser Has Entered The Chat Room.
Junofan14342: hi halo
Rusty: hlo
Halo_kisser: hi yall
Goth*Lolita: it was preem
Goth*Lolita: I was nr teh guy who got her hat grrr. Missed it.
Goth*Lolita: Juno looked sooooo good. I [heart] her!
Halo_kisser: u were there? OMG OMG sooo jealous!
Rusty: G*L lives in Honk Kong
Rusty: sorry Hong Kong [grin]

Goth★Lolita: number 1 fangirl!

Junofan14342: how did JQ look? She not on ZBC Pulse.

Goth★Lolita: beautiful!

Rusty: did u see pix from airport? She was v.moody

Halo_kisser: not. How would u feel after NO crazeeness?

Rusty: seem weird 2 me.

Goth★Lolita: everything weird 2 you rusty!

Junofan14342: yeh rusty sez secret messages on junos discs!

Rusty: TRUE

Halo_kisser: is not, you R looped, rusty!

Goth★Lolita: I posted pictures from my eyecam on my site - [link]

Junofan14342: cool. Swipe 4 my wallscreen!

Rusty: did ne1 read netfeeds about NO concert? Mad reports off samizdata grids

Junofan14342: [frown] that stuff is jagged, rusty! Illegal u should not read!

Rusty: just want to know about juno

I_Witness Has Entered The Chat Room.

Goth★Lolita: was ne1 at NO concert?

I_Witness: me. I was there w my sister

Junofan14342: bet it was good

I_Witness: r u high? Concert was psycho! They freaked us out!!!

Rusty: I heard it was AAAA screw w lasers

Goth★Lolita: yeh they h8 all j-pop

I_Witness: not AAAA. Thatz bull[censored]! I saw monsters in there!!! My sister is coma'ed!!!

I_Witness: corp cops told us to be quiet!! It was insan@~}{*%£$£....

I_Witness Has Been Suspended.

RWB_Moderator Has Entered The Chat Room.

RWB_Moderator: Hello, friends! Please don't be alarmed, but our records have flagged the user identity [chatname=I_Witness] as a known alias for a convicted sexcriminal.

Junofan14342: OMG! pedo!

Rusty: WTF?

RWB_Moderator: Because of this intrusion, this chat room must now be closed for a reboot. Please feel free to log on again at the central JunoFans nexus. We apologise for any inconvenience. Juno thanks for your friendship!

Halo_kisser: w8 stop what about
http://junofans.rwb.vnet/r584923921/chatroom_TERMINATED

7. sex and zen

THE RED TAXI hurtled along Nathan Road at a speed that seemed far faster than was sensible. On the dashboard, a warning clicker snapped at the driver like an angry cicada. The small man behind the wheel had stuck a piece of adhesive tape over the illuminated display that read "Slow Down Now!"

Fixx took it in his stride, at every intersection where the chorus of horns serenaded the wild turns the driver made. On the sunshade there was a photo of the diminutive cabbie in his younger years, grinning out from under a Kevlar army helmet on the bonnet of a burnt-out North Korean jeep.

The blocky cityscape of Kowloon seemed to go on forever, flat towers of pastel-painted apartment blocks and multi-level shopping plexes crowding in over the street. He peered up through the plastic bubble roof. The gaps between the buildings were festooned with huge signs folded out like clipper sails, some of them holographic but most made from steel plate and old-fashioned neon tubing. The riotous glow of advertising vanished up into the night sky. Here and there he could see where the uppermost levels were being used as apartments – long strings of washing dangling out, dropping soapy rain on the streets far below. According to the signs he could read, there were schools and churches up there too, even a public swimming baths. Most of the neon was directed at more commercial endeavours, though. At the ten to twenty floor mark there were restaurants, nightclubs, casinos and vircades; it was only on the levels that were in sight of the ground where the constant marketplaces of the megastores roared, day and night streaming out goods of every stripe. Fixx wondered where all the money came from, where all the purchases went. There were only so many consumers in this city, he imagined. The cab vaulted into a side road and down a narrow chasm between two massive city blocks. The constructs loomed overhead, layered with retrofitted floors in stripes like the layers of sediment in a rock face. The cab turned and turned again, jarring Fixx in his threadbare seat. He was having difficulty keeping track of where he was, the warren of alleys challenging his sense of direction.

The vehicle screeched to a halt in the sullen glow of a shuttered door. Fixx saw the street number he wanted over a caged lamp and he swiped a creditchip across the pay-sensor. The red car was gone before he reached the doorway.

The entrance led him downwards. The basement was uncharacteristically cool, a welcome change to the blood-warm Hong Kong night. He came across a thick hatch, the kind that submarines had to keep out the crushing pressures of the ocean. It spat out gusts of air and opened just as he was about to knock on it. Fixx ran a fingertip over the SunKings in their holsters, just to be sure, and entered. The first thing he noticed were the mixed scents; ozone, a faint whiff of old meat and cat piss.

"Hey, Fixx." The voice was slow and agreeable. "Just hold still a moment."

It was dim down here, hard to see anything beyond racks of skeletal metal shelves and the giant seedpod shapes of NeoSoviet bio-matter processors. Fixx noticed a wall of stripped TFT screens, some of them showing television channels, others with grainy feeds from street cameras. An emerald laser fanned the room, washing across him.

"Say something," said the voice.

"How's retirement treatin' you, Lucy?"

There was a chuckle in the reply. "Joshua. It *is* you. That's lovely. Come closer."

Fixx relaxed – but only a little – and did as Lucy asked. He had the distinct and slightly unnerving sensation of walking into the centre of a web. Cables as thin as hair and as thick as his arm snaked along every surface, disappearing into holes laser-bored through the walls. They terminated in banks of glittering LEDs, arranged in a ring around a single object. Roughly the height of a small child, it was a khaki green cylinder made from heavy impact plastics. The glow from the machinery revealed hooded boxes holding numerous litter trays and pop-top cans of cat food. Fixx became aware of lazy slitted eyes studying him, maybe a half-dozen felines lounging on the warm spots atop the processor stacks.

"Spider to the fly…" The words came from a vocoder welded to the cylinder's outer casing.

Visible along the surface of the object were a string of letters: *USAMRID* and then *Mod.# LU(c)*. Panels had been removed since the last time Fixx laid eyes on the unit, and components removed.

"You lost weight?"

"Charmer. Just some modifications."

Fixx found a folding chair and sat himself in front of the screens. He fingered a low-hanging wire. "Nice place you got here."

"Better than where I grew up."

Fixx nodded. Lucy's origins had been in a blasted wasteland in the Dakota NoGo, assembled by government techs with a budget too large and a shortfall of morals. They'd made her software self-aware in order to create better and more horrifying bio-toxins, but Lucy had other ideas.

She sent invites for her coming-out party to some sanctioned operatives who could help with her "confinement issues". Fixx scratched his thigh absently, in the place where a bullet from that night's work had raked him as they exfiltrated. Poor Haley Joel had died out there to liberate Lucy's mainframe core. "You're keepin' busy?"

"Yes. This part of the world is data-rich. The Chinese have a thing about numbers. It's a good fit for me, small beer for the most part but then I like the low profile. I'm trading information for wattage and bandwidth, plus my special projects."

"Like the cats?" He gestured at a ginger tom that ambled past him with an air of regal disdain.

"I'm doing some research, collating data. I hope to Uplift them in a couple of years. In the meantime, I use local talent for any legwork."

"Right." Fixx noticed a replay on one of the screens: Juno Qwan stepping off a bus and into a glare of publicity. His eyes narrowed.

"Joshua," Lucy began, "You didn't come halfway around the world to reminisce. What are you doing out here?"

"Following an inklin'," he said, still watching the screen. "I need to call in a marker."

"Okay."

"I need a vehicle and some walkin' around money."

A couple of lights blinked on the khaki box. "I can do that for you. Give me a second, I'll talk to the boys in the Wo Shing Wo." She paused. "This have something to do with that planeload of women who landed in Zhuhai?"

He flicked a glance at the machine. "You know about that?"

"Male-to-female ratios on the mainland are off the gauge, Fixx. Fem-smugglers are coining it in up country, so naturally folks will talk about it when a C-5 full of girlflesh goes rogue."

"They deserved better. This way, they get to pick and choose when they have kids, not get locked in a breeder farm."

Lucy chuckled. "Same old Joshua. Fighter for the underdog."

Fixx looked away. "It ain't about the women. That was just what you might call an ellipsis. I'm lookin' for something different." His eyes strayed back to the screen.

"I pay my debts," said Lucy. "Car's outside now."

"Merci, mademoiselle." He gave the cylinder a pat.

"Hey, you like her?" Lucy brought the images of Juno on to all her screens. "I'm running hacks of her new album for the Temple Market pirates. You want a copy?"

Fixx shook his head. "I prefer to listen to the real thing." He tickled the ginger cat and wandered away toward the door. "Stay well, cheri."

"Watch your step, Joshua," called Lucy. "This place, they do things differently here."

"You know," said Frankie, "I think every man in the room hates me."

Juno smiled, watching as his face wrinkled a little as he spoke, watching the look in his eyes that reminded her of a playful child. "Oh really? Are you such a bad guy? Should I not be dancing with you?" She let him lead her around the room, orbiting the musicians on their dais.

He returned the smile. She liked it. He had an easy way about him that came through when he stopped being nervous. "No, it's just that every one of them wishes they were me, and they'd love to see me trip or impale myself on some potted plant."

Juno laughed. "If it makes you feel any better, every woman in the room hates me too."

"Maybe. But that's because you're the most gorgeous person here, not because *you're* dancing with *me*."

She gave him a mischievous look. "Are you sure?" It was strange. She'd met him tonight and yet she felt like they had been friends for years, that she knew all about him. The moment she stepped from the elevator, she'd wanted to be with him.

He laughed back at her, and it made her feel good to share that. "Aren't I supposed to be flattering you?"

Juno shrugged. "I hear it every day. It's nice to be nice to someone else for a change."

Frankie swallowed hard. "You, uh, you can do that any time you want."

And she was smiling again. There was something about this man, something that hovered at the edge of her thoughts, ephemeral and ghostly. He drew her, and Juno couldn't be sure why. She tried to probe the impulse but it fell away, down into dark places where she didn't want to follow.

He saw the shadow pass across her face. "Are you all right?"

She shook her head. "A little tired. It's been a busy few days."

"I'll say. I'm surprised to see you here, straight off the plane and up for a party. I thought you'd rest a while first, get over your jet lag."

"There are pills for that," she said with an airy wave. "And I wanted to celebrate coming home." They swung past one of the windows and she took in the city beyond the tower with a sweep of her hand. "I love Hong Kong so much. I feel like I'm seeing it for the first time."

Frankie followed her gaze. "Yeah. I… I know how you feel."

"I'm just so glad to be back." She felt it like an ache in her chest. "I don't ever want to leave again."

He frowned, and it spoiled his face. "I heard at your last concert… There were problems."

"Would you mind if we didn't talk about it?" she replied automatically. "I don't want to dwell on… on dark things." The gloom at the corners of her mind shifted and she blinked it away. Remnants of memory, faint and fading like afterimages, glistened in her thoughts. The droning murmur of the jetliner engines. A grey numbness. Water on her lips and face. Juno shuttered the pieces of recall, turning away from them. Back here. Back to Francis.

She let herself fall into his gaze. He had kind eyes.

"What's wrong?" he asked, the words catching in his throat.

"You're not happy," she said. "Tell me why."

And he did; he spoke about Alan, about the way he'd been torn from the comfortable-but-mundane life he knew in America and spirited back to his homeland, about his fears and uncertainties. It spilled out of him in a rush, and Juno listened to it all. Frankie needed someone to confide in, and she found herself touched that he chose her. On an impulse, she leant in and stole a kiss from him.

"Wah," he managed. "Uh. Thanks."

"You seemed to need it."

He smiled again. "You're not what I expected. In Los Angeles, I dealt with people from the entertainment sector sometimes, stars. They were always so hostile, so anxious. But you… You're alight. It's like you're radiating warmth."

"There's that flattery," She blushed. "Those people? I feel sorry for them. They're afraid – of losing, of falling out of favour, of wearing the wrong clothes. But not me. I have exactly what I want. I get to do what I love." Of its own accord, her hand traced his cheek. "Make people happy."

Frankie coloured. "It, ah, it's working on me."

"Juno, darling," The music came to a gentle finale and Ropé was there, nodding politely. "I hate to press you, but there are people here–"

"Oh, of course," said Frankie, disengaging. "I, uh, I'm sorry if–"

Juno drifted away from him, and sent him a dazzling smile. "Don't be. We'll talk more later."

FRANKIE WATCHED HER melt into the partygoers and blew out a breath. He licked his lips. His palms were sweaty and his pulse was racing. The moment Juno was gone from him he felt almost a physical need to have her close again. He shook off the sensation and snared a drink from a passing waiter. The tumbler of Glen Fujiyama went down in a single jolt.

"Quite something, isn't she?" Mr Tze crossed his line of sight, four girls in unfocussed disarray following him in a loose gaggle. "It's hard not to fall for a woman like that."

"She's a fantastic dancer," he said lamely, bereft of anything better to say.

Tze laughed, a brusque bark of sound over the music of the string quartet. "Of course she is." The executive gestured at the girls with him. "Francis, some of us are retiring to the private suites. Perhaps you'd like to join in?"

"Are you Mr Tze's protégé?" asked one of the women, the hint of a predatory smile on her doll-like face.

"He may well be, Nikita," said Tze. "Francis has a shining path set out before him."

Frankie gave a shallow bow. "Thank you, sir. I'm, uh, grateful for the opportunity."

The girl, Nikita, extended a hand to him. "You're coming, then?" The other women giggled.

His stomach knotted with disquiet. Tze's women looked at him with calculating eyes. Frankie felt like he was beneath a microscope or pressed on to an auction block. "Perhaps later," he mumbled. "I'd, ah, I'd like to enjoy the party some more."

There was the very smallest flash of annoyance in Tze's expression, but then it was gone so fast Frankie wondered if he had imagined it. "Of course. Later."

Nikita tossed a last look at him as the group vanished into the depths of the atrium, to the chambers and rooms hidden in the shadows.

He watched the party diffuse, the people drifting away or coming together into small knots of murmured conversation. He spotted Juno's manager but each time he crossed the atrium to find him, Ropé was gone when he got there. The pillars of creamy green jade and the artfully strewn furniture made the chamber difficult to navigate.

As Frankie crossed and re-crossed the room he became aware of a shift in the mood around him. The melange of genteel conversation and light amusement had faded, and in its place was a shady ambience, a sense of secrets and harsher humour. Startled, he happened on a couple in one of the booths engaged in slow, mechanical sex while a dozen silent spectators watched. Both of the performers were blindfolded with silk ties that bore the YLHI corporate logo, and their hands were fixed to a seat frame in the same manner. The spectators were breathing in a chorus of rhythmic, gasping breaths. One of them offered Frankie a tray of blue capsules and he shook his head, backing away.

He stumbled into Alice and half-stuttered an apology. She eyed him. Somewhere along the way she'd lost her ornate jacket and the red silk blouse she wore was open, revealing a glimpse of breasts beneath.

"Hungry?" she asked. Her eyes were glassy but there was a challenge in her flat tone.

"No."

"Liar." She pushed into his personal space, crowding him. "You want something more plastic, is that it?" Alice walked lazy fingers over his jacket and pulled his glass from his hand, swigging the contents. "Go on then," she snapped, turning her back on him. "Go play with your dolly." Alice wandered away, unsteady.

Frankie glanced around. Suddenly it seemed everywhere he looked, there were bodies pressing bodies and the taint of drug haze in the air. He felt flushed and uncomfortable. Sure, he'd been at corp raves dozens of times, seen drink and drugs and sex tossed around like party favours, but here it seemed... *darker*.

Cautiously, he walked out of the atrium proper and into the shadows.

Tze closed the door behind Nikita and nodded at the other girls. They had been here before and they knew how things were going to play out. Nikita flashed him a look, a heady mixture of fear and arousal in her dull eyes. He showed her where the suite's small bar was and ordered her to make some drinks. She did so, eyeing the door now and then, thoughts of bolting warring with her baser, more avaricious instincts.

He wandered about the room as the other trio took items of equipment from the hidden compartments beneath the wide, burgundy-coloured sofas. Tze feathered the dimmer control on the discreet lighting control panel – he liked the gloom to be thick and warm – and started the recorders concealed in the walls and the ceiling.

There was a bowl of blue capsules on the low table in the corner, and next to that a flat metal case the size of a hardcover book. It was cold to the touch, condensation speckling the surface. Tze tapped it lightly and the lid sighed open, letting a waft of white vapour escape before he reached in and took out two glassy rods. He glanced up. The girls had the rig fixed up, straps and spars dangling from the rings fixed to the ceiling. They played a quick game of rock-scissors-paper and the blonde was the winner. Nikita returned from the bar with two highball glasses and she stopped short as she took in the scene. The other two girls were stripping the blonde, binding her into the cruciform support frame.

Nikita blinked and backed away a step as Tze crossed to her and took his drink. "Hard to know what to think, isn't it?"

The other women giggled, and began to toy with one another, taking capsules from the bowl.

Tze rolled a blue caplet between his fingers, and despite herself Nikita licked her lips when she saw the glittering Z3N embossed on the side. There were hundreds of the pills in the receptacle.

"Don't be shy," Tze smiled, offering her the tablet. The smile turned into a laugh as her free hand shot out and snatched the Z3N capsule. She washed it down with a sip of her drink.

"Good," he said. "We're getting somewhere." He nodded to the other two women. They opened a cabinet on the far wall to reveal a dozen mirror-bright arcs of surgical steel within. Giggling, they each selected a curved blade, wicked and sharp as a raptor claw. Eyes glinting, they descended to the blonde's bare flesh and began to cut on her.

THE PRIVATE CHAMBERS ranged away along the darkened corridor. Each had lights above them, some dark but most illuminated. When Frankie pressed his ear to the doors, there was nothing but silence. A chill went through him. The rooms were soundproofed. Anyone could be doing anything in there and nobody would know. He turned in place, his hand trembling, and then at random he tugged at a handle. To Frankie's surprise, the door opened without resistance, and brought with it a draught of potent human scents. He peered in and his throat went dry.

The room was so dimly lit that it was barely possible to be sure of what he was seeing, but he could make out the forms of men – one of them was one of the APRC officers he'd seen before, wearing nothing but his uniform jacket – coiled on the floor and snarling like animals. He saw flashes of female flesh in there, and violent rutting caught between the motions of sweating, scratched bodies. Someone was crying, and the sound of it drew Frankie's attention to the ceiling. There was a man up there, ebony screws as fat as a finger holding him in place where they punched through his ankles and wrists. Skin hung off him in flayed strips, wet red meat showing in the half-light. The unfortunate's face was twisted in agony, tracks of black tears crossing cheeks laced with complex scars. Frankie recognised the man: Ping, from the airport, the careless one who had lost the escort car.

He retreated in shock, forcing the door shut, and his heart almost stopped when he realised there was someone towering over him in the corridor. A hulking mass of a man, it was another of Tze's masked guardians.

"Participants only," rasped the figure. The Mask was white and black, hanging there like an apparition. The stylised face belonged to Judge Bao, a character from the Peking Opera stories of the Song Dynasty.

"In there—" Frankie gasped.

"What are you looking for?" said the guardian.

"Juh-Juno—" he managed.

Judge Bao pressed a hand into the small of his back and guided him away. "Over here, sir. I'll take you to her."

Frankie stumbled on, his mind reeling, the healing scratches on his hand stinging.

NIKITA'S FACE WAS waxy with shock underneath her make-up. She was aware that her lip was trembling, and in the back of her skull she could feel the first cool tendrils of the Z3N hit unfolding. It seemed unreal, some horrific vidshow instead of a real performance happening in front of her. Tze's women were opening up the skin of the blonde in turned petals of pale flesh. When the stink of copper touched her nostrils she gagged and stumbled back a step.

Tze's broad hand shot out like a striking cobra and enveloped hers where she held the glass. "No, no. You're not going to leave."

She tried to deny him, but he closed his hand tighter, crushing the skin and bones. The glass made a cracking sound.

"Don't lie to me." He squeezed and the glass shattered. She cried out as the fragments bit into her palm.

Nikita looked to the others with a pleading stare, but they were busy drawing intricate shapes on each other in spilt blood, a confusion of lines and symbols.

Tze took a handful of her blouse and ripped it off her. He drew his finger through her cut hand and used her vitae to draw a design on her trembling breast, just above her heart. Two discs, one larger than the other, connected by a line that was in turn bisected with an arc. Tze unbuttoned his shirt to show her the same shape rendered as a tattoo on his chest. The lines were made of dragons, eating each other's tails.

"Please don't kill me." She forced out the words.

He smirked and showed her the glass rods. They were long and thin, rough-hewn. Nikita was reminded of icicles. Inside each of them was a reservoir of actinic blue liquid, glittering like stars. In spite of everything, her mouth immediately flooded with saliva.

"Pure," said Tze, seeing the reaction in her eyes. "A thousand times more potent than the weak tea you're used to." He jerked his head at the girls, who were scooping handfuls of capsules into their mouths, crunching them down like candy.

Then he moved, quick as lightning, and buried the first of the needles through the middle of the pattern he had drawn on her. Nikita crashed to the floor, a white-hot shock rushing though her. She glanced up, hovering on the edge of awareness, in time to see Tze stab himself with the other rod.

Nikita's world broke open, drowning her in floods of chilling blue. Tze loomed over her, a towering god wreathed in noxious smoke and shimmering darts of painful colour. From behind him, tendrils of liquid night emerged and snaked over and around his body. They stabbed out and penetrated her, rushing through her flesh and savaging her mind. She could not speak.

Tze displayed a terrible aspect. "Greedy child. You wanted to taste my air, dared to know the glory of my world, yes? It will be my pleasure to give it you. Shall we see if your pitiful cattle-mind can grasp such beauty?"

He dominated her senses, blotting out everything. Tze opened the stygian halls of his psyche, and let the horrors within rush to fill her.

Nikita looked at the truth of him in the eye, and she shattered.

JUNO BLINKED AND realised that she hadn't heard a word of the twittering platitudes of Phoebe Hi. She found herself staring into the depths of the champagne glass in her hand, locked on the shifting shapes of the rising bubbles. They shaded black as she watched them ascend, turning into tiny ebon pearls.

"Juno?" said Phoebe. "Did you hear what I said?"

She nodded, tearing herself away. The conversation area, raised up above the main level of the atrium, was secluded and quiet; but the singer suddenly felt enclosed in there, the long shadows around the delicate lightstands growing even as she watched them. Her stomach turned over and she shivered. Juno's hand wandered to the back of her neck, where her skin felt cold and clammy to the touch. There at the corners of her vision, dark motes swarmed, just as they had when she tried to touch her memories of the disastrous concert. She shifted uncomfortably, the wide sofa too big around her. Juno felt lost in it, tiny and small.

"I... I'm sorry." She forced a smile. "Perhaps it's just travel fatigue." The words seemed like a lie. Colour was bleeding out of her vision in little increments, and there was a pressure in her ears. There were only a handful of people in the room, but she felt like there were thousands crowded around her.

"Can I get you something?" Hi was watching her carefully.

"Juno!" She turned at the sound of Frankie's voice – and for a moment, the gloom around her retreated. He saw the look on her face as he approached, and his kind eyes clouded. "Are... Are you okay?"

"Better now," she said, with genuine feeling. On an impulse, the singer put the half-full glass down on a table and stood up. "I think I'm going to retire for the night."

"I'll arrange transport to your hotel—" said Hi, but Juno shook her head.

"No. Frankie's taking me home." She took his arm and guided him away.

"I am?" he said, nonplussed.

She almost ran as she led him by the hand up towards the helipad levels. The shroud of unease dogging her retreated, and she gave Frankie a brittle smile. "I want to go," she said. "Please?"

"Of course," he replied, sensing her disquiet. "But I don't have, uh, clearance for a spidercopter."

"I'm Juno Qwan," she said. "I get anything I want."

Hi frowned as Ropé sat in Juno's vacated seat. He toyed with her glass. "You're not going to intervene?"

She sneered. "Why would I? It was my idea in the first place. It's an ideal way to expedite two problems at once."

He shook his head. "You haven't lived with the talent as closely as I have, Phoebe. You don't see the variables, the off-pattern behaviour."

"This is a necessity," she said, an edge in her tone. "The talent will do what it is told to do."

Ropé covered his derision with a sip of champagne.

When it was over, when the women began to clean themselves down, Deer Child entered and dutifully handed Mr Tze a fresh robe.

"I have ascertained the origin of the stolen smartcard," said the Mask. "It belonged to a grade three accounts executive in Section F. What manner of severance package would you prefer me to implement?"

Tze gestured at the bloody walls. "Bring him up here. Keep him for our next recreation."

"As you wish." Deer Child gave a slight incline of his impassive porcelain face toward Nikita's pale, trembling form. "Disposal for this one?"

Tze considered the question for a moment. "No," he said finally. "Throw her back. An object lesson to be seen and considered by any other pickpockets or grade three executives with poor judgement."

"Your will." Deer Child picked up the catatonic girl and carried her away.

Tze watched them go, fingering the spot where the wound in his chest had already healed.

See these mighty buildings, all shall be torn down, shattered, splintered, split.
   [static]
The Earth herself will tremble and the masses will go hungry.
Their bellies bloated, skins hanging in folds.
The sky will open upon itself unto darkness.
These are the birth pains. No flesh will be spared.
No flesh will be [static]

No lives will be spared but for the Elect. No lives but the Cabal.
And they will know The Coming.
And the Beast will task his agents to a mission to gather together their cohorts.
The city of the sleepers will dream in their name.
[static] war between the agents of blood will conclude.
The new void will rise to smother the old.

Intercepted transmission #5932-02, recorded by Maritime Offensive Force submersible Ameratsu, broadcast location unknown.

8. young and dangerous

Ko had the small of his back pressed into the corner of the holding cell, legs pulled up on the foam cot, knees to his chest, his head flat against the cold wall. With mechanical boredom he was ripping pea-sized balls of material from the mattress and flicking them across the short distance to the stainless steel toilet bolted on the far wall. The dots of foam landed in the murky, stinking bowl one after another. The plastic-coated sides of the cell were made of some kind of wipe-clean germicidal supersynthetic that was way past the need for replacement. Decades of enterprising criminals had whiled away their confinements scoring their names into the plastic or leaving obscenities that railed at their petty injustices. Mostly, the graffiti was of the kind that suggested certain law officers engage in anatomical impossibilities, or attempt sexual congress with their mothers.

The depressing familiarity of the narrow room weighed down on the young man, and he masked a heartfelt sigh with a move of his hand, letting his fingers wander across his face and through the dark spikes of his hair. Ko carefully probed the places on his ribs and legs where the coppers had struck him.

There would be a colourful horde of bruises there to greet him when he undressed.

He considered Second Lei for a moment. How badly had he punished that half-witted fool for his arrogance? Something had opened a floodgate to every jibe and ridicule Ko had ever turned a blind eye to. He'd always thought he was big enough, cool enough to rise above that sort of thing; Ko imagined that the slights and snipes just rolled off him, vanished into the air. But that wasn't how it went at all. On some level, deep in his marrow, he remembered every one – and when the moment came, they returned in a hurricane of fury. Even now, here in this small place, hurting and cramped, a faint smile came to Ko's lips as he thought of how much he had enjoyed beating seven shades of shit out of that fat prick. The smile faded as he imagined what Poon and the Cheungs and the others would say about it, though. Ko had broken a Rule. Quite how or where the Rules got codified or created was beyond him. Somehow, the group would unconsciously come to accept that a certain thing was just the way it was, that certain words or deeds would not come to pass within the sphere of their tribe. Mouthy, over-confident Second was a living avatar of that mindset. He was the self-styled big dog of the Pak Sha Road Posse, a braggart whose only real superiority over the rest of the gang was that he had slightly more money than the rest of them. Truth be known, if Second was so damn cool, then why the hell was he hanging out on street corners, fucking kogals and hustling Z3N? Second's ambition ranged to getting recruited into the 14K triad and that was about it. Ko didn't dwell on the fact that his own life goals were even less defined.

The weird state of grace in the group, the idiotic dynamic of it, the whole thing seemed progressively dumber the longer Ko thought about it. Second didn't deserve to be the top gun. He had a good car, sure, but he wasn't that hot on the road; he was like the annoying kid who owned the ball when you wanted a kickaround. You had to let him play and throw his weight about, just because he could take it home if he wanted to. Everyone just turned a blind eye to it, they just let it go because it was easier to eat his shit and ignore it than it was to deal with the alternative. And now, Ko had crossed that line and extradited himself from the only friends he had.

"Friends? That's a joke."

He saw it now, plain as daylight. It was inevitable that one day the button would have been pushed, that Ko would lose it and turn the kung fu he'd learnt under Sifu Lee's tutelage on the supercilious asshole. Second hadn't even put up a good fight. If the police hadn't come along, there was no telling how it might have ended.

He glanced up and there was Feng, rail-thin and glum, standing in the opposite corner of the cell. "Those people are worthless," said the swordsman. "Be glad you've left them behind. You were wasting your life with them."

Ko wanted to be; but instead Feng's words annoyed him. "I don't want another bloody lecture from beyond the grave."

"You know it isn't a lie. Those fools were all wastrels."

"And you're not?" Ko snapped, the anger of the evening returning to him. "The proud, noble ancestor, warrior of the ancient days?" He mimicked Feng's voice. "Things were better in my time. We had honour and courage. Did you shit! You're just as bad as me, greedy and self-indulgent!"

Feng's face clouded. "Don't take it out on me because you're a failure, boy!"

"Why? What are you gonna do, haunt me some more?" Ko shook his head. "You ain't gonna do that, who would you get to buy you smokes?"

In spite of himself, the swordsman licked his lips.

Ko's head drooped, his anger fading. "Ah, screw it. This is it." He prodded the ragged mattress with a finger. "Enough is enough. I'm getting out of here. I'm sick of living like this."

"What are you talking about?"

"This place, Hong Kong. I'm done. I'm going to escape from this city even if it kills me." He leaned forward. "I'm going to get money and go, take Nikita and leave it behind."

"How will you do that, exactly? You've got, what? A dozen yuan to your name?"

Ko gave Feng a hard look. "I'll find a way."

The warrior's head snapped up to face the heavy steel door. "Company."

The observation slot in the metal hatch irised open to reveal a bored-looking trooper in APRC fatigues behind an inch of armoured glass. "On your feet, citizen."

FRANKIE ROLLED OVER as gently as he could manage, keeping his eyes closed. He wanted to make sure that it hadn't been some kind of strange fever-dream, a weird melange of fantasy created by too much jetlag and too little sleep; but no, as impossible as it seemed, there she was at his side. Her chest, unblemished like newly fallen snow, rose and fell above the edge of the silk sheets, and gentle breaths escaped the pursed flower of her lips. Juno Qwan lay naked beside him, as stunning in repose as she was on the billboards around the city.

"Wah." Frankie whispered, and a grin emerged on his face as the evening rewound in his mind's eye. They had fallen into the apartment entwined around one another, a peculiar hunger for human contact compelling them. Her kisses were electric on his lips and her skin, her perfect flawless skin, rose up under his touch. She discarded clothes worth more than a year of his former salary in ragged heaps as they crossed the lounge. With steady hands, she steered him toward the bedroom. They fell into each other, and with the lights of the city cast through the windows of the chamber, Frankie and Juno had made love, orbiting the room until they set down on the bed and began again.

He saw it in snapshots: the strobe of a passing advertisement blimp painting red and blue across her breasts as her back arched. Her hands on him, guiding him in. Juno's hair, free and wild, crossing his chest. The taste of her. The sparkling chemical impact as they met orgasm together, synchronised and stormy. Everything else but her seemed faint and pale in comparison, faded images held against a vivid holograph.

Frankie felt the lazy beginnings of an erection as the fresh memories surfaced; but there was more to it than the sex. He felt strange, a peculiar sense of ease here with her, a realisation that there had been a missing piece to his life and now here she was, completing him. He shook his head and looked away, smirking. *Where did that come from?* he wondered, *I'm mooning like some love struck idiot!*

Dawn was coming up over the skyline of Hong Kong Island, turning the mirrored towers honey gold. The light moved across the walls of Alan's former apartment, illuminating his tasteful Mondrian prints. Carefully, Frankie slid himself out of the bed without disturbing Juno's sleep and padded across the room, grabbing a dressing gown. He gave her another look before he went into the bathroom, watching her at rest there. Man, she is gorgeous!

But what was going to happen next? Was it possible that a guy like him could actually have some kind of a realistic relationship with a woman like her, a pop star whose face was on the bedroom walls of a million teenagers? Hadn't he seen something last month on Tiplady's screamsheet, about Juno dating Brook Beckham? Maybe this would be a one-night thing for her, an amusement park ride, there and then gone. Something for him to tell his grandkids about — yeah, Juno and me, we had a thing — but nothing real. When he thought of it like that, it made Frankie's chest ache. He didn't want it to end that way, wham bam thank you salaryman. He thought of the look in her eyes when they kissed, the melancholy, the loneliness. It made him want to hold and protect her. She wanted more than that, he was sure of it. He saw the mirror of his own isolation in her, the same disconnection, the same darkness.

Darkness. Frankie looked into his reflection over the bathroom sink and frowned. Now he found his thoughts drifting back, past the thrills of last night and into disturbing recollections of the party at the YLHI tower. The sense-memory of blood came back to him with such force, for a moment he gripped at his hand, convinced the knife cuts had opened up again. Half-seen things began to unfold at the corners of his vision, and Frankie snapped his fingers to halt them, shaking the thoughts away. Forget that. I'm here now. With her. Not my business.

He went to work washing his face, then halted when he couldn't locate any soap. There was a cabinet within arm's reach and he peered inside. Rooting through dozens of bottles of expensive aftershave and skin balms, his fingers closed around a plastic disc. He brought it to eye level and peered at the object.

Inside the coin-sized case was a memory spike, and on the flag of its tail was a single word printed in tiny characters.

Brother.

THE POLICE TROOPER walked Ko through the detention section and up the broad stairs to the main level of the precinct house. The place was alive with the morning shift, young men in green uniforms and slow-eyed older guys who had the paunchy, ex-boxer look of career detectives. The actinic glow of dozens of monitor screens gave the place a chilly look at odds with the sweat-warm temperature. It was a single open room fenced off into threadbare cubicles with proper offices boxed off around the outer walls. Watery sunshine leached from skylights across the ceiling. The station was a mess of retrofitted Twenty-first century technology and clumsy beat cop hardware from the Eighties, fat plastic telephones side-by-side with datascreens.

A squad of Special Duties Unit constables were gathered in front of a stuttering holotank as he passed them by. The men were all featureless beneath full spectrum gas masks and the blank bands of optical rigs. They wore matte black clamshell armour festooned with snap-clips for ammunition packs, grenades, heartbeat sensors and leaflet dispensers. On their backs were the sponsorship logos from their corporate partners, a pattern of symbols like those on the jumpsuits of arena drivers but rendered in discreet grey-on-black. They carried guns that blinked and whirred in standby modes. The heads of the SDU men bobbed and moved as they talked among themselves, but Ko heard nothing; their helmets were sound-sealed and they communicated on encrypted radio frequencies.

By contrast the trooper who nudged Ko along the way was at the opposite end of the spectrum. He had the puppy-fat and slightly moronic look of a mainland country hick, filling out the dull khaki uniform of the Army of the People's Republic of China, Incorporated. There was a holster at his waist and in there, Ko knew, was a palmprint encoded CNI 10mm revolver. He'd seen the damage those pistols wrought on human flesh more times than he liked. The copper stopped him outside an office and rapped smartly on the door. A voice inside called out and the trooper jerked a thumb. Ko sighed and entered.

The man behind the desk wore the same uniform as the bored trooper, but his epaulets showed the silver badges of a chief inspector. The officer waved Ko into an empty seat across from his desk as he finished something on his screen. The teenager didn't need to study the face of the inspector. He knew it well. The jowls where he was getting old beyond his years, the false tightening of skin from treatments at the NooYoo Clinic. The man had the sort of schoolboy face that seemed better suited to a funnyman on the vid than an aging cop.

Ko held a contrite look on his face as at last the inspector looked up at him. "Hey, uncle. How are you?"

The policeman frowned. "Don't call me 'uncle', Ko. You're not a child anymore, even if you do act like one, picking fights in the street."

"Sorry, sir," he said with a nod. "Inspector Chan, sir."

"Better," replied Chan and shook his head. "Ko, what are you doing? I thought you were smart enough not to get caught? I know what you're up to out there, boy, don't think that I don't. But I can't turn a blind eye if you're right here in my damn precinct!"

"Sorry," Ko repeated. "Things... got out of hand."

Chan made a noise of agreement and Ko saw a blink of images on his monitor: streetcam shots from the road showing the fight, stills from Second Lei's juvenile arrest records. "That's one way to describe it." The older man blinked slowly and gave the youth a level stare. "You were eight years old the first time you saw the inside of a police station, do you remember?"

Ko sighed. Here we go again...

"Your dad brought you in to show you what he did for a living. I locked you in a cell just to give you a scare and you punched me in the gut for it." He looked away. "Next time I did that, it was nine years later and you'd run a police cruiser off the road in Wanchai. And here we are again. How many times is this, now?"

"You tell me, uncle. Uh, inspector."

A scowl passed over the police officer's face and he threw up his hands abruptly. "Ah, fuck it!"

Ko blinked. He'd never heard his father's old partner swear in all his life.

Chan shook a finger at him. "I'm tired of giving you the same bloody lecture every time we cross paths, you delinquent! I don't want to hear it again!"

"That makes two of us," said Ko.

The older man moved faster than his years and dealt Ko a savage slap about the head. "Don't get cocky, boy! The only reason you haven't been sent down a dozen times over is because I owe your father my life! I promised him I'd look out for his kids... I can't do anything about that wild sister of yours, but you..." He leaned closer. "What kind of man are you growing up to be, Ko? You're a disappointment!"

"More than you know," said the teenager quietly.

"I know you got good in you. I see the flowers you leave on the old man's grave." Chan sat back down, fuming. "Your father forgive me, but this is the last time. I'm not covering for you any more. From now on, you're just another go-ganger punk to me, understand?" He rapped on the desk. "You need to get your head straight. You should be looking after your sister, not wasting time on the roads."

Ko felt something shift in his chest; he thought about what he'd said in the cell and there was a sudden surety inside him. "You're right, uncle. I'm getting out."

Chan's face darkened. "And Nikita? You're not just going to leave her in the hospital?"

Ko's blood ran cold. "Hospital? What are you talking about?"

The policeman's face shifted. "Oh, hell. Don't tell me you don't know..."

"Know what?" His voice rose in panic.

Chan's pleasant face turned sad and compassionate. "Nikita was admitted to Saint Theresa's. They said it was a drug overdose. She's critical."

ALICE HAD YET to provide a replacement d-screen for the one Frankie had lost in the car, so he had bought a basic tourist PDA from the In-Shop Micromall in the apartment block. His throat went dry when he input the spike and a security program began a regimen of questions; it asked about people he went to school with, about where he'd hidden his copies of *Playboy* as a teenager, the name of the first girl he ever slept with. Things that only Alan would have known the answers to. He locked the door to the toilet and sat on the edge of the bowl, hunched over the book-sized screen, growing anxious with every passing moment.

Finally, the programme was satisfied and it opened to him. There were gigs of data on the memory needle, and he flicked experimentally through them. Most of the files had warnings promising censure and contract termination if they were viewed outside a Yuk Lung Heavy Industries database. Frankie understood that his brother had plundered proscribed levels of the company's deep storage, illegally copying a king's ransom in sensitive data. Even from a cursory examination, he could see that there was enough here to earn billions of yuan on the open market. If the spike fell into the hands of a rival like Eidolon or GenTech, YLHI would be destroyed.

Frankie swallowed hard. Alan, an industrial spy? It hardly seemed real. He was set for life in his upper tier posting at Yuk Lung... There was nothing any other corporation would have been able to give him that was better. There had to be another reason why he had been collating data...

A sudden, chilling thought struck him. The label on the spike. *Brother*. Alan must have left it for Frankie to find, a message of some sort. Had he known he was going to die? And what if...

The palmtop shook in his hands. He could hardly bring himself to think it.

What if Alan's death wasn't an accident?

The knock on the toilet door made him jump with fright, and the little PDA slipped out of his hands and across the tiled floor. "Wait!" he piped, "Just, uh, just a second!" Frankie flushed the toilet and gathered up the PDA, stuffing it into the pocket of the gown. He wiped sweaty hands on the towelling and forced a smile as he opened the door. "Juno, hey–"

"Mr Lam, good morning," Monkey King filled the doorway before him, steady as a statue. "My apologies for disturbing you."

Frankie utterly failed to keep the shock from his face. "What…?"

"Miss Qwan has an appointment at the Ocean Terminal Mallplex. I'm here to escort her."

"Yes. Of course."

Juno emerged from the bathroom wearing a man's tracksuit ensemble. She gave him a deep kiss and smiled. "I'm borrowing this, hope you don't mind."

"No. That's fine. It's, uh, was my brother's."

She traced a finger over his cheek. "I have to go." Her face softened. "See me again, Frankie? Say you will?"

He nodded, unable to find the words. Juno kissed him again, and followed the masked man out. On the threshold, she tossed him a jaunty wave and was gone.

Frankie stood there for a long time, his mind in turmoil. The palmtop in his pocket felt like lead, heavy with terrible possibility. Alice had told him that Alan's death had been a mistaken assault, but now a tide of suspicion was rising.

I have to know for sure.

His hands tapped at the air. But where could he turn for help? Hong Kong was an alien place to him now, and he had no doubt that Tze's people would never give him leave to investigate on his own. He needed someone on the outside. Someone who knew the street.

Someone who had connections.

KO FELT THE colour drain from him in a sick rush. In the hospital bed, Nikita was barely visible beneath a network of plastic tubes and sensor wires. Machines painted in the same leaf-green as the walls were clustered around the girl's sallow face, chiming in time to her heartbeat. His sister's chest rose and fell in ragged jerks, her breath disordered through the oxygen mask clasped over her nose and lips. Beneath closed lids, her eyes fluttered and moved.

He staggered forward, some part of him wondering if Dr Yeoh had brought him into the wrong room by mistake. This pale thing in front of him hardly seemed real enough to be Nikita, dear Niki with her explosive temper and her flashing I-dare-you eyes. The woman on the bed was a faded copy of his sister, washed out and thin as tissue paper. This was some weak facsimile.

"She was admitted in the early hours of the morning," the doctor said, her voice calm and measured. "A police unit found her in Kowloon Park. She was very lucky. A few more hours and she would have died."

"Lucky." Ko repeated in a dead voice. He reached out and ran a hand over her cheek. Her skin was clammy and cold. Nikita's mouth was moving, and he bent close to hear. She was whispering.

"Your sister's medical records are patchy, Mr Chen, but it's clear she has a history of drug use. I'm afraid this is very serious."

Ko moved the oxygen mask and placed his ear to her lips. He felt tears welling up as he made out the peculiar litany.

"Mountain and the blood, screeching cats. Where are the masks talking? Can't see the lines on his chest, ropes and cutting knives." The words came in gasps. "No zen. Invisible hands. Know zen. Demons, pieces that smell like dark."

"What's wrong with her?" Ko turned, his fists balling.

The woman's brow furrowed. "She's suffered an overdose of a hallucinogenic. Her mind is struggling to make sense of it, but the drug effect tampers with conscious recall and perception, it creates a synesthetic overload." She sighed. "It's like the book of your sister's life has been jumbled up. She's lost in it."

"The worms gathering, the mirror sea," whispered Nikita, "Mirror see. See mirror. Mirror. Bubble in a stream. Jade. The Jade Dragon."

"Can't you help her?" he demanded. "Can't you... fix her?" Ko blinked furiously, impotent and frustrated.

Dr Yeoh's kind face set in a frown. "Nikita has suffered severe neurological damage. There is a possible remedy, but it's beyond my skills. I can give you a referral but you must understand, the cost is very high. Have you ever heard of the Zarathustra Clinic?"

Ko gave a bitter laugh. "Do I look like millionaire? I don't have the kind of yuan they charge!" He gave the doctor a hard look. "Who did this to her? I want to know!"

The woman was silent for a long moment. "This isn't the first case I have seen like this. Your sister's reaction is to a street narcotic, zee-three-en. Do you know it?"

"Zen." He screwed his eyes shut, remembering the tingle of the spilt drug on his fingers.

"Other users haven't been so fortunate. But it's difficult to stem the flow of this poison. The police look the other way. The corporates…" She spread her hands in a gesture of helplessness. "Yuk Lung and the others, they help proliferate the drug but their high-level government connections put them above the law. All we can do here is pick up the pieces." Yeoh turned away. "I'll give you some time with her. Talk to her, it may help."

Ko stood over Nikita, vibrating with pent-up anger. "You motherfuckers," he said to the air. "I'll kill every last one of you for this!"

Feng rested against the window. "Ko. You can't help her that way."

He rounded on the swordsman. "Look at her! She's a mess! One of those cashwhore bastards made that happen to her, just for shits and grins! Don't try to calm me down, dead man! I'll give them payback, a hundred times over!"

"Look to the girl first," said Feng. "You get yourself killed and who will care for her?"

Ko's angry retort died in his throat as the sound of a nightingale rang through the air. His hand wandered to the pocket of his coat. The cellphone. It was still there, forgotten after the events on the expressway.

He flipped open the device, illuminating the miniscreen and the camera pickup. "Who the hell is this?" he snarled.

"Remember me?" said Frankie, pressing himself deeper into the public phone booth. "We had a little chat about cars a couple of nights back." He squinted at the screen, making out the shape of a well-lit room and what looked like a pile of machines on a bed.

"You," said the youth on the other end of the line, pouring burning hate into that single word. "You got balls calling me."

"Listen," Frankie said. "If you weren't just bragging about being hooked up with the triad societies, I could have a deal for you. I need a job done."

"The fuck?" spat the other voice. "You piece of worm shit, you do this to my blood and then you call me up trying to play me? I'll fucking ice you!"

Frankie blinked. This wasn't going how he had expected it to. "Wait, what are you talking about?"

The camera view wobbled and rushed in close to the bed, and with a start Frankie understood what he was looking at – a haggard woman on a life-support machine. "What was it, huh?" snarled the car thief. "Is this your way of getting your own back on me for jacking that Vector? You pump my sister full of that blue poison and leave her to die?"

A cold trickle of recognition shot through the executive. The woman's face was familiar to him. "I know her… I saw her at the party…"

"What d'you say?" snapped the thief. "Tell me, damn it! Where did you see her?"

Frankie stuttered, wrong-footed. "Uh, with Mr Tze. At the Yuk Lung tower… But she seemed fine then."

"Tze? I know who he is," came a growl.

"Wait, no—" The screen went dead, and Frankie was left there in silence.

Ko snapped the phone shut and pocketed it.

Feng gave him a narrow stare. "Boy, don't do anything foolish."

"I'm going to get a weapon," he said, his voice low and loaded with menace. "And then I'm going to kill a man."

Next on ZeeBeeCee Ultrasports Daily, we go live to Sao Paolo for the World Series of Celebrity Cockfighting. But first, live coverage of the day's endorsed highway combat matches in the Denver Death Zone, including the triumphant comeback bout for John Knoxville and the surprise result on the Hasselhof Memorial Circuit—
CLICK…
I don't care what you think, Susan.
But Bill, it's just unnatural.

Love is the most natural thing of all, damn you! And Flippy and I are going away to the sea together and you can't stop us! I love her!

sob Oh Bill, how could you—

CLICK...

Hey kids, it's Pepe The Robomule!

CLICK...

I promise not to kill you—

CLICK...

In a statement released earlier today, British Prime Minister Peter Mandelson said that he was "fully confident of the support of the nation" and that he felt that challenges to his recent policy statements by the Liberal-MetaMarxist-Democrat leader Edward Izzard were nothing more than blatant electioneering. Izzard was unavailable for comment, but his second-in-command William Bailey said—

CLICK...

Stay tuned to The Arthaüs Channel for our retrospective on the works of stud actor Billy Priapus, following a hypertext-enhanced screening of his masterpiece Shaven Ravers IV—

CLICK...

And coming in at number ten on the Billboard Chart, the new single from Bombs Not Burkas, "Jihad My Ride"—

CLICK...

Now, the fourth season finale of Firefly, only on Wave-Net, followed by back-to-back episodes of Sundowners. Next: on a very special CSI: Baghdad—

CLICK...

Sea of stones, sand waves. Harmony, come with me. Taste the blue—

CLICK...

This gorgeous photodiamante necklace and nose-piercing set, only twenty left now and numbers are dropping fast. If you look here you can see a lovely crystal colouration. Call now, the number is on the bottom of your screen, we accept all major creditchips, indenture warrants and PRC-certified viable transplant organs—

CLICK.

9. days of being wild

There were entire microcommunities living within the confines of Ocean Terminal. People crammed into the spun ferrocrete dorm blocks retrofitted to the upper decks, if they were rich enough, and beneath the waterline if they were the poorer folks. Parts of the terminal were turned over to maintaining the armoured corporate liners that rolled in from the South China Sea bristling with anti-pirate hardware, or the exclusive submersible party boats that sailed about the Golden Triangle on endless loops of debauchery. A liner was there today – the *NeoGen Delphi*, out of Osaka. Her decks were crammed with salarymen and their one-partner, one-child families, forbidden from disembarking but free to observe the city from their sealed viewing bubbles. While the NeoGen wageslaves looked down, the people who lived and worked in Ocean Terminal looked up. Almost everyone in the terminal was an employee of the Chinese State Corporation, never without the subtle red bracelet on their wrists bearing the happy face of the CSC's Panda spokestoon Di-Di. The smiling bear beamed down from the walls of the dorms, above the school clutches and the clinics, inside the toilets and shared washrooms. The Panda provided; the terminal complex was a city-within-a-city, wrapped around the edge of Tsim Sha Tsui on Kowloon side, extending out into the bay like a giant growth of smooth white fungus. The Panda didn't encourage people to quit life inside the terminal, once they'd been born into it – after all, why venture outside when the place you lived in had it all? It wasn't uncommon for people to be born, to live and work and then perish without ever having crossed outside the boundaries of the massive mallplex. Ocean Terminal had grown so large that it had its own microclimate, its own emerging subculture. People living outside the 'plex in Kowloon called the residents "termites" and made fun of them on the late night comedy vids; the Panda's people in turn watched the rest of Hong Kong go in and out of the thousands of stores and entertainment centres, and laughed amongst themselves as they took their money.

There were a lot of stories about Ocean Terminal; that it would one day break off and become an island, or expand to smother the whole southerly tip of the New Territories; some said there were gangcults on the lower levels who traded in human cargo, and indeed the APRC would make vague but unspecific comments when the question of abductions came up; others said that the Panda salted the drinking water in there with chemicals that made you need less sleep, so you could work more. But the story that kept circulating on the screamsheets, the one that had recently risen to the surface and failed to fade away, was about Juno Qwan.

She kept her private life private, and in interviews Juno would often give a coy smile and ask people to respect her wishes. That did nothing to deter the armies of stringers and newsnets eager to fill vid-time and fax pages with every iota of data they could unearth about the pop star. The rumour was that Juno was a former Panda Girl, a termite chick spotted by a talento hunter from RedWhiteBlue during a shopping expedition. The young Qwan, bussing tables at a Burger König and singing in that crystal clear voice, had been plucked from obscurity and thrust into the global spotlight.

It made for great copy and it played big with the natives in Hong Kong, that whole "local girl does good" angle. The odd thing was, there were forty-three Burger König franchises within the mallplex, but none of the managers had ever admitted to having the pre-famous Juno on their waitstaff. Reporters who tried to track down the fast food joint she worked at got dissimilar answers, conflicting shots of different yellow and blue storefronts for their webcasts; and if you scratched the surface, dug a little deeper, it was hard to find anything about the girl before her explosive debut at the top of the charts. But then the termites were terrible that way, weren't they? Not very talkative to outsiders, a bit slow. They trusted in the Panda, and like everyone else who cheered Juno's limobus as it slid to a halt on Canton Road, they had short memories. They didn't remember the other performers that had topped the charts two, three, four years ago. Lisle Yep; TriniTriniTrini; Cressida; the Lovely Angels. Musichips bearing the names of these idols didn't even appear in the bargain bins anymore; they'd been crushed and used for landfill.

Juno stepped out into a chattering swarm of camera drones and photographers, beaming her smile and casting out handfuls of kisses to the crowds. Heywood Ropé hovered at her side, the careful look on his face never changing, the distance from Juno's shoulder never lengthening. Every gallery and balcony was packed, and below piezoplastic barriers corralled the fans that had been there since the night before, hands clasping the rails, on tiptoe, desperate for any breath of her. A CSC agent from the terminal manager's office presented her with a bunch of flowers and a plush toy version of Di-Di. Juno gave it a coquettish hug and twirled it around in her arms. Her audience ate it up.

No one thought of the others who had gone before her, who had played the same kinds of songs and offered the same kind of hopeful distraction to the same kind of people. They loved Juno today, and in that moment it seemed like they would love her forever.

FIXX HAD A sour taste in his mouth, and his lip twisted. It wasn't the mud-coloured slurry that Burger König called coffee. There was a taint on the air like rancid meat. He pushed the half-finished drink away from him across the cracked plastic table, suppressing a shiver even though the interior of Ocean Terminal was always a summery thirty-five degrees. For a moment, the ghost of the sensation he'd felt at the Hyperdome was about him, there and then gone. He glanced around at the laughing, clapping people. Their faces were the same as the fans in Newer Orleans, they shared the distant look in their eyes, desperate to capture some tiny fragment of Juno Qwan.

On this level, the view of the singer was decent. She was talking into a handheld microphone and waving. The crowds called to her, and even the cocky cluster of go-gangers drifting near the open patio couldn't help but crack smiles. Fixx shifted to get a better angle and adjusted the gain on his espex. He took a breath, one hand dipping into his pocket to finger the bones, collapsing his view of the world down to the space between him and her. Fixx let Juno's aura find its way to him, gentle and slow. He forced away the ill scents in the air, concentrating on the woman.

He'd had one of the waking dreams again. It came as he took the tunnel beneath the bay, the car dipping into the red-lit corridor, torrents of colour streaming over him. In there he'd seen webs come from nowhere, the reaching arms of things distant and older than space. They were gossamer, vanishing when he put his full attention to them; in among the ghosts he heard a woman screaming, tasted the bitter scent of things dark and alien.

"Juno," he rumbled. It kept coming back to her.

She was singing, dancing through a rendition of "Capsule Lover" while overhead screens displayed directionless, watery vistas all blue and inviting. The waves became words: *We Are Free*, *Break The Dark*, *Unstoppable*. Fixx saw the aurora of Juno's spirit, the faintest Kirlian glow about the woman. It was different.

He worried the bones a little more. *Wrong. That is wrong.* Fixx looked her in the eye at the Hyperdome, in that second of connection he had *known* Juno Qwan. That was the gift the loas gave him, the Sight. He could see a man and find the colour of his soul, turn it one way to mark a quarry or another to know a man's intention. It had never failed him.

But the woman, the starlet down there wore a different aura from the morose girl he had faced in the stadium. Fixx frowned. It wasn't like she was an impostor or someone disguised – no, he would have seen through that. Even a twin would have been visible to him. The colours of her were the same, but just *wrong*. Altered. Different. The experience was so new to him he couldn't frame it in his mind. He knew with sudden conviction that he had never laid eyes on the girl on stage before.

"Who are you?" The words slipped from his mouth. Fixx shifted, for one instant his attention elsewhere, and bumped into one of the go-gangers, a skinny kid with a wired look and a wifebeater top.

The punk made a face and cocked his head. "Watch it, gwailo."

There were three others, two who were obviously brothers. They exchanged loaded looks and the bigger one sneered. "Never saw a 'white ghost' as dark as him."

"Break the dark," mumbled the shorter one, tracing his fingers down to a bulge in his jacket pocket.

Fixx was back in the moment now. There was ample room on the terrace of the burger bar for trouble to unfold, if things went that way. He watched the first punk carefully; he would be the one to start it.

"You like Juno, huh?" said the skinny kid. "You like looking at our girl?" He stepped closer, looking Fixx up and down.

The sanctioned operative stayed very still. In the past, he'd seen what happened when a man made the mistake of underestimating packrats like these. In Mexico City, Fixx saw a rival gutted by a horde of Little Zulus, a fellow twice his weight taken apart by children under the age of ten. What kids lacked in experience they tended to make up for with speed and enthusiasm.

The last of the four finally spoke. "You know what I think? I reckon this guy doesn't like Juno at all."

Fixx, with slow and careful movements, stood up and smoothed the front of his coat. There was a flicker of concern on the face of the younger brother as he came up to his full height, but the other three were stone-faced. This was not going to end well. Nonetheless, Fixx felt compelled to try. "I'm a big fan," he said. "She's a dream come true."

Big Brother made a flicky gesture that failed to get a reaction from him. "Gau's right. This hwoon dahn, I bet he's A4." He approached. "Am I right, hwoon dahn? You here to mess with the gig like you did over there?" He jerked his thumb in the direction of the ocean.

Fixx showed teeth. "I know what those words mean."

"Yeah?" snarled the skinny one, getting into the swing of things, pointing his finger. "Do you know what these ones mean too? Fuck off ni–"

He moved. The troublemaker was suddenly on his knees and smothering a scream, his index finger pointing the wrong way where Fixx had snapped it like a twig. "Now, boys," he said. "Let's not say anythin' we might regret."

The brothers came at him, the one called Gau blinking in surprise. From out of nowhere they materialised wicked balisong knives and cut high and low. For go-gangers, they were quick.

Fixx had the SunKings on him, but it was a safe bet that Ocean Terminal's security would go wild at the sound of a gunshot. The mere fact that these boys had been able to freely enter with edged weapons told the op that the Panda probably turned a blind eye to the odd stabbing, as long as the shoppers weren't deterred. Similarly, the flexsword would be too showy, would draw too much attention. He decided to remain barehanded. It would be good practice.

The big brother's knife was one of those ostentatious toys with the faux-tribal laser etching on it, a blade with candy-colour anodization. Fixx caught his wrist and held it there for a moment while he used a sharp side kick to hobble the younger brother. Gau was pulling a spike-chain from his belt as Fixx turned the big brother's hands the wrong way. He lost the knife and the op heard it clatter away across the table.

Skinny was getting to his feet, his face all puffy and crimson. Below them, Juno had gone into a powerful rendition of "Shade Me", the crowd clapping along with the beat. "Unstoppable!" said the kid. "Break… Break the dark!"

Fixx drew the big brother in and crossed over his free hand; his elbow collided with the punk's face and broke his nose with a solid *crack*. A fan of blood issued out of his nostrils and dribbled down his chin. Fixx reversed his grip and hit him again, this time with the back of his hand. He pulled the blow – but only a little – and sent the big brother down.

Gau threw the spike-chain at him, a glittering arc of mercury cutting air. It made a low whoop as it crossed the space before him. Fixx dropped and spun, ducking under the reach of the weapon, and stepped closer. Gau reversed the move, whipping the chain around his neck and swapping ends. Clever.

The skinny kid was using his off-hand to finger a lanyard around his neck; he wasn't a threat for the moment. The younger brother was turning, trying to keep on Fixx's periphery while Gau used the chain to lash him. He was limping where he'd been kicked and it made him slow. Fixx saw him telegraph a move, the lunge coming in his shoulders before he did it. The op swept his hand across the table, catching the cup of disgusting coffee. He tossed it and a steaming streak of fluid spattered on the punk's face and chest.

The chain thrummed at his head and Fixx shifted. All at once he felt his amusement with this little diversion fade. He snatched the end of Gau's weapon out of the air, ignoring the bite of pain from the cobra-tooth head, and yanked it. Gau didn't let go quickly enough and was reeled off his feet. Fixx met him with a hammer blow punch that broke ribs and set him on the deck, choking.

Wiping searing hot coffee from his face, the remaining brother was distracted from the dark shape that came at him, coat flaring open in black raptor wings. Fixx used a throat grab to choke a lungful from the kid and then dropped him into a vacant chair. He took the boy's knife – another gaudy weapon that looked like it came out of an arcade gatchapon game – and snapped it in two.

Skinny had recovered a little and stood blinking owlishly, waving a spade-shaped push dagger. "Ghost you," he spat, pain making his voice rise. "I'm unstoppable…"

From the corner of his eye, Fixx caught sight of one of the glowing billboards, the trains of gossamer words fading in and out. He paused, turning his Sight on the punk; not the full strength of it, mind, just a little inch's worth. The go-ganger was heavy with pollution, an oily blue swirling down deep in the wells of his irises. He'd seen the same on people in Newer Orleans, and sometimes, in the daydreams. He could sense it there running through his veins, the indigo taint of Z3N. The boy wilted under the hard-eyed gaze, the dagger drooping.

Fixx mulled over the idea of putting him down; but then in the distance he spotted the floating blobs of CSC security mobiles coming up for a look-see. He left the punk behind and melted into the crowds.

On the giant datascreens, Juno came to the end of her set and the adulation from her audience echoed around the mallplex atrium like captured thunder.

MR TZE HAD a private elevator set into the corner of the Yuk Lung Tower that faced the city proper and the span of the bay. Through thick armoured glass he could view Hong Kong as he ascended or descended the gleaming flanks of the corporate skyscraper. He liked to take a place just an inch from the bowed window; there, it seemed as if he were some powerful ghost-lord coming down from heaven, the city rising up to meet him in supplication. Such a conceit amused him, it brought the semblance of a smile to the hard lines of his warrior face.

Tze allowed no one to speak during the elevator journeys. He made it a point of law that there be silence for the short duration, keeping the moment as an oasis of tranquillity wherein he could marshal his thoughts. The Masks, as inventive as ever, would communicate with one another via sign language if the matter required it. Behind him now, Deer Child and Blue Snake, one of the female guardians, discussed the CEO's security protocols with efficient twists of finger and arm motions. There were many things that clamoured for his attention, matters pressing as diverse as the effects of an arctic earthquake on YLHI's seabed oilrigs to the issue of a local triad leader who was not showing the proper level of deference. But he found it hard to dwell on such trivia, not when the Great Pattern was coming together.

If he concentrated hard enough on it, Tze could find a small knot of boyish anticipation hiding the depths of his soul, past his careful, most serious persona. After so long spent in service to the core goal of the Cabal, at last he would see it come to its fruition. The idea was as breathtaking now as it had been when he first understood the scope of it, when the members had taken that first meeting in the ruins of a small town in the Gobi Desert. In that place, as they walked about inside hazmat suits turning over glassy fulgurites fused from sand, finding the bodies of couples merged into dead amalgams of flesh, Tze had been touched by truth. The knowing had set him free.

There, they picked through the remains of the failed summoning, they read the cantrips and reviewed the splinters of tape that had not been obliterated in the thermal bloom. They came to understand the mistakes that had been made. Tze, in particular, had embraced the challenge with the fresh, untrammelled zeal of a convert. It was nothing less than the key to the mastery of the human soul that was being offered to them. It dwarfed the dreams of empire that Tze nursed. The Great Ones offered not just the earthly powers of prowess, of wealth and influence – those Tze had earned already – but more. The road marked out by the King of Rapture was the gateway to lordship over the most primal of human emotions; desire.

Tze felt that now, a need so great it made his blood ache. It was sweet, a perfect salve for the ills that had coloured his existence. Oh, his had not been a life of tragic circumstances and terrible hardship, far from it. Tze had grown to manhood in the bosom of a moneyed mainland clan, fed and educated with the finest that could be bought. It was there he had come to understand the full might of intemperance, that the majesty of a man flowed not just from the breadth of his appetites, but also from the extremes to which he would be willing to take them. It was only on the edges of what lesser types called "morality", beyond abstract, foolish concepts like "ethics" where a man could honestly know himself. And in that knowing would come mastery, not just of the self, but of others. All others.

He had no words for it then, in the days when they called him Black Tze behind his back, and scattered like birds when he came to take prey. But it made him strong; and eventually Tze came into the orbit of people who could open the way to him. The Gates of Sensation unlocked to his touch, and the ennui that had threatened to engulf him was wiped away. So much had changed since then. Tze's marriage to the Cabal was a second birth, a gift giving that he would soon repay with the lives of the world.

He pressed his hands to the window. It was fitting that it would begin here, birthing from the skies above this city. When it was done, when Hong Kong was ablaze as New Gomorrah, he would be the one to ride the Jade Dragon's back and take the first succulent taste of the world's fresh terror.

The light outside the lift vanished as the elevator dropped past the lobby atrium and through the basement sublevels. Tze caught a warped glimpse of his own face in the darkness beyond the glass and paused to wipe a thin line of drool from the corner of his mouth with a silk handkerchief.

With a chime, the lift doors opened and the Masks moved with him into the underground car park. Tze took three steps from the elevator before he stopped abruptly. "Intruder..."

IT WAS ONLY when he hid himself in the back of the delivery truck that Ko realised Feng wasn't with him. He threw a worried glance up at the gap beneath the roller door and saw the swordsman as the vehicle pulled from the kerb. Feng turned his face away, like he was sad and angry all at once.

For a moment Ko was upset, but then he mashed that feeling down with the hammer of his churning rage. One thought of Nikita beneath the webs of life-support sensors and he was high with fury. The anger had shifted and changed since he left the hospital. At first impotent and directionless, the call from the salaryman had provided him with sudden, perfect clarity. Now Ko was aimed like a laser, he had a name to give form to his pain. This Mr Tze, this phantom creep with his cashwhore flunkies, he was where the blame lay. That the guy on the phone from the expressway might have been playing him, maybe lying to Ko to get him jumping through hoops, that was something that the go-ganger never gave a moment to consider. This was not a matter of careful reflection and thought. Ko was a loosed missile, homing in on a target. He could not see past the moment of his rage's release, destruction looming large in his mind. The thief had never felt the urge to commit murder so strongly in his entire life. Every other consideration was secondary to that.

Vengeance. This man is going to pay.

In a back street lock-up in So Uk, he turned over crates of old engine parts and cartons of fake Peacefuls cigarettes, dragging an oily toolbox from a shadowed corner. Inside there were two Beretta automatics and fistfuls of hollowpoint bullets rolling loose. Generally, guns were a last-ditch tool for go-gangers, the street punk code short on firearms and long on bare-hand fighting or bladed weapons. It was a holdover from when the gun was seen as a badge, something you earned the right to carry only when you stepped up to join the Bamboo Union or the 14K as a Red Pole. The triads and the cops didn't like the gangers having guns; those were toys for the big boys. Ko loaded all the clips he had and weighed the weapons in his grip. The gun oil smell reminded him of his father, but he forced away any thought of that before the man's face could fully form in his mind's eye. In the back of the truck, he took out the guns again and looked at them. They hadn't been fired for months, lying there in the dark wrapped in greasy rags, and now it was too late to test them.

Ko raised the weapons to shoulder height and sighted down the barrels. He had seen a picture of Tze, just once, on the cover of the *HK Herald*. He remembered it clearly because it was such a rarity, some photographer catching a split-second glimpse of the man. There had been a story that the guy who took the still vanished off the street the following day; so it went, the *Herald* had been sent more pictures, this time of the photographer, but not in the kind of state they could print in a national newspaper.

Ko's face was a mask of concentration. He drew his focus inward, waiting. Now he lived on a clock from second to second, his mind framed on that face and nothing else. The robot truck rumbled through the security gate of the Yuk Lung tower and rolled down the incline to the lower levels.

"Tze!" Ko burst from the shadows of a concrete stanchion close to the CEO's idling limo and opened fire, the pistols slamming out shots.

Deer Child reacted instantly, dragging Tze behind him and stepping into the line of the fire. Many of Ko's bullets went wide, smashing into the walls and skipping off the limo, but a handful of rounds struck the chest of the bodyguard and a single shot fractured the perfect sheen of Deer Child's porcelain opera mask. The guardian stumbled backwards, bleeding heavily.

One of the Berettas made a high-pitched noise and jammed. Ko let it drop and kept on firing, brass casings glinting as they ejected into the air.

Blue Snake produced a series of throwing knives from concealed wrist holsters and threw them at Ko. The kid was quick enough to dodge one, but not enough to avoid the second. The lightweight stiletto hit Ko in the sternum and threw him to the ground with the force of a freight train. Ko lost the other gun and lay there, wheezing.

Seconds had elapsed. Tze disentangled himself from Deer Child's twitching form and found the duty security officer; neither he nor his men had got off a shot.

"Sir, I–" he began, his face flushed. Blue Snake had another knife, and she slit the man's throat with it. Tze walked on to where Ko had fallen. He paused to brush a speck of lint off his suit as Blue Snake hauled the youth off the ground.

Tze examined him. "Ah, the folly of youth." He leaned closer. "Do you know why no one ever tries to take me out, boy?" He smiled. "Because no one is that stupid. Except you, of course."

"Go," Ko managed. "Fuck yourself." He spat a mouthful of blood and spittle into Tze's face.

The older man carefully wiped it away, and then licked his fingers, smiling. "That fat fool running the 14K… I think perhaps he can earn his way back into my good graces with this little urchin."

"Sir?" said Blue Snake.

"Take this interloper to the docks and tell Hung I want an example made of him."

FRANKIE STARTED AS his car rolled to a halt. He saw someone being bundled into a vehicle, bodies under sheets, and blood on the tarmac. "What the hell?"

Tze approached, smiling. "Don't be concerned, Francis. Just a small security incident. A trespasser."

He saw a face, just in the instant before the car door slammed, heard a string of gutter swearing. Oh shit. I know that voice. The car thief.

Tze patted him on the shoulder. "Take care of things here, will you? I have some business to attend to in the city."

Frankie watched them go, the stink of fresh cordite and violence in his nostrils.

The distinctive colourations of Chinese Opera masks have a series of layered significances that go beyond the mere portrayal of a given character. A blue face (such as that seen on Xia Houdun) is indicative of someone possessing the traits of dedication, ferocity and shrewdness; a green face (like Zheng Wun) means the character is reckless, likely prone to sudden violence and a surly nature; figures like Guan Yu (a noted Chinese warrior) bear a red mask, which highlights the soldierly traits of fidelity, valour, heroism and decency; yellow (such as Tu Xingsun) indicates a level-headed person but also someone with the qualities of ferocity and determination; black masks like that of Judge Bao Gong indicate selflessness as well as a coarse, aggressive manner; white (traditionally a colour associated with death in the Far East) marks the villain of the piece, highlighting the sly and the wily, the underhand and treacherous (such as the fiendish Qin Hui); finally, the special colourations of gold and silver are employed only on characters who come from beyond the human realm, such as gods and ghosts. The function of the mask in these plays is not only to provide cultural cues to the audience but also to establish a palette of known archetypes, in stories that form a key part of the myths of the Chinese people. On some level, the masks create an aura of power for the performer wearing them, a way in which they can subsume themselves into the role and tap into the pure strengths of the character.

Excerpt from *Painted Faces, Swords and Gods: The Mythology of Chinese Opera* by Georgina Golightly.

10. warriors two

THE EXECUTIVE OPERATIONS suite was decorated in the style of a stately English library, heavy with polished teak and mahogany, rich with deep oxblood leather chairs and brass lamps. Ornate desks lined the walls between subtle privacy dividers. Only the screens seemed out of place, and even those had been disguised in wood mounts similar to portrait frames. The keyboards were hidden in the leather blotters on the surface of the desks, illuminating from below when Frankie took his seat. The other men in the room were subvocalising into hidden microphones, but Frankie disabled the voice circuit and got to work typing.

Under his cuff he had a piece of tissue on which he had scribbled a dozen strings of numbers. Code keys copied from the data spike that Alan had left concealed for him, these were permissions that allowed entry into parts of the Yuk Lung mainframe that would normally be far outside of his sphere of influence. Frankie had not dared to bring the precious needle with him, or even to upload the smallest part of its contents to another computer. He was afraid to contaminate himself with the material, at least until he had a clearer idea of what his brother had been doing with it. It seemed quaintly low-tech of him to actually jot the codes down on a scrap of paper instead of entering them on his PDA.

The files. What he had glimpsed in there made him shiver. Alan appeared to have been making two distinct collections of information. The largest of the two was broad in scope, a collation of details on YLHI's corporate battle plans, notes on what investments they would be buying and selling in the next year. It held highly secret reports on the performance of the conglomerate's subdivisions, the sort of data that a rival like Eidolon or NeoGen could easily use against them. The second, smaller file was more eclectic. It consisted mostly of laboratory reports from Yuk Lung's genetics labs on the mainland, some peculiar transcripts from ancient tablets, metallurgical scans of meteor fragments, even audio samples that sometimes seemed like music, other times like voices. Frankie had almost given up with paging through it until he saw his own name amid an indecipherable block of medical-speak. Alan's name was there too, along with a couple of other people from their graduating class. The others, he had heard, were dead now. Something about an accident in the wilds, a company team-building exercise that went badly wrong.

What were you doing, brother? Frankie asked the question over and over. The planning files, that was the kind of stuff that a man would assemble if he were thinking about jumping ship. With that information in his hands, Alan could have struck a deal with any of the Big Six Multinats, got them to exfiltrate him from YLHI and set him up somewhere with a new identity and a billionaire lifestyle. But why would he? Yuk Lung had been very good to Alan Lam, so why would he ever turn on them? Frankie was sure that the answer to that question was in the second set of files, if only he could comprehend it.

He entered the codes, licking dry lips. On the screen, pools of information filled, presenting themselves for his examination. If the data on the spike had been the first trickle, then this was the flood. Frankie cast a look around, fearful that he would be seen for what he was doing; but none of the other men paid any attention to him, all of them engaged in their own private infospheres.

Frankie pushed on, beginning a search protocol using himself as the subject. Layers of files fanned open, some of them the ones on the data spike; but there were others. He started to read.

Ko's FACE MET asphalt and he rolled into it, grit scraping the skin of his cheeks. He tried to right himself, but with his hands strapped together behind his back it was nearly impossible. A random boot met his thigh with a shocking impact and he let out a grunt of pain. Strong hands took hold of his arms and dragged him off the ground. As much as he tried, his attention was fixed on the three inches of stainless steel protruding from his breastbone. Each breath he took was a lungful of razors.

All at once his hands were free as they flapped uselessly at his sides. Ko wobbled unsteadily, taking in what he could through eyes gummed with dried blood. Blue Snake's associates had not been careful with the youth as they stuffed him into the back of the town car.

He smelt saline, diesel oil, the faint stinks of old rot and rust. He could make out boxy shapes all around in bright primary colours, the building blocks of some giant toddler. Distantly, the rumble of robo-trucks reached his ears.

A familiar voice crossed him. "Ah, Ko. What did you do this time?"

"Rikio? That you?" he asked thickly. Blood was working its way back into Ko's hands and he wriggled them, fighting off pins and needles. By painful inches, his vision began to unfog.

Rikio shook his head, the same Ushanti SMG still glued to his side. "I warned you about this. I told you, you don't get with someone, you're against everyone. Out in the cold."

Ko shivered involuntarily. "Didn't 'spect you to understand. About honour, see? Man drugged my sister!"

"You're an idiot. What, did you reckon you could just tippy-toe up to a zaibatsu warlord and pop him like some yokel right off the ferry? That's your problem. You don't *think*."

"Got close," he said lamely.

"Yeah. You go right on believing that." The Red Pole looked away to where the woman in the suit and the blue opera mask was holding an intense conversation with Big Hung. The old man had a rock solid expression of displeasure. One of Hung's men approached and pointed at Ko.

"Boss is sick of looking at this maggot," snapped the guy. "Put him in a can for the time being." Rikio began to march Ko away, but the other man halted him. "Just a sec." He reached down to Ko's chest and jerked the knife out. "She wants her blade back."

Ko fell in a heap, pain flashing through him and blood spreading under his fingers.

"What we gonna do with him?" he heard Rikio say.

The reply was disinterested. "Probably just some waste disposal, nothing serious."

AT FIRST IT seemed like bloodwork, more medical stuff, the kind of paperwork that any corporation would keep on an employee. But there was just so much of it. Frankie found the reports from his quarterly health checks at the LA office, all of them stretching back to his very first posting there – but there were layers of other files, dates that didn't tally up to visits to the clinic or the dentist. He saw reports that spoke of "bio-surveillance" and found fluoroscopes of hair samples, soiled chopsticks, stool samples and Band-Aids. In the most recent he came across a polymorphic scan of a used toothbrush that had gone in the trash a couple of weeks back. Some anonymous lab somewhere had dismantled it and done intensive DNA sweeps of the cell material he'd left behind. There were workups on women that he'd dated, spectrum analysis of their physiology and intensive scrutiny of their sexual histories.

Unnerved, he read on. Frankie expected the file to end with his very first medical at the corporate academy, but it was the tip of the iceberg. The data went back and back and back, through his teens and his childhood, every broken bone and skinned knee, every schoolboy illness and sick day; and still it did not stop. There were bloodline charts, great multileveled things spread like inverted trees, root systems of birth, death and marriage unfolding down through the generations. He stopped, trying to steady the shaking in his hands. Yuk Lung had not only tracked every living moment of Frankie's life, but that of Alan and the whole of the Lam family ancestry. He flicked down the scroll bar, hopping decades in an instant, rolling back hundreds of years. Still the pages unfurled, through the dynasties of ancient China and into the haze of pre-history. He halted the file with a gesture and swallowed hard, the acid taste of bile burning in his throat.

His own company, his own corporate faction had been shadowing him to a level far beyond the bounds of normality, like some omnipresent stalker peering back into the past. He felt naked and sickened.

After a moment Frankie's eyes focussed on a pop-up window at the side of the screen. It was more of the same, layer upon layer of G-T-A-C coding, but the form of it was different. A blinking tag linked this separate page with Frankie's, some vague connection that he couldn't read from the reams of medical jargon. He recognised the name at the top, though. There was no way he couldn't have.

"Project: Juno."

He wiped the screen and entered those words, using the highest code from Alan's secret records.

"Access Restricted."

For a second he could smell her there in the room with him, the warm flowery scent of her perfect skin, the feel of it under his fingertips. Frankie savoured the moment of sensory recall before it faded. If someone was keeping such a close eye on him, it wasn't hard to imagine that the same would be true for Juno... but why? What possible purpose could there be for such a thing? He and Alan, they were just two unremarkable salarymen, two Hong Kong brothers who'd pulled themselves up off the streets to make a better life. Nothing about either of them warranted such scrutiny...

Or did it? What if Alan had found something he shouldn't have? The spectre of his brutal, pointless death cast a chill over everything, magnifying the guilt Frankie felt at their estrangement. If there was a chance that the triads had silenced his brother for a reason, not because of some blind error, then he had to know for certain. He owed Alan nothing less; even after all the distance between them, he was still his blood. Someone wanted him silenced, Frankie thought, and they had him murdered.

The only question was: how far did it go? Whose finger had been on the trigger?

The trilling of his phone made him start, and he grabbed it clumsily from the inner pocket of his suit jacket. The motion drew some arched looks from the other execs; it clearly marked him as a new boy.

His vu-phone was the latest model, a replacement for the one he'd lost, with top-of-the-line encryption and executive level pass codes. On the readout was a name he hadn't expected to come across again. "Incoming Call: Burt Tiplady."

"Yes?"

"Frankie?" It was rare to hear that tone in Burt's voice, his usual braggadocio replaced by nervous indecision. Digital whispers across the satellite link to Los Angeles fluttered under the words of his former superior. "Or do I have to call you Mr Lam, now you got yourself promoted?"

"No... Burt, what do you want?"

"Been trying to get you for the best part of a day. Seems all your baggage ain't caught up with you yet."

Frankie sighed. "Burt, this is a bad time. I'm right in the middle of something."

"Uh, well," Tiplady's voice wavered, and Frankie knew what was going through his mind. He wasn't sure how to react. Lam had been his subordinate for a long time and he was finding it hard to take on the notion that their roles were now reversed. "It's just that, there was a comm that came in on your old office email here. One time signal, couldn't forward it." An embarrassed cough. "The thing is, I kinda accidentally opened it."

"Accidentally," Frankie repeated.

"Yeah. Uh. Sorry."

He frowned. The last thing he wanted was this dolt wasting his time with trivia. There were bigger things at stake than some lost piece of junk mail.

"It must have got held up in that big server outage last week, delayed in the system I reckon. It... It's from your brother."

Frankie felt his blood turn to ice water. "Read it to me."

"It's not much, just a couple of words. It says, uh, 'Don't ever come home.' Did you piss him off, or something?"

The room suddenly seemed tight and confined. Too late, Alan, said a voice in his head, I'm already here. "Burt, listen to me. Erase it and close down the line, okay?"

"Sure, sure," said the other man. "Say, listen, I was wondering if maybe you could put in a good word for me with head office, now you're there? Y'know, if you might–"

Frankie folded the phone shut and sat there for long moments in the darkness, surrounded only by the murmuring of the other users. After a while, he toggled the datascreen's security protocols menu and asked it to locate Blue Snake for him.

She was at the docks, it replied, conducting an unspecified errand for the CEO. Frankie studied the area on a digital map, and with careful deliberation, he began once again to dial his old phone number.

RIKIO SHOVED HIM into the dark interior of the cargo container and Ko stumbled on the metal floor, his sneakers slipping on damp patches. The cold and rainy weather made the inside of the container feel like an icebox. The youth bounced off a wall and coughed. Every physical exertion made the injury in his chest hurt like fire. The front of his grey shirt was stained purple with blood.

"I'm bleeding…" he said.

At the doors, Rikio threw him a pitying look. "That's the least of your problems right now."

Ko shivered, at last a real sense of the depths of shit he was in coming to him. "Are you gonna kill me?" The words came out in a scared little boy voice. Rikio's lip curled but he didn't reply. "Dude, we used to play on the street together. You know me. We were friends."

"We were never friends, Ko," the gunman said sadly. "We were just kids. Doesn't mean I owe you anything."

Ko started back toward the doors. "Riki–"

The Ushanti's nickel-plated muzzle came up. "You stay right there. You just be quiet and you stay right there." Rikio stepped out of the container and closed the hatches, throwing the bolt shut.

Even though he knew it was pointless, he tried the doors. Ko opened his mouth to call out, but the words died in his throat, escaping as a faint whimper. No one would hear him. No one would care.

He slumped to the floor and sat against the wall. Chinks of light from rust holes provided illumination as Ko went through his pockets, in lieu of having anything better to do. Scraps of paper and an old matchbook from the Dot. A couple of loose bullets – fat lot of good they would do him now – and a wallet with a handful of yuan. And…

Ko's fingers closed around the cellphone in the instant it rang. He snapped it open in panic, suddenly terrified that Hung's men would hear it.

"H-hello?"

"Is THAT YOU?" Frankie frowned the moment he asked the question. It was a dumb thing to say.

"Yeah." The kid was muted and fearful. "This how you get your laughs, huh? Fuck with me and my family, and then phone up to gloat about it?"

"Where are you?" Frankie had the digi-map of the docks open in front of him. "Where did Blue Snake take you?"

"Dancing Dragon Pier. Big Hung's docks. Like you don't know."

Frankie nodded to himself, running an image transform program. The satellite image became an infrared pattern of cold blues and moving orange blobs. One peculiar shape – green instead of human-red – was standing among a group of others. Tze's guardian? "Tell me where you are. Exactly."

"Inna cargo pod. Freezing an' bleeding to death. Why are you asking me this shit?"

Frankie took a breath. What had they taught him in the academy? The best time to negotiate with a hostile source was when you had them on the ropes. "Remember what I said before? I have a job for you."

"HUH." DESPITE HIS dire predicament, Ko felt the urge to laugh. "You got great timing, mister wageslave. Pretty soon, I ain't gonna be in any shape to do anything for anybody." The soft glow of the phone cast faint shadows around the gloomy interior.

"I had nothing to do with what happened to the girl... Your sister." The voice on the other end of the phone seemed genuine, or at least as far as Ko could tell. These corps, they lie for a living. "I could help."

Ko fought off a shiver. The cold was leaching into his fingertips and toes. "What do you care? I'm just a thief, neh? A streetpunk for you suits to roll over like some bug. You don't know me. What d'you want, huh?"

"You said you had connections with the triads, yes?"

"Yeah," he nodded woodenly. "I know people in the Wo Shing Wo, the 14K, others. Not that it has done me any favours." Ko coughed and spat out blood.

"I can get you out of there," said the voice, "if you trust me. In return I want you to get some information. There was a hit... I need to know who ordered it."

"You can't do it yourself, mister big shot?" snorted Ko.

"I can't take the risk of investigating myself. I need someone like you. I can't be connected."

"Like me," murmured Ko, masking a wheeze. "Oh yeah. I see where this is going. You want some no-namer to do your dirty work, someone... disposable?"

"That's about the size of it, yes."

Ko forced a smile. "Yeah. You got yourself problems you don't want your boss knowing about, so you gotta come down to the gutter to deal with it." He shifted, fighting down the pain. "Sure. I'm your man. But I want something else."

"I'm going to save your life," insisted the corporate. "That's not enough?"

"No. I want money. After what that rat shit Tze did to my sister, it's gonna take some heavyweight paper to make her well again. You clean that mess up, too."

FRANKIE CHOKED BACK a laugh. "You're in no shape to be setting terms."

There was a dry, painful chuckle. "I gotta guy ten metres away from me with a machine gun gonna drill me any second now. I got nothing to lose. Pay up or get some other chump to be your errand boy."

In spite of himself, Frankie smiled. This kid's nobody's fool. "Okay."

There was a long pause. "Fine. Now how you gonna spring me, mister wageslave?"

A plan began to form in Frankie's mind as he examined the data traffic streaming in and out of the dockyards. "Can you swim?"

"Uh, yeah, but—"

"Be ready. And don't lose that phone." He stabbed the disconnect key.

"OH MAN," Ko breathed, staring at the silent cellphone. "What did I just do?"

The steel doors answered him, opening with a clattering squeal. Ko staggered backward, reflexively trying to make himself a smaller target; but there was no cover at all inside the cargo pod. The hatches opened wide and there was Rikio and another one of Hung's boys, scowling from underneath a sepia-toned punch-perm. Rikio's face was expressionless.

"Look," Ko said, "there's no need for this."

Punch-perm nodded at Rikio. "That blue-faced bitch wants this tyke aired out. You gonna do it, or do I gotta tell Hung you're not up to the job?"

"Hey," said Ko. "Wait."

Rikio licked his lips. "Naw. It's okay."

Punch-perm kept talking as if Ko wasn't even there. "So, then. You wanna use my gun?"

"Naw," Rikio repeated, flicking off the Ushanti's safety, "I got it."

Ko heard a rumbling sound, getting louder by the second. Was that death, bearing down on him? "Please," he implored, tears spiking his eyes. "Just let me go—"

Rikio raised the machine pistol; that was about the moment the robo-truck slammed into the side of the container and rode right over the punch-perm guy, wheels grinding the man into the asphalt.

The empty metal box shifted with ear-splitting shrieks, fat yellow sparks flying from the doors. Rikio tumbled into the cargo pod, narrowly missing the same fate as the other enforcer. Ko slipped and fell, his hands crusted with a film of dried blood.

He saw the front of the robot six-wheeler as it retreated back a few feet, huffing like an overworked dray horse. Written across the blank-faced prow of the truck were three words: "Yuk Lung Haulage."

The vehicle came at the pod again and this time the impact threw it back two metres, pushing it back over the edge of the dock. The machine shouldered into the container and began the slow and steady process of tipping it into the bay.

FRANKIE WORKED THE controls, licking sweat from his lips. On the thermal scan he could see the shapes of a dozen men sprinting across the cargo apron toward the truck, the cold shapes of weapons in their grips. It had been simple to open up the automatic navigation controls on one of the many YLHI drone haulers, and reprogramme the dog-smart drive brain to do his bidding; but now Frankie was having second thoughts about his impulsive choice of exit strategy. He could make out the two flailing orange shapes inside the box, so he knew the kid wasn't dead – not yet. Pinpricks of bright white showed where the triad gunsels were firing on the truck. Behind them, the alien shape of Tze's Blue Snake stood and observed, motionless.

The robo-truck smashed into the cargo pod one last time and drove it over the lip of the concrete dock. Vehicle and all, the pod struck the waters of the bay and vanished, the shape fading away into the blue sheen of the cold.

KO AND RIKIO collided with each other and the walls, bouncing around like stones in a rattle. Rikio tumbled underneath him and Ko felt something break inside the Red Pole as he softened the impact against the steel box. Water gushed into the container, buoying up Rikio's body. Ko noted the new angles in his arms and legs, the freakish tilt of the neck, but found it hard to summon any sympathy.

Ko pushed at the undertow of the seawater, but the icy cold and the searing bite of the wound in his chest bled the energy from him. Tilting, the box dropped beneath the surface, the tiny pocket of trapped air inside bubbling out in whooping breaths. He tried to swim, but there was nothing in him, not a drop of energy to spare.

I'm going to die. I'm sorry, Nikki. I let you down.

"Stupid, weak city boy." The voice hammered into his head. "You're not dead yet." Something tugged at him through the chill water and Ko saw a shape drifting at the mouth of the container, leather cords and a long ponytail floating around him. "Swim, damn you," snarled Feng. "The drowned never know peace! You want to spend eternity haunting this concrete cesspool? Come on! Swim!"

Ko's leaden limbs moved, dragging him forward. The container dropped away toward the dark, and with agonizing slowness Ko felt himself rising toward the bland grey light of the surface. Feng beckoned him from the shadows of the dock stanchions, speaking without moving his lips. "This way! Come up here, quickly!"

He burst from the depths through oily water, sucking in great wet gasps of air. Ko's fingers found a rusty rail and he pulled himself hand-over-hand, up and on to the concrete pier. Behind him on the next dock over, he could hear shouting and curses. A gunshot rang out, and a divot of stone cracked near his leg. He felt hollow inside, but somehow there was a secret reserve of energy coming from a place he'd never known of, and it propelled Ko forward, gasping and spitting up acrid water. Ahead he saw a chainlink gate lying open, and beyond that, a service road.

On the road was a parked car. The speedgeek part of his brain identified it immediately as a Korvette Impulse, one of the '23 models that had the puny touchlocks on the doors. Ko felt a weak smile forming on his lips just at the sight of it.

Wild…
WILD…
WYLDSKY!
One Night Only! Victoria Peak!

The greatest concert of the decade, with the hottest bands and NO RULES!
There's no ticket – the only thing you need to get in is freedom!
Come together and stand your ground!
Show the world that music can't be caged!
It's not about the green! It's about the BLUE!
WYLDSKY!
Featuring performances by JetSlut! Charlie Fish! Yellow Dancer!
And a SPECIAL guest star – Who Knows? YOU KNOW!
The biggest free gig in the PacRim!
WYLDSKY!
The future starts here!

11. saviour of the soul

Fixx let the road do the driving, allowing the turns and changes to come from the world around him, travelling without moving, conscious but unseeing. The black Korvette seemed to understand its new master, and behaved as a good horse should, cantering unhurried through the canyons of the city. Lucy had done him proud.

There came the point, just as Joshua expected, when the road ended, and there he turned off the motor and let the surroundings talk to him. Hours passed without his notice, instead his mind dwelling on the fragments of time from the mallplex; the pieces of sensory recall from there and the same moments from the Hyperdome collided and merged in his mind, an ocean of floating jigsaw pieces connecting, disconnecting, seeking patterns in each other. In the car, in the service road between the concrete warehouses, in the place of silence-such-as-it-was, Fixx recovered the deck of cards his sainted grandmother had bequeathed and began to play out a reading on the empty passenger seat beside him. The patterns started to emerge, and he chewed his lip. All this time, and still Fixx felt like he was unready, like he was waiting.

"Stage ain't set," he said aloud. "Players ain't ready yet."

His mind was so focused on the tarot matrix that the shadow crossing the window by his head was a sudden surprise.

The Korvette had one-way surrounds of black glass, and with the car dormant as it was, a person might be forgiven for thinking it was empty. Fixx paused, an unturned card in his hand, and studied the raggedy youth working at the door lock. The Chinese kid had his tongue pressed between his teeth in serious concentration. He looked strung out and wasted, a nasty blossom of blood down the front of his shirt, constellations of bruises on his face and neck. He was wet through, his clothes plastered to him; but most of all the fear was coming off him in waves.

In spite of all that, Fixx took a look at the card, even though in that moment he knew exactly what it would show. The sanctioned operative flipped the latch and the Korvette's gullwing door rose.

The thief jerked in shock as he realised the car was occupied. "Oh. Shit." He blinked and skipped back a few steps as Fixx got out. "Hey, uh. This isn't my car!" He faked a frown. "What a silly mistake!"

Fixx handed the tarot card to him. "Here. This seem familiar?"

The kid read the name on the bottom, eyes narrowing. "Knight of Wands. Huh. He kinda looks a little like me."

"How 'bout that?" Fixx grinned. "Yeah. Curtain's going up now."

There were footsteps coming and they turned to see a group of men in spaciously cut suits approach at a run. All of the new arrivals were carrying guns, and they exchanged confused looks at the sight of the black man and his car.

"Hold it, Ko, you little punk!" snapped one of them. "You brought this on yourself!"

Fixx raised a hand. "A moment, gentlemen. If you'll just allow me…" He drew the bones from his pocket and scattered them across the Korvette's bonnet. The op bent low, examining the turn and placement of them. He glanced at the youth. "Ah-yuh." In a flash, he gathered the bones back up again. Papa Legba had told him what it was he had been waiting for.

One of the men came close, reaching out a hand. "Keep out of this—"

Fixx broke his gun arm and the enforcer's pistol fell at Ko's feet. As the kid scrambled for it, Fixx punched the triad gunsel off balance and bounced his head off the Korvette's roof.

The other men opened fire, and Fixx cut low, the SunKings leaping into his hands. The boy was letting off wild shots, doing the best that he could. Fixx went for short, controlled bursts from his silver pistols.

Close misses keened off the bulletproof windscreen and the dirty concrete. Fixx drilled each enforcer in turn, going for disabling hits when he could, outright kills when he couldn't. The kid, this Ko, emptied the revolver and then ducked in cover behind the car.

Fixx shot the last man in the leg and strode back to the Korvette, reloading as he went. Mercifully, no stray shots had gone into the vehicle's electronics. The op took his seat and opened the passenger door. "So," he said conversationally. "You need a lift." It wasn't a question.

"I'll take my chances, thanks."

"No you won't. You're smarter than that."

The youth gingerly got in. "I'm Ko," he coughed.

"Joshua Fixx." The op shook his hand. "Pleasure."

Ko still had the tarot card. "You, uh, want this back?"

"In a while." The sports car growled into life and raced away.

FATIGUE ENGULFED HER in a slow, warm wave, drawing Juno down on to the bed and into the cool embrace of the silken sheets. She had a brief moment of sense-memory, there and then gone, just the quickest taste of Frankie's musk upon her lips; she wanted to hold on to it, but it disintegrated beneath her scrutiny, the way that ancient paper became dust when you crushed it in your fingers.

Was it daylight outside? She couldn't tell any more. After all the travelling, every rootless moment of motion inside and outside, she had gone beyond a point where she could reckon herself against a watch. She lived on Juno Time now, where every hour was Me O'Clock, her needs fulfilled as long as she never stepped outside of the bubble. And why would she? Out beyond the safety zone that dear old Heywood and the nice men at RedWhiteBlue granted her, well, she knew there were people there who loved her, but there were also the scary ones. The ones that posted dead animals to the fan club, or sent her emails of themselves wearing clothes of hers that her maids had stolen to sell on iBuy.

Still. At times she felt the urge bubbling inside her, the need to go and walk in the real world without legions of cameras and men whose only jobs were to plot and scheme over the content of her every breath, her every move. She could get out if she wanted to, *really* wanted to. Juno knew a way.

She shifted and felt the bed move with it, gently closing around her. She blinked, trying to shake away the dark shades hovering at the far edges of her vision, there in the pools of inky shadow behind the hotel suite's curtains, or in the places where light didn't fall beneath the furniture. Her mouth was suddenly arid. She felt... she felt... She felt *wrong* somehow, uncomfortable no matter how much she moved, as if it were her skin that fitted her wrongly, not the cloying touch of the silk.

The woman kicked at the bedclothes with sudden violence. She wanted them off her, but they refused to budge. Juno rolled over and pulled. The bed shifted back with tendrils of gossamer material and dragged her down. Juno opened her mouth to cry out, but her lips, her dry lips were stuck together.

Outside the window there was the sound of cats yowling, the whispering of voices that came from placid porcelain faces, hidden eyes under unmoving masks. Juno flailed for the edges of the bed and couldn't find them. Her hands sank into pools of brilliant blue capsules, glittering candy-coloured shapes that tingled when she touched them. The dusty interior of her mouth craved them, begged for the refreshing bursts of fluid inside.

Invisible hands. Know zen. Bubble in the stream.

The room had become dark while her mind was elsewhere. The curtains, thick and heavy brocade flapping in a pre-storm breeze, they came open now and then to show her glimpses of a distant green mountaintop, and beyond it a purple sky lit by silent lightning. Where was the thunder? Why wasn't there any thunder?

Juno pushed very hard at her lips and forced a word out of her mouth; it came apart in fragments, blue and black and green and yellow. She spoke in colours and not sounds, rainbows of light erupting. It made her cry.

Balling the slick sheets in her grip, Juno forced her way up. Her eyes would not close, no matter how hard she tried to seal them. By chilling inches, the contents of the room began to haze over and change, turning from wood and paper and cloth into glass and glass and glass. Everything had edges like razors, all of them pointing inwards to scrape at her eyes.

Mirrors. Everywhere there were mirrors. Talking mirrors that screamed and cried or made sounds that could have been songs.

And here came the shapes again, the moving things in the shadows under the glassy madness. The Angels of Pain. The serpents and the worms, and over her head, somewhere in the rafters kilometres above, a dragon made of dark jade, watching. Waiting for something. Waiting for her to sing to him. The Lord of Bliss ready for her to serenade…

Juno forced herself up and curled her hands around her naked, shivering form, fighting to shake off the dream; but it clung to her like a film of oil, coating every surface, reflecting pieces of her life back at her.

Ocean Terminal, the screaming crowds. The upturned faces in the Hyperdome. Outside the Yuk Lung tower. Heywood's hands around her throat…

She choked, her back arching with pain; and suddenly she saw that moment, watching it unfold from a place behind the frosted door in the upper deck of the limobus, the lights of the Lantau Expressway flicking past outside. She observed…

Herself? Juno Qwan, behind a pair of Minnuendo sunglasses, the Inverse Smile chapeau, the Dior dress, the Westlake pumps. Her face taut and morose. Juno Here watching Juno There, detached, an observer.

The Other Juno is irrational and she's making high-pitched noises that could be words, but she sounds like she's underwater. Other Juno reaching for a bowl of the gorgeous blue pills, so many of them. Heywood stops her, there's a blur of motion and those Minnuendos, a two thousand yuan limited edition from the Fall Catalogue, they fall from her face as he strikes her with the base of his hand.

She bleeds. The sunglasses are smashed into broken mirrors under Ropé's shoes. Ropé puts his big white hands around Other Juno's throat and he begins to twist and turn her head. This Juno, Watching and Observing Juno, touches her neck in reflection, detached, distant, not understanding.

How can this be happening? How can I be here and there at once? Why is she dying? Juno is a star. I can't die.

And the Other Juno's face turns florid and then slack as Ropé twists and twists, he's laughing a little as he does it, eyes wild and enraptured as he makes the kill last, teasing it out. The slow, slow cracking pops as vertebrae snap. The meat-sack thud as the body falls from his clawed hands. Juno. There dead. Dead.

Mirror is broken.

Heywood brushes back stray hairs made unkempt by the murder, straightens himself, calms down his arousal. He looks at her with kind, fatherly eyes and beckons Juno Here from behind the door. So she comes, because that's what she must do. And This Juno sloughs off the shapeless plastic oversuit and gently undresses Other Juno, Dead Juno, Pallid and Forever Not Juno…

SHE WAS IN the shower beneath a hot spray of water when she finally recovered enough to stop weeping. The needles of liquid massaged her body, pain making the dream fade. The punishing heat reddened her skin, but it forced the thoughts to retreat back into the dark pools and the black places. Juno shut it off and crossed to the full-length mirror, wiping away the patina of condensation, examining herself.

"Just… a dream," she said aloud, her words taking on a peculiar echo in the cavernous bathroom.

Juno padded out to the suite proper and studied the display on her comm. It was still ringing, the call unanswered. Francis Lam – Temporarily Unavailable.

The girl swallowed the beginning of a sob and dressed, taking the most shapeless, the most basic clothes she could find. The room was tight about her, strangling.

Juno donned an eyeband and concealed her hair beneath a baseball cap. She slid out over the lip of the balcony, and edged over into the neighbouring room, where a fat billionaire from Minsk was sleeping off a binge on the sofa. She picked her way past him, and out.

FROM THE OUTSIDE, it had appeared to be just one more in a line of nondescript lock-up in a back street full of rusted roller doors and gates cut from corrugated steel. Somewhere a block or two back was the main crossroads of Mongkok, the constant rumble of traffic and the sounds of distant metro trains under everything, ebbing and flowing like waves. Ko found the gateway with the ease of someone who had done it hundreds of times, and Fixx ducked low to follow him inside, past hand-painted signs in unreadable characters and layers of flyposters.

Within it was a different story: an oasis of old history nestled there, a small courtyard and a couple of low buildings in an ancient style. The place was a little shabby around the seams but still impressive in its own way. Fixx mused on the fact that the space taken up by the temple could have easily been enough for a housing tower. Whoever owned this place had influence, money, or both.

There were a few boys and a couple of older teens, spinning out tightly trained katas with lionhead swords or halberds.

"A dojo," Fixx said aloud. He glanced at Ko. "You train here?"

The thief gave him an uncomfortable look. "Not for a while."

Ko made him wait outside while he went into one of the buildings, and the op watched the other pupils. They were very good, and their kung fu was something new to him. Fixx picked out elements of a dozen Oriental fighting styles, but all modified beyond their rigid origins. The kids with the halberds flowed like water, the pikes meeting with hollow clacks, never passing close enough for anything but a glancing blow.

He orbited the perimeter of the courtyard and came across a corridor. Along it there were framed photographs, glass cases that were home now only to spiders and nameplates where trophies might once have stood. He found a yellowed newspaper article and there in a dulled image was Ko, younger and happier, between a whipcord fellow in a yellow tracksuit and an older man in police uniform. The boy held up a medal. Further down there were other items that seemed out of place – a stained film script with the title *Blood and Steel*, and old movie posters, their lurid colours and vivid blocks of text all faded shades.

The op looked up as a figure appeared in the shadows. "Joshua Fixx," said the man. "Who might you be?"

"Just passin' through," said Fixx. "Following an inkling, you might say." The man walked into a pool of light and he saw the same face from the paper; the muscular cut of his posture was less than it had been back then. He had grey hair and that kind of wispy beard the old guys in this part of the world seemed to like. "The kid?"

"Ko." The man shook his head. "Such potential. It saddens me to see him squander it on fast cars and street fights. Ah Sing will see he's patched up."

"He'll be cool. He's tougher than he looks."

The old man cocked his head. "You can tell that from just meeting him?"

Fixx showed his teeth. "I'm what you might call a good judge of character."

He held out the tarot card. "Ko asked me to return this to you." The man examined it. "You a fortune teller, Mr Fixx?"

"I have my moments." He paused. "I'm not responsible for Ko's state, if that's what you're thinkin'."

The old man shook his head. "I know that. If you were, we wouldn't be having this pleasant conversation." There was an edge of challenge in the words that gave Fixx pause. "These are dangerous days for the unwary. The streets of my city are filled with foolish men and easy roads to jeopardy. Ko, and the others... I try to teach them to seek a path of enlightenment, not darkness." He came closer, and Fixx saw the subtle cues in his posture that showed he was ready to take things to another level, if that was how it played out. "But I am asking myself, why would a man like you rescue a streetpunk like him from out of nowhere?"

"Like you said, the lad's got potential he don't even know about yet." Fixx took the card and returned it to the pack, careful to remain easy and unhurried. "Kid's got a role to play, neh? Like all o' us." He tapped the dusty glass, reading the only English text he could find on the movie posters. "*The Silent Flute*. I never seen that flick. That's you there, right? The leading man?"

"Long time ago," admitted the old fellow. "Times change."

"Yeah," said Fixx, sensing a kindred spirit. "Not always for the better."

Ko's teacher beckoned. "We should talk, Mr Fixx."

"Call me Joshua."

The old man smiled. "I'm Bruce."

THE INTERIOR OF the church was silent when she slid between the heavy oaken doors. Her footsteps made gentle tapping sounds on the tiled floor as she moved deeper into the building, passing the ranks of oaken pews, empty of worshippers. The chapel seemed strange and out of place in a city of towering glass and steel, a tiny knot of ancient beliefs crowded out by the new temples of the corps.

Juno tried to clarify the impulse that had brought her here and found nothing that could explain it. It was the silence that drew her in, the sense of tranquillity inside the ancient building. In here, the rest of the world seemed far distant. She thought of the old ideals of sanctuary on hallowed ground.

At the altar there were constructs of gold and painted plaster; saviour and cross, seraphs and saints. They appeared stern and unforgiving, and Juno kept her head down, the bill of her cap pointed at the floor.

Someone nearby took a breath. "It's traditional to take your hat off inside the House of God." There was gentle admonishment in the voice.

Juno looked up to see an old priest. He had a pleasant face with concerned eyes that peered from a dark cassock. "Would you mind if I didn't?"

The priest smiled. "I'm sure we can let it go this once."

"Can… Can I sit? I'm not…" Her words trailed off. This was all new to her.

He found a place on one of the pews and gestured around. "It's a slow day. We have plenty of room."

She sat on the bench behind him, perched on the edge in case she felt the sudden urge to escape. "Thanks."

"First time?" he asked, and got a nod in reply. "Well, we never close." The priest patted the wood. "We're always here." He offered her his hand. "I'm Father Woo."

There was the sound of fluttering and she looked up. Birds moved in the rafters, caught by shafts of light through the stained glass windows.

"Doves," explained the priest with a wan smile. "They roost up there, despite my best attempts to entice them to leave. We have an understanding now. They behave themselves and I don't chase them with brooms."

Juno found herself warming to the old man. He was the last thing she expected to find in a city as ruthless and as rapid as this one. "Is it always this quiet?"

Woo sighed. "We've never been the busiest of branch offices, if you take my meaning. These days... many people are finding other idols to give their love to."

She swallowed hard at his choice of words. "It's peaceful."

He nodded and steepled his fingers. "How can we help you, child?"

"Why do you think I need help?"

Another smile. "I've been doing this job a long time, my dear. I've developed an eye for my visitors."

"I have dreams," she began haltingly, "bad dreams, about death and destruction. I see terrible things."

"Dreams can't hurt you," said the priest, "a nightmare is just your mind ridding itself of waste."

"This is different," she insisted. "These visions... I think I see the future, sometimes the past. But there are memories of things that seem out of place, like they belong to someone else." Juno took his hand, her eyes glistening. "Father, I think something terrible is going to happen to me, to all of us. I've seen it."

The priest said nothing for a moment, surprised by her words. "We can't grasp the future, child. That's not for us to know. All we can do is look to what is right, to try and do the proper thing when the choice is laid out in front of us." He squeezed Juno's hand. "Life is about choice. That's the gift God gives us. It's how we use that choice that makes the world a better place."

"Or a darker one," she added.

"Yes," he said sadly. "But if you do what is right, and trust in God, your soul will be saved."

A gasp escaped Juno. She felt hollow inside. "But, Father... What if I don't have one?"

The priest blinked. "Juno, everyone has a soul—"

She bolted up from the pew, clattering against the old wood. "You know who I am?"

"Of course I do. I'm not blind, child, I have a television. Your face is on billboards everywhere." He frowned. "That doesn't mean we can't talk—"

"I have to go." Juno scrambled away down the aisle. Above her, the birds left their roosts, disturbed by the sudden commotion.

The old man was still calling her name when she crashed on to the street and wheeled into the roar of the living city.

IT WAS EVENING when Ko awoke. The watery day had given way to a drowsy sunset, pregnant with humidity. "Typhoon weather," his sister always called it, glaring out of the window of the apartment and fanning herself furiously, as if that would lessen the chances of a tropical storm.

He frowned as he thought of Nikita and rooted through his clothes. The Sifu had got one of the younger pupils to wash his gear and hang it up in the corner of the meditation cell where they'd put him. The poultice of herbal remedies and treated bandages across his chest was moist and tight, but the pain from the wound was far less than it had been before. Quietly, so as not to draw any attention, he searched until he found the corporate cellphone. Despite the damage he'd done to it, the thing was still working, and – he hoped – the sat-locator circuits inside were still dead to the world. As he flipped it open, he heard a rough chug of laughter from out in the courtyard, and Ko leaned close to the window to take a peek. On the stone steps, his erstwhile rescuer was chatting amiably with his teacher, the two men grinning like they were old friends.

Ko watched Fixx. The way the guy had moved out there at the docks, and the hardware he was packing... He had to be a sanctioned operative, no question about it. But ops were rarer than virgins in this part of the world. The mere fact that Fixx was here in Hong Kong and that for some reason he'd chosen Ko to save from certain death was unnerving.

On the drive to Mongkok, he'd questioned the man. At first Ko thought Fixx was someone that the corp guy had recruited to get him away from the triads, but the op showed genuine confusion when Ko mentioned it. He insisted that somebody called "Papa Leg-bar" had sent him, and Ko had no clue who the hell that was.

But Fixx seemed to know things. Not like names or exact details, but he gave Ko a cool-eyed stare and told the youth that he knew he was looking for revenge, that he was in search of reparation for his blood. And however you sliced it, Fixx had saved his life out there. Ko wasn't sure if that should make him pleased, or more wary.

He dialled Gau's number; just before they stashed the Korvette, Ko had forwarded a file he found in the phone's memory. Mister Wageslave had transmitted a copy of a police record about a hit-and-run in Mongkok during their phone conversation.

Gau answered on the second ring. "This is gonna cost you," he said without preamble. "If Second knew I was talking to you—"

"Fuck him," growled Ko. "You owe me, Gau. Remember Shek-O?" There had been a gang rumble on the beach at Shek-O a year earlier, when a Sabre Girl left Gau concussed. Ko had stopped him drowning in the surf and got him home alive. "What you got?"

There was a sigh. "I looked at the pix. I asked around. Spoke to my cousin."

Ko nodded. Gau's relative broke heads for the Wo Shing Wo, who ran most of the action in the Mongkok area.

"This guy who was clipped? It wasn't a mistake like the cops say it is. Cousin says, it was ordered. Bought and paid for. The lie was so the corps didn't lose face."

"Who paid for it?"

Gau hesitated. "Listen, Ko. Once I tell you this, once I hang up, we're done. Your name is poison, man. Second wants to cut you up, and anyone you hang with."

"Gimme the name!" snapped Ko. "That's all I want!"

"Cousin says she was some fat little bitch, big shot music corp or something. The boss called her Miss High."

Feng watched from the shadows, glowering at him.

teh Jade DRAGON gonna rule HK
enda the world

>> Graffiti seen in Lok Fu Metro Station.

12. to Live and die in tsim sha tsui

THE KORVETTE GRUMBLED along Nathan Road in the stop-start evening traffic, a black shark drifting between the slab-sided hulks of double-decker buses. The street was lit with gaudy neon and blinking holos, dancing over their heads. Ko caught a glimpse of a flickering dragon in brilliant green, but it was gone before he could focus on it.

In the driving seat, Fixx glanced at the dashboard navscreen. "Couple more blocks." He looked up at the youth. "Still time to change your mind."

Ko's eyes flicked to a passing street corner. Feng stood out there, arms folded, shaking his head. "Just drop me off outside," he insisted, turning back. "I'll handle it."

Fixx made an amused noise. "I don't think I'll be doin' that."

"I can take care of myself."

"Didn't seem that way at the docks," said the op. "Or perhaps I was just readin' the situation wrongly."

Ko's lip twisted. "Look, this isn't one of those things where you save a guy's life and then it belongs to you. That's the Apache who do that, not the Chinese."

"The old guy, the Sifu. He asked me to keep an eye on you for him. Says you're reckless, impulsive-like. Could get you into trouble."

Ko looked away and smoothed down the jacket he was wearing. The clothes were nondescript and traditional in cut, and they reminded him of a school uniform; but that was all they had to spare in the dojo, and there was no way he'd get into The Han in his go-ganger colours. "There's only one ticket on the door, and it's in my name."

Fixx smiled. "You let me worry about that."

The thief blew out a breath. "Don't get me wrong, I appreciate what you did for me, but the Good Samaritan thing, it's getting a little old now. Why don't you just go on about your business and let me deal with mine?"

The sanctioned operative's eyes flicked to him over the rim of the espex. "Maybe you *are* my business, kid."

He slapped his hands on the dash in exasperation. "Why? What the hell do you want with me, Fixx?"

One hand left the steering wheel and dipped into a jacket pocket. It returned with the tarot card, the Knight of Wands. Fixx held it up.

"That's it?" Ko snorted. "'Cos of some stupid card trick you suddenly gotta stick to me like glue?" He tried to snatch the card from the op's fingers, but Fixx did a magician's flourish and made it disappear. "That's jagged, man! You think your freaky-ass cards and your pocket full of chicken bones makes you some kinda wizard?"

"Houngan," corrected Fixx, but Ko wasn't listening.

"Whatever you think you know about me—"

"Ain't about you," the other man said. "Nor me neither. It's about the way things come together. We got parts to play."

Ko's face flushed with annoyance. "Who told you that, huh? Some voodoo hoodoo? Some—"

"Ghost?" Feng was there in the back seat. Ko could smell the dry scent of his leather armour.

Fixx saw the fractional glimpse he gave the rear-view mirror and looked as well, eyes narrowing. He sniffed.

Ko was still talking, the words spilling out of him. "Maybe you don't see nothing, huh, did you ever think that? Maybe people are right when they call you spooky and weird, maybe the phantoms are all in your head and you're just too looped to know it..." He trailed off, silenced by his own words.

Fixx gave him a quizzical look. "You all right, kid?" The navscreen chimed. "We're here."

Ko's face darkened, and taking care not to let his eye line cross the back seat again, he popped the latch as the vehicle halted at the kerb. "One thing," said the youth, "if you're coming with me."

"Yeah?"

"Quit calling me 'kid'."

Fixx tabbed the autodrive control and set the Korvette to take itself somewhere secluded. "Whatever you say, slick."

THE DEAL, SUCH as it was, came together in a flurry of text messages, back and forth in the dimness of the meditation cell. The wageslave was waiting for Ko's call, and he could taste the man's anxiety even through the strings of letters and numbers. There would need to be money, real yuan cash and not some fairy gold eDollars that would vanish from the account the moment the transaction was done. The corp made promises, and the thief turned the screws on him.

Not just cash, wageslave. More than that.

This chance would never come again, Ko was sure of it. He made the man secure stratojet transfers, nameless and no-questions-asked tickets that would get Ko and Nikita out of Hong Kong and to any major city in the world. The thief thought about the Zarathustra Clinic, the glossy brochure of the clean white buildings in Zurich and Aspen.

Ko laughed off the corp's attempts to get him to meet on Hong Kong Island. Nah. That was the corporate heartland over that side of the bay. Ko wanted the meet to go down on his turf, Kowloon side, the domain of the Street. He thought about how Hazzard Wu had dealt with a similar situation in *Cat Street Killer*, the last reel was the nightclub duel. Yeah...

They'd meet at The Han. The place was high profile and exclusive, catering to top echelon corps, media types and the richest members of Hong Kong's criminal dominions. You had to have an AmEx Plasma card just to get in, so he'd heard. Wageslave could make that happen, he promised. Ko's name would be on the guest list. Of course, he hadn't reckoned on needing a "plus one".

Feng still did not speak to him, silent since the incident at the docks, and he seemed to be there less and less. Ko had lost the last few Peacefuls in his pockets to the waters in the bay, and couldn't even give the swordsman the smallest of offerings by way of apology. The warrior retreated to the shadows and faded.

Fixx and the Sifu caught him trying to sneak out. He heard them talking in riddles, something about "black skies over the peak", the old man's voice tight with anger as he spoke of "monsters on the streets" and "poisoned blood".

He told them, after a fashion, how it was going to go down.

"Smells like a trap," Fixx noted. "More at stake than you know."

But Ko didn't care. He wanted out, him and Nikita gone. The city, his life, everything he knew had turned on him, piece by piece.

"I'm done here," he told them, and he meant it.

ANY OTHER NIGHTCLUB, and the red carpet outside would have been crammed with paparazzi and camera drones; but the management at The Han had a discreet flicker-field screen extending out to the street. It formed a tube of runny air, appearing like smoke hazing through glass, fogging the image of anyone who passed inside. Coupled with an EM frequency jammer, discretion was assured.

Most people didn't even know exactly where the club was. There were no advertisements for it, no address listed on the matchbooks. It was a stealth venue, sandwiched between two equally nondescript buildings. Rumour had it that there were even fake entrances dotted all around Hong Kong, just to throw off the riff-raff and the uninvited. If you didn't already know where it was then you had no business being there.

The doorman was aptly named. He was as large as one, dark aged oak. He held up a hand the moment he got a good look at Ko's clothes. The AV feed in his monocle had a programme embedded that served solely to judge the fashion index of those who wanted to enter the club. "Name?" he rumbled.

Ko thought himself clever when he told the wageslave what identity to place on the guest list, but now it came to say it out loud, he felt a little silly. "Uh. Hazzard Wu."

There was the very smallest raise of an eyebrow, and the man nodded, ticking off an item on an embedded d-screen. "Good evening, Mr Wu. Nice to see you again." He beckoned Ko with one hand and warded off Fixx with another. "And you are?"

"A gatecrasher." The sanctioned operative stabbed out with a single finger and struck a nerve point near the doorman's clavicle.

"Ah," was all the big man could manage, as his muscles seized up and left him twitching there, rooted to the spot.

Fixx uncurled a hundred yuan note and slipped it into the doorman's jacket pocket as they walked past. "Thanks, bro."

THERE WERE BARS that dealt drinks and food, oxygen and pills. Boys and girls in costume drifted through the clientele distributing orders in stone cups or rough-hewn glasses that looked like cubes of ice. Music and drugfog hazed the air, weaving around the flaps of ceiling fans worked by nubile girls. Ko walked in deliberate slow motion, keeping to Fixx's right, working hard not to be dazzled by what he saw around him. The club was modelled on the interior of a warlord's grand hall from ancient China's feudal past, but in a weird neo-tech style that blended lunar steel with resin statues and old tapestries. The "historic fusion" look was very *now* among the PacRim incrowd.

Some part of him, the core of his working-class streetkid soul, felt so utterly and completely out of his depth that the tingle of a flight reflex shuddered through his legs. One look at the opulence inside The Han and Ko had never felt so *common* in his whole life.

"Can almost smell the riches," Fixx said out of the corner of his mouth.

Ko nodded, watching men at the bar with yakuza electro-tattoos emerging from their collars. No money appeared to be changing hands; the staff at The Han obviously knew whom they were charging.

A girl, maybe a year younger than Ko, drifted up to them. She wore stylised magistrate's robes cut to reveal legs and cleavage. "Mr Wu? Mr Lam will receive you upstairs in the gallery." She pointed to a hooded balcony on one of the upper levels.

"Lam, huh?" Ko glanced at Fixx. "He's not expecting two of us."

The operative nodded, a curious, distant expression on his face. "You settle what you gotta."

"You just going to stand here and sniff the air?"

Fixx walked away like he knew exactly where he was going. "Don't worry 'bout me. I'll be around."

In the depths of the shadowed booth, Juno sipped her drink and gave Frankie an artificial, purse-lipped smile. He met her eyes and hesitated.

"What's wrong?" he asked, leaning in. "If you don't like it here, we can go someplace else after—"

"It's not that," she said. "I'm just... just tired."

Frankie's expression didn't change, and Juno felt cold inside, as if something was pushing at the cage of her ribs but couldn't get to her throat. *Why can't I tell him?* The question burned in her, the embers of her dreams and the echoes of the conversation in the church still drifting around her mind like windborne ash. Her mouth opened and closed, but each time she tried to frame the thoughts, speech fled her. Juno could not make herself tell him, as hard as she tried.

"I'm sorry, I shouldn't have asked you to come if you weren't up to it."

She forced another smile. "No. No, this is a great club. The Han is one of the few places I can go where I'm not hounded by drones and people who want autographs." Juno squeezed his hand. "Can we just not talk about it? Just be together for a while?" The moment the words left her mouth and she turned her mind's eye from the darker thoughts, she felt calmer, tension ebbing.

"Sure," he said, a frown threatening to form at the edges of his expression.

It was Juno's turn to be concerned. "What about you? What's bothering *you*, Frankie?"

He seemed on the verge of telling her, but then a screen set into the top of their table lifted itself up and chimed. "Your guest has arrived, Mr Lam," it announced.

"I, uh, have to—"

She waved him away. "That's fine, go ahead."

He reached out and gave her hand a squeeze, as if he needed to make sure she was still real. Frankie stepped out of the booth, straightening his tie.

A boy cruised past, bearing a tray with dozens of small jewelled containers. Juno caught his eye and he paused. She threw a glance to make sure Frankie wasn't looking back at her and beckoned the waiter closer. "I need some blue," she told him, the sudden need licking at her gut. The words felt new and strange, as if she had never said them before.

The boy gave her a beautiful cloisonné box in green and gold; inside were dozens of dot-sized tabs, glistening like sapphires.

ON THE UPPER galleries there were rows of doors leading off to VIP suites and chillout rooms. Frankie kept his attention away from them as he passed, memories of the activities in the tower returning to him in blinks of smell and sight.

There was a figure arched over the balcony, tapping the brass rail with nervous energy. Turning to face him, the executive saw the youth's drawn, serious face and almost smiled. *Hell. He's a damn kid.*

"Mr Lam?" he drawled, the affected sneer on his lips just failing to give the effect of cocksure arrogance he was aiming for.

Frankie shook his head. "Steal any good cars lately?"

The thief's face soured. "Fuck you, wageslave."

He nodded. "Right. Guess that proves who you are."

"You got the, uh, payment?"

He pulled two smartcards from his pocket. "Here. All-access flight vouchers for Raümhansa Transcontinental. These'll take you anywhere but orbit."

Suspicion bloomed on the younger man's face. "Where's the money? No cash, no deal—"

"Relax," said Frankie, as much to himself as to the youth. He produced a ticket. "The money is in a case in the cloakroom. This is the check for it."

The kid began to back away. "That's not what we agreed."

Frankie stood his ground. "Hey, I got no reason to trust you either. How do I know that what you've got for me isn't bogus?" He wiped his hand across his brow. The tension in the gallery was draining him. He sat heavily in a chair. "Ah shit, look. Just give me the name and you can take the stuff and go. I'm not interested in anything else." He put the ticket and the cards down on a table. "I don't have time to play these games, kid."

"My name is Ko," said the thief, with irritation. He stood his ground, tense and ready to fight. Fists balled, shoulders set, ready to go to the mat with anyone.

Frankie studied him, and saw the mirror of himself there, a decade ago, standing in the corridor of a detention centre...

Brother, listen to me! If you don't do this, you'll go to prison, and you know what will happen in there: indentured work service on the mainland, maybe even sending you to the rad-zone reconstruction projects! You won't survive in there! Look, my supervisor at the academy knows the judge and he's willing to put in a good word for you. I vouched for you, Frankie. I told him you didn't want to be in a gangcult, you just fell in with the wrong crowd! Come on! If not for me, then for Mum and Dad! I have faith in you, I know you can be more than this.

I don't wanna be a damn corp, Alan! I'm not like you, the good boy with the great grades.

It's not about that, Frankie! It's about surviving! You gotta trust me, brother! Please!

"Why the hell should I trust you?" said Ko, and abruptly the executive realised he'd been thinking aloud.

Frankie eyes him. "Because, I'm guessing here, that both of us have something to lose. Am I right?"

"Yeah," came the reluctant, distant reply. "I got someone... something to lose." Ko took the cards and the ticket. "The dead guy, his name was Lam?"

"Family," said Frankie, staring at the floor. He could hear the blood singing in his ears.

Ko nodded gravely. "It was a couple of Wo Shing Wo hitters. It wasn't mistaken identity, an accident or any of that shit. They were paid to do it."

"The name?" Frankie felt sick with anticipation and dread.

Ko told him.

THE COOL, CRYSTALLINE hit was coming on strong when the apparition rose into her vision. Juno stiffened with fright as he took solidity there, at the mouth of the alcove. He blocked the light from the rest of the club like an eclipse dulling the sun.

"Miss," came a voice, rich and smooth. "Might I presume to take a moment of your time?"

Juno nodded woodenly, and the man shifted into the booth with her, taking the place where Frankie had been sitting. She felt very small in his presence – or was that just the Z3N? The capsules were supposed to make her feel better, make the shades and dreams go away. Lately they seemed to do the opposite.

He said something and she caught only a little of it; was he asking if something was broken, asking to share the hit? Looking for a, a *fix*?

"But you can call me Joshua." He took off his shades and studied her in a caring way, a brotherly way. "You remember me, Juno? Newer Orleans? Under the 'dome?"

She had that memory somewhere, but it shrank from her whenever she tried to hold on to it. Confusion creased her face. "I... am not sure we've met."

"I know the feelin'," he admitted. "That's why I wanted to talk to you. I won't hurt you, you understand that?"

She nodded; the mere idea that he would harm her seemed laughable. It seemed to her that she'd always known that about him. "Of course not. That's not why you're here." And if Juno thought very hard, she could just about understand why he had come. What it was he wanted. What it was he was offering her.

"The dreams, they happen in the day," he said, careful and matter-of-fact. "Angels in the glass and the snakes, sometimes." He gave a shudder. "Stronger now."

Juno's hand reached out and took his. It seemed like the right thing to do. "The days... When I'm in the now it's all so clear and vivid, but the days before are cloudy and dull. The further back I try to see, the darker—" Her breath caught. "I don't want to look back."

Fixx pressed a card into her hand. She ran her fingers over it. "The High Priestess. Is that me?"

"Could be. You have the look of her." He reached over and took the green and gold box. "Will you do somethin' for me, Juno? Make me a promise?"

"If I can…"

He rattled the box, the pills whispering inside it. "No more. Don't take the blue anymore. That's where the dark is coming from. It's not helping."

Juno heard herself speaking, as if someone else were animating her. "I believe you."

He smiled warmly. "That's a good start. Now, you gave me trust so I'm goin' to give you a thing in return, okay?" He gently cupped his mahogany fingers under her chin and met her gaze. Juno felt the material real of the club become gossamer and faint. The depths of his amber eyes held her transfixed. "I'm gonna give the past back to you, girl. It'll be slow and it won't come easy-like, but in the end… You'll know who you really are."

"I want that," she breathed. More than anything, she wanted that.

"Then, child, listen to me. Listen to me. Listen. Listen. Just listen."

PHOEBE HI, THERE under the glow of the lamps in Tze's library. Her plastic smile, the too-perfect face on the dumpy little body. *I worked closely with your brother. I hope to do the same with you.*

"Bitch…" hissed Frankie, half in anger, half in shock. "Why? Why the hell would she do that?"

Ko chewed his lip. "Happens all the time in HK, man. You're a corp, you know how it is." He made a fist. "Like in history, when guys in the palace did shit to each other so they'd look preem in front of the Emperor, make the other sucker take the rap."

Frankie got up in a rush and he wobbled, the revelation making him dizzy.

Ko grabbed his shoulder to steady him. "You all right?"

He shook off the hand. "Don't..." He tasted bile in his throat. "I... I gotta think..." Frankie could barely hold the thought of it in his head. His suspicions had been raging for days, and while he knew that YLHI were no strangers to dirty tricks, it still hit him like a sucker punch. It was one thing to sanction something on a rival or apply pressure to a client – but to hire criminals to kill a high level executive in the same corporate clan? On some level of denial, Frankie had been hoping that the obfuscation of the truth was some attempt to protect him from a darker threat, something that had cost Alan Lam his life; but now his certainties rocked around him. Hi had ordered Alan's murder! Had she done it alone? Who else might be involved? Alice? The Masks? Even...

"Tze?"

A round of clapping came from the lower floor, drawing their attention. The clientele were toasting a new arrival, a gaunt figure flanked by a broad man in a dark green suit and a woman in a white strapless dress. The man and the woman wore shimmering Peking Opera masks.

Frankie's heart shrank in his chest. "Speak of the devil..."

Ko spat. "You set me up."

"No, no," insisted Frankie, "I didn't know he was going to come here!"

But the thief was already moving, snatching up his reward from the table and sprinting for the spiral stairs to the lower level. When Frankie looked back from the balcony, Tze was staring up at him. The older man gave him a nod and knowing smile.

Ko HAD THE case in his hand when the cloakroom floor rose up to meet him. He rolled, the black attaché skating away from his grip.

"Hello again." The rasping voice came from behind Deer Child's mask, newly repaired after the melee in the car park. "Remember me? You have unfinished business with Mr Tze—"

Ko did a scissor-kick that put a boot in Deer Child's crotch, and spun, coming to his feet in a rush. He ducked to dodge a salvo of fast blows to the chest and head, marvelling at the speed of the bodyguard.

One punch shattered an oil lantern and in a whoosh of sound, a tapestry flooded with hungry flames. Ko moved to avoid more attacks, on the defensive as The Han's clientele began to panic and flee.

He was a second too slow, and Deer Child snared his throat, one large hand choking the life from him. "Teach you about pain," said the guardian.

In the confusion of the crowd bolting for the door, Ko saw motion, predator-quick and deadly. The glitter of a nickel-plated handgun. The muffled roar of a heavy gauge bullet.

Then the pressure was gone, the grey mist fogging his brain receding. Fixx was carrying him out into the humid, screeching night.

Ko saw flickers of Deer Child's face though shattered porcelain. Flayed flesh, dataprobes pressed into optic jelly, lipless mouth over shark teeth.

"Wait, the case..." he coughed. "The cash..."

THERE WAS A moment when Tze made the briefest eye contact with the black man who rescued the presumptuous little thief. His breath caught in his throat; the dark face, the hooded eyes. This face was *known* to him. He had plucked it from the songbird's mind while little Juno slept. At the time, Tze had dismissed the moment as a spasm of random memory, bereft of any meaning — but his presence here, in the city, on the eve of the ascendance? Tze knew there were no coincidences, only synchronicity. Did the little doll sense something that I did not?

The palpable aura of threat the dark man radiated made his jaw clench, but he had no time to dwell. The Masks would have to deal with this new variable, and swiftly, before it could expand to alter the pattern. He turned, sniffing archly at the commotion. "How disappointing. The standards here fall lower and lower." He studied Frankie's flushed countenance. "Francis, you look perturbed. Is something wrong?"

The anger and frustration overtook any good reason in Frankie's mind. "Alan's death wasn't a mistake," he snapped, "he was murdered!"

The older man's face became sad. "Yes, son. I know. I was hoping to keep this awful truth from you, but you seemed so determined to find out for yourself."

"You... you knew?"

"Francis, there's more to this than you understand. What happened to your brother, who was responsible... There's a pattern to these things that you are only now becoming aware of."

He rocked on his heels, giddy with emotion. "But Hi, what she did—"

"She's at the tower, right now." Tze leaned in closer. "Blue Snake will take care of Juno. Perhaps you and I should have a word with Phoebe, yes? I'd like you to get a better handle on things."

Francis felt his hands coiling into fists, a sudden and potent fire kindling inside him. "Yes," he said. "I want that."

"Come," said the CEO, and pressed him toward the door.

The Statue Park at Victoria Peak is one of the city's most popular tourist attractions. The park is a fantastic fusion of the modern and the ancient. Using design elements from Hong Kong's stunning skyline combined with actual stonework and statuary dating back more than two thousand years, the Statue Park brings past and present together in one place.

The layout of the park is based on astrological charts from the Qin Dynasty; those of you walking the route follow runes drawn by Chinese magicians, so breathe deep and you might take in a little "qi" of your own! The exhibits at the Statue Park include stone temple guardians from the northern provinces, a troupe of authentic terracotta warriors and the preserved wood beams from a Ming warship. The park is free to all, funded by generous donations from corporate sponsors such as Buell Tool Inc, GenTech East, Yuk Lung Heavy Industry, and Lan Ri Foods.

The Peak Rail Tram operates a half-hourly service. Tickets are available at the terminus in Garden Road. Gangcult activity, while at a minimum across the city, is distinctly possible late at night or during periods of activity such as concerts, festivals or eclipses. Passengers travelling at these times are advised to consider a personal defence device for peace of mind. The terminus gift shop sells a range of semi-lethal deterrents, including tanglers, taser-touch gloves and Nauseator™ gas dispensers.

Excerpt from *The Hong Kong Highlight Guide*
[2026 edition].

13. time and tide

"Miss, wait a moment—" Juno ignored the voice and kept walking, her feet clacking across the polished granite of the Yuk Lung tower's atrium. She was aware of the guardian at her side, the woman Tze called Blue Snake. "Perhaps we should return to your hotel."

Juno stopped suddenly and stamped her foot. "No. I want Frankie. Where is he? Mr Tze brought him here, I know it." She rocked as she shouted at the bodyguard, feeling flushed and faint. In one hand she was still clasping the tarot card the dark-skinned man had given her. It was hot against her fingers.

Blue Snake hesitated. Juno knew the woman was trapped by her orders from her master, and like a robot with conflicting commands, the guardian stood watching her rather than initiate a choice that could be the incorrect one. Juno looked at the blank eyes inside the azure and gold mask and thought of the other one, the big man with the green faceplate. She had heard the gunshot, saw him falling with a trail of ruddy matter streaming from the back of his head. Then the fire, the screaming. Calling out for Frankie…

"I want Francis Lam!" she snapped, her voice pitching up. "Now." Her throat felt dry. "I'm giving you an order."

"Perhaps I can locate him and bring him to you at the hotel," Blue Snake tried again, cocking her head like a dog.

"No!" Juno shouted like a petulant child and slapped the guardian, the unexpected impulse of anger shocking her. Her hand connected with the mask and she staggered back a step, her palm stinging. Blue Snake flinched, unsure of how to proceed.

Bile bubbled in Juno's throat and she swallowed metallic spittle. "I… I have to…" She ran for the washroom concealed behind the banks of elevators and crashed into a stall. Juno was barely over the steel bowl before she vomited, a thin purple fluid of spent cocktails and half-digested food streaming out of her.

The girl slipped to the cool white tile floor and shivered. Her clasp bag was somewhere out in the limousine, but in her hand, there was the card. Burning her, even though she couldn't dare to let go of it.

Juno looked at the careworn image, the priestess in her courtly robes, hands open and cupping arcane energies. The card shimmered, as if she saw it through tears.

"What did you do to me?" she piped, licking tainted lips.

I'm gonna give the past back to you.

Fixx's words rumbled in her bones, as loud as if he were there inside her skull. She was afraid, trembling on the toilet floor. She wanted Frankie to be with her, to hold her, to tell her it was all fine.

Instead, there was a rising tide of terror. It welled up from a secret place in her heart, and there came an awful moment when Juno realised that it had always been there, always waiting. The man with ebony skin and dark, deep eyes, he had known that. He unlocked something in Juno, just with a touch and a word. With a picture and a card.

High Priestess. High. *Higher…*

The ink from the card was staining her fingers, stinging them, passing through her skin. Memory came upon Juno in a tidal wave and she choked.

Sunglasses smashed. Ropé's hands around her throat. Slow, slow cracking pops. Vertebrae snaps. Body falls dead. Beckons her from the door. Gently undresses the dead. Taking her clothes. Becoming her. Becoming the dead. Reborn. Renewed.

I am you now.

"Fuck!" The word came out in a tight animal screech. Juno scrambled from the toilet stall and slammed into the rack of glass sinks, the room swaying around her, her balance hazy and faltering. She could *not* release the card. He had done something to her, like the street magicians who made people sleep with a snap of their fingers. The dark man had reached into her thoughts and pulled out the stops.

Juno hung on to the sink, the room spinning about her so fast she was afraid that gravity would throw her off if she let go. She raised her head and saw mirrors.

There were silver ovals on every wall, perfect and flawless reflections of her pathetic scarlet face and eyes of smeared kohl. In each her irises glowed amber, staring back at her. The mirrors ranged away into a curved tunnel of infinity. She was here and she was there; she was dead and she was living. Image and real. Reflection and reflected.

She was one and she was many. The girl tasted alien fluids in her gut, for one phantom moment feeling the distant sensation of tubes in her mouth, probes in her nostrils, thick oils dragging on her naked skin.

Her equilibrium returning in slow, painful ticks, Juno discarded the coat about her shoulders and pushed out through the doors. There were jade pillars dotted about in this part of the atrium, and with slow, careful progress, the girl kept herself from the line of Blue Snake's sight, finding an elevator to the tower's upper levels. She seemed to be escaping, but to where she had no idea.

PHOEBE HI LOOKED up and started as the doors to Tze's library opened. She was cleaning the ornate bowl in the centre of the room with a sanctified cloth and a vial of tainted blood plasma supplied by an operative in a Kowloon children's hospital. "Mr Tze! I, ah—" Her words faded as Frankie crossed the room toward her, his face murky with anger. The vial slipped from her fingers and rolled across the oaken table. "Francis?"

He loomed over her, his fists balling and uncurling, his lips moving but no coherent words emerging. He was so utterly furious that his capacity to speak rationally had vanished. Hi shot a worried look at Tze. Frankie released a powerful backhand blow that knocked the woman off her feet and to the floor. "You fucking bitch, you killed my brother!" he screamed.

Hi's hand came to her lip and traced blood. She looked at Tze again, confused.

"Francis deduced the train of events himself," Tze said sadly.

"Doesn't he understand?" wailed the woman. She glared at Frankie. "It was necessary. He was going to destroy the great work. He was defecting."

"You didn't have to kill him!" roared Frankie. "You didn't have to do that."

"Yes, I did." Tze's words cut through the air.

Frankie turned. "But the 14K said she—"

"Phoebe brokered the hit, yes, but on my authority." He let out a small smile. "Did you not think that I would have some say in the disposal of so valuable an asset, Francis?" Tze shook his head. "I regret what happened, I really do. Alan was like a son to me. We are so close to the ascendance. Perhaps I could have overlooked things if only he'd kept faith with us."

"What?" Frankie rocked on his heels, a sick churn in his gut. "Why...?"

Tze frowned. "Your brother was flawed, Francis. A bright man and very good at his job. Ruthless in the right places, careful in others. But there was a certain inner strength he lacked. The capacity to subsume himself to a greater cause. Alan did not have the courage to embrace self-sacrifice."

Hi was picking herself up, attempting to gather her dignity. "He couldn't see the reach of the pattern."

The CEO of Yuk Lung Heavy Industries took off his jacket and began to unbutton his shirt. "The time is not right. We are early. But I see that rigid adherence to the letter of the pattern has only brought us grief. We must be flexible and adaptable, like our King."

And very suddenly, Frankie felt the world shifting around him. The nagging doubts, the faint fears, the splinter in his mind that screamed something is not right. All of it crystallised in this moment. He knew that these people were going to kill him, just as they had his sibling. His eyes flicked to the doors; Judge Bao stood there, the mask glaring back at him.

"Few men have a sense of their own worth, Francis," Tze said. He had his spidersilk shirt off now and the suntanned skin beneath seemed murky with lines of writing and whorls of colour. "Fewer still of their own destiny. I am blessed because I have both, and by that token, it is my gift to know your worth as well."

"Wh-what the hell are you talking about?" Frankie stuttered.

"Hell." Tze smirked. "Yes, indeed. My meaning, lad? It is no less than this. I know the colour of your blood, Francis Lam Cheung Yee. By the grace of the Dark Ones, I've tracked the threads of your bloodline across the weave of history." He made a sweeping gesture. "Your family, your brother too. In both of you it runs thick." The man came into the light and there on his chest one brand burned brighter than the others, a connection of circles, lines, arcs.

Hi snorted. "He still doesn't comprehend. He's no better than the other."

Tze silenced her with a snap of his fingers. "There's never been a time when we haven't watched you, Francis. Even before your birth, the King's Men observed, measured, tracked. And waited."

"The files," Frankie blurted. "I saw them."

The other man nodded. "You and your kindred have something I could only dream of possessing, son. You are touched by Him. Your bloodline bares the mark. You are living avatars, the keepers of the Key to the Great Pattern, scattered across the world like seeds. Waiting to bloom." He touched a hidden control on a wooden lectern. "Let me show you."

A d-screen dropped from the ceiling behind Hi and flicked into sharp reds. Frankie recognised electron microscope images of blood platelets, of twisting ropes of DNA. The view crawled closer.

"Do you not see?" grinned Tze, pointing.

At a size visible only on the highest magnifications, Frankie saw shapes that seemed embossed on the very matter of his flesh and blood, imprinted there like a maker's mark: the repeated icons of a star with eight points and the same shape that was burned into the chest of Mr Tze. His stomach twisted.

"Spilled blood marks the way," intoned the other man, "and it must be of a vintage that the King prefers." He snapped his fingers and Monkey King was there, strong, iron-hard arms snaking around Frankie's torso. "Don't fear Him," murmured Tze, "embrace Him. When your veins are opened and the Jade Dragon drinks of you, you will become a part of His Glory. You will seal the pact for us." Tze's eyes glittered with rapture and he pointed up at the ceiling. There were carvings of serpents and cruel angels up there, shadows writhing in the dim lamplight. "Alan perished too soon, he forced my hand. That error will not be repeated."

"You, every damn one of you, are absolutely out of your fucking minds," said Frankie.

Rope stopped dead in his tracks at the sight of Blue Snake, standing there in the middle of the atrium, her slender and dangerous hands moving in front of her chest like leaves in a gentle breeze. The bodyguard was watchful, patient.

"Where is Miss Quan?" He demanded, striding toward the guardian.

"She became unwell." Blue Snake nodded blankly at the restroom. "She required privacy."

"How long ago was this?"

She cocked her head. "Elapsed time: four minutes, thirty-six seconds."

Rope sneered and went into the toilet. Blue Snake walked warily behind him. The guardians were useful tools in the correct circumstances, but they were flawed. Drained of their humanity by the Masking process, they sometimes became slow, confused by emotions and reactions that they had lost the means to process. Tze's ridiculous attachment to them had been shown for the idiotic affectation it was in the club tonight, his personal bodyguard downed by a mystery assailant; and now this, the female one failing to understand the mindset of the girl Juno.

He slammed the stall door with his hand, kicking at the discarded coat with the tip of his boot. The smell of cooling puke tickled his nostrils; Blue Snake examined the remains, analysing them in a vague attempt to grasp the error she had made.

Ropé prodded her in the chest. "Seal the building. Locate her. But be *discreet*."

Blue Snake padded out into the hall and halted. "Tracking reports... target is ascending. Destination is Research and Development level."

He swore and pushed the woman out of the way, dragging a smartcard from his pocket. Ropé entered a lift and gave chase.

The chamber began to unfold. Where they stood in the centre of the room, the circular section of the stone floor remained static; but the rings of smaller flagstones around the edges of the hall folded back upon themselves and allowed twisting wooden pillars to emerge. Some of them were wet and they smelt coppery in the thick air. From the ceiling, extending from the carved bodies of snakes and worm-headed abominations, metal arms ending in the glass eyes of holojector lenses fell into place and emitted coherent light. Frankie saw the shapes of people forming in some of the glowing haloes beneath them, others showing black monoliths that reminded him of obsidian tombstones.

Hi completed cleaning the bowl and allowed Tze to cut himself into it. The CEO removed the same silver box from beneath the oak table and Frankie suppressed a shudder. Out came the knife of manifold blades, into Tze's hand with casual, dangerous motions.

"You're not going to die tonight," Tze said in an offhand manner, whispering so that the other players in his sick little theatre did not hear. "Your bloodline is the most potent, the most vital. We have to be economical with it." He smirked. "I am not a man for wastage."

Frankie struggled in Monkey King's grip. "This is nuts! You're telling me, my whole family is some line of sacrificial lambs for some psycho cult?"

"Not just you. There are others." Tze nodded at the holos. In one, Frankie saw a general in the uniform of the APRC carefully stabbing an elderly man; in another, a woman in a blue shipsuit was coring the eyes from a screaming child. He turned away, reeling. "It is just that your blood is the superior strain." Tze took the knife and made shallow, stinging cuts on Frankie's wrists, catching the ejecta in the bowl.

Hi made symbols in the air and bowed. Tze waited for her to have her face over the basin, and in a single sweep, he tore the blade across the bare white flesh of her throat. Dark arterial spray fanned into the air and the music executive perished with a wailing, streaming gurgle. There was something like rapture in her dying eyes.

Tze gave a pious nod to the other members of the Cabal. "The altar is anointed. As the pattern speaks, we will allow the stone and wood to drink their fill, preparing themselves. We Open The Way."

"We Open The Way," came a chorus of voices from hidden speakers.

"In the wastes of America, a fool tries and fails. So-called Elders with their petty, limited ideals bark like dogs believing they have the attention of men. They have nothing but the contempt of the Dark Ones. It is only we who will succeed. We, who light the path. We, who will thrive where Seth fails." He showed a mouth full of white, razor teeth. "The Jade Dragon rises. It is ordained."

JUNO HAD NEVER been here.
She had been here many times.
She had no idea what number to key into the security keypad.
The code was 7-9-5-7-3.
Juno remembered the glass and steel rooms with floors of hollow plate.
She was terrified at her first sight of the facility.
She was scared the security drones would see her.
She knew where to stand to avoid them.

The tarot card in her hand. It seemed to merge with her flesh, become insubstantial. The image of the High Priestess was a brand, a tattoo done in acid inks. She let it lead her in, muscle memory taking Juno deep into a place of quiet, patient machines and liquid glows.

Inside, the laboratory was lit in a watery yellow, a series of light bars set in the floor casting shadows around a collection of large spherical modules. The orbs were transparent, and in each of them was a naked human body, coiled and floating in a green ocean. Juno recoiled, almost falling over a low console. The sphere closest to her held a child, a girl, and as she watched, Juno could see the slow movement of her chest and the occasional twitch of fingers and toes. A flat mask covered the girl's eyes, and a pair of thick, semi-organic cables extended into the liquid medium. One was attached to her navel, and the other disappeared into a fluffy matt of hair at the back of her head. Juno felt her stomach turn over again and put out a hand to steady herself, inadvertently touching the wall of the sphere.

The sensation was instantly familiar, and her mind swam with the faintest recollection of a thick, warm sea. She retched, tasting plastic in her mouth, the horrible memory of pipes snaking down her gullet and into her stomach.

Behind her the door hissed open again, and a gust of warm air wandered into the chamber with Heywood Ropé at its centre.

"Oh dear," he said, lilting and mocking, unconcerned and hateful. "Don't you know it's wrong to peek behind the curtain?"

Juno began to cry. Her world was coming adrift, huge icebergs of her personal reality breaking off and sinking.

Ropé came close, snatched the tarot card from her stiff grip and shoved her down. "What have we here?" He raised it to his nostrils and took a long, deep sniff. "Where did you get this?"

Juno shook her head, backing away.

His face twisted. "It doesn't matter. It doesn't matter what you know. There's no time for the pattern to be altered. You're going to do what you were made for, you little bitch."

Tears streaking her face, she glanced at the glassy spheres, the sleeping girl and the other, unfinished things. Ropé answered the unspoken question.

"Them? Oh, they're just leftovers, darling. Remnants and remainders. Understudies, you might say."

She found her voice again. "I'm not… going to help you. You kill people."

He laughed and the sound made her whimper. "I've murdered you in a dozen different ways, each sweeter than the last. So know that. Know that you will do what I tell you. You don't have a choice." He rolled a Z3N capsule between his thumb and forefinger, and she wanted it more than anything in her life.

"I hate you," she wept, collapsing in on herself.

Ropé knelt by her, the horrible façade of his outward face coming to the fore again. "Don't," he said mildly. "I'll give you what that witch doctor offered. You want to know yourself, Juno? Here you are."

He bent close to her ear and whispered a word. The command made a post-hypnotic suture in her RNA tear open and bleed memory. Juno went into quiet shock as she remembered…

The songs fading. The channel into her sealed and dark; disconnected, the world ending.

Around her, the slow thick ocean pulling, dragging as she turns. New sensations of movement and direction, and the ocean falls away.

Muscles spasm. A burning stream of pain from her belly, out in a plug of expelled jelly. Weight pulling her into places and directions she's never known. Cold hardness pressed into the length of her, light flooding over, coming in some impossible way from outside of her head. Fluids dripping out of holes in her body.

Something digs into the skin of her face and the light blazes inward like the ignition of a supernova.

"Eyes are open."

Convulsing. Burning coming up again, a million times worse.

"Got your smock?"

Out in a rush, a torrent of agony.

"Aw, shit!"

"I told you, always point the head towards the drain. Stupid."

Voices? Moving her mouth, pushing and pulling at her muscles. The slow waters are gone, a cold, invisible ocean around her. Wet hiss from her lips.

"Meat's awake. Dose it, then."

"There's a lot of blood in the ejecta. Shouldn't we—"

"Just get it done."

Light breaks apart into shifting pieces, growing large or small.

"Uh, okay." *Something at her neck. Hard. Sharp.* "Full dose." *It bites her.*

Sound like a pressure leak sings out of her mouth, dropping into a thick gurgle.

"Juno Seven decanted at fourteen-forty. No anomalies, cleared for processing."

"Let's go, hurry it up."

Movement. Light falls away. Touching her belly, there's a fleshy stub, crusted with drying fluids. The cord is cut! She spits out bone-jarring coughs, ejecting droplets of dark colour from her mouth...

"Do you understand now, little doll?" whispered Ropé. "Little plastic girl?" He took a handful of her hair and pulled her to her feet. "You're nothing but a wind-up toy, the ballerina on the music box. We made you."

"Yes," she cried, her body shaking with fear. "Oh, yes..."

FRANKIE SHIVERED, FEELING scattered droplets of Phoebe Hi's blood cooling where they had spattered on his face. Monkey King's inviolate grip held him erect, and all he could do was turn his head away as Tze came closer. "I want you to comprehend, Francis," he said. "I want you to appreciate how special you are. Those others are just the first morsels of the banquet; you are the delicious feast. The gift you are given will be sweeter than anything the rest of us can imagine. The King of Rapture will take you into himself...." Tze shook his head. "Such a glory."

He used the fluids in the bowl to write shapes on himself. One of Tze's other minions, a man in a spotlessly clean laboratory coat, offered up a tray bearing a stone bottle and cups. Tze poured out equal measures of thick syrup. The fluid was sparkling blue.

Frankie saw what was coming and struggled, but the Mask tipped back his head. Tze threw back the liquid Z3N and tipped the other cup into Frankie's mouth.

He tried to cough it out, but the fluid tingled like cold fire in his gullet and it surged into his body. Monkey King let him go and he fell to his knees.

Frankie's vision swam, his senses became woolly one second, ultra-sharp the next. Tze crouched down to face him, grinning. "Yes. Don't fight it."

He'd done drugs before, but the stories that came with the Z3N caps had always scared Frankie away, of how it was used at sex parties and bloodclubs, of the mad psychedelic high and the weird way it made people speak alike, act alike, think alike. Something about the blue had always seemed *invasive* to him.

Tze started laughing, and Frankie felt the echo of it in his chest. He couldn't stop himself from joining in, the bitter humour overtaking him. In the haze of his vision he could see dark tendrils unfolding from the old man, whip-fast and sharp. They penetrated Frankie's skull and wormed into his mind. Tze was in there with him, sharing his thoughtspace.

You see? boomed the mindspeech. *This is His gift to us, the means to unchain the psyche and marshal it to our cause.*

He heard Juno singing, somewhere very far away. *Touch my thoughts and flow. There's no world we can't know.*

Tze roared, and Frankie had no choice but to shout with him.

ROLL CREDITS
ANNOUNCER: Live! From Ocean Terminal in Tsim Sha Tsui! Panda-Vision presents Musical World, with Xing Xing Xing!
FX: APPLAUSE
PANNING SHOT: AUDIENCE
ESTABLISH MEDIUM ANGLE
XING: Hi-hi-hi! It's my super-happy pleasure to introduce my special guest! Let's hear it for Juuuuuuuuno Qwaaaaan!
FX: WILD APPLAUSE
JUNO: Hello Xing, how are you?
XING: Better-better-better now that you are here! Phew! She's ice-hot, huh guys?
FX: MALE LAUGHTER

JUNO: You're making me blush!

XING: Ha-ha-ha. Juno-Juno-Juno, China is happy-wild to have her famous singer-babe home at last. Did you miss us, bwah?

JUNO: Every day. America was fun, but—

XING: Whoa-whoa-whoa, those crazee 'merrikins! Too much red meat and too much drinky-winky!

FX: LAUGHTER

XING: Pop-pop-pop, I gotta six-gun! Jack Daniels and Cola! Ah shaw thunk yoo's a reel purty laydee, missuh Juuunoo!

FX: LAUGHTER

JUNO: Some of them are… a little… intense. But I love all my fans.

CUT TO CLOSER ANGLE: TWO-SHOT

XING: But-but-but to be Mr Serious for a moment. Hmmm. It was a trying time.

JUNO: Yes. America is such a fantastic place, but many people there are living day by day. I hope that my music can bring some light to them.

XING: Hmmm. Yes, yes-yes. I bet they wished they could live in China!

JUNO: Well, maybe, but—

REACTION SHOT: AUDIENCE
BACK TO ANGLE

XING: Big question for you, Juno-peach. Wotta bouta Wyldsky? Are you gonna-gonna-gonna be there?

JUNO: Well, Xing, I'm not sure I should say anything…

FX: AUDIENCE CALLING OUT

XING: Pwease-pwease-pwease? Pwetty pwease wid sugar on it?

JUNO: The answer is yes. I've agreed to headline the Wyldsky show, even though some people have advised against it…

FX: RAPTUROUS APPLAUSE

JUNO: I just want to sing to Hong Kong—

XING: Super-super-super cooool-a-rama! Yay! Wow! Zee! And now we're gonna hear Juno perform her hit song 'Capsule Lover'!

GO TO WIDE SHOT: CENTRE ON JUNO: ZOOM IN.

14. the east is red

KO SAT IN the corner of the empty courtyard, drawn as far as he could into the shadowed space beneath the arched beams of old wood and peeling red paint. It was raining lightly, and the gloomy clouds overhead matched the glowering, morose cast of the young man's face. He watched the growing spread of a puddle, the patterns of ripples made by the raindrops, desperate to lose himself in the simplicity of it. The rush of the downpour was still not enough to blot out the recriminations echoing in his thoughts.

"I hate my life," he said in a small and heartfelt voice. He wanted to be angry, or scared, to feel *something*, but Ko's world felt hollow and cold. He was empty. He needed... a purpose.

Feng stood a short distance away, amid the rain, untouched by it. He rested one hand on the hilt of his lionhead sword, watching the teenager. "What are you going to do now?"

He didn't look up. "I... I'm not sure. That cashwhore Tze knows Big Hung's boys didn't waste me like they were 'sposed to. I'm marked. I'll be lucky to see out the week... And Nikki will rot away up in that hospital."

"It pains me to tell you this, but–"

"Then don't," growled Ko. "Don't say 'I told you so' or 'you screwed up again, Ko' or whatever you're gonna say. I don't want another damn lecture." He sniffed. "All I ever get. Lectures."

"Wallowing in sorrow wins no wars." Feng walked over, holding out his hands to cup the rain, the drops passing through unhindered. "A man is only without power when he believes it."

Ko shot him an acid glare. "Why don't you just fuck off and die?" he said miserably.

Feng tapped his chest plate. "I cannot. I am already dead."

"No, but you *can* fuck off."

The swordsman whipped out his blade and swung it at Ko's neck. The thief reacted instantly, the prickly sense of the phantom sword making him flinch backwards. "You are such a weakling." He sniffed archly. "I smell the stink of mother's milk on your breath, mewling little baby." Feng advanced, rubbing at the stubble on his face. "Do you know how many men I had killed by the time I was your age? How many battles I had fought in?"

"I'm sure you're gonna bore me with the story," Ko replied, his ire starting to rekindle.

Feng looked up at the grey sky. "Heaven, tell me what crime I committed that this wastrel must be my companion?"

Ko came to his feet. "Eat shit, you corpse! I never asked to be saddled with your prehistoric ass! Why don't you go haunt a museum or something?"

"If only I could!" Feng snapped back, "But you're my penance! My stinking, worthless luck to be tied to you."

"Luck?" Ko said bitterly. "You don't know bad luck! You're dead, how much worse could it get? But I'm still breathing." He stabbed at his chest. "Every damn thing I do blows up in my face! Every choice in my life is always the hard one. There's never an easy day for Ko, is there?" He pointed angrily at the sky. "You got a hotline to those fuckers up there, you tell them to cut me some bloody slack!" Ko shouted into the clouds. "You hearing me, you bastards? Are you happy now you made everything go wrong? I got no money, I got no future! I got nothing!"

"You got the tickets." Fixx said from the shadows.

Ko reacted with shock and spun around on the wet stones. His face flushed crimson. "I, uh…" The stratojet vouchers were still in his pocket.

The sanctioned operative stepped into the light and gave the empty courtyard a curious look. Ko waited for him to ask who he been talking to, but Fixx did not. As ever, Feng had made himself scarce.

"What good would it do?" Ko said, after a moment. "I could take her away, but she'd still be sick. And the corps would still come after me." He shuffled out of the wet. "That's how they work. It'd never end."

Fixx nodded. "That's right. Still. A lesser soul, he might take one o' them rides, cash in the other and use it to get off the grid."

Ko's face betrayed the revulsion he felt at that idea. "I'm not leaving my sister in some nuthouse."

"No, you ain't. You may not have any luck to speak of, but you got what they call strength of character, slick. You got that in spades."

The youth sagged. "I just wanna get out."

Fixx's eyes narrowed. "That ain't gonna happen. Not until the story has its end. Not 'til the storm's blown over."

"What storm?"

The op nodded in the direction of the dojo, where the elderly teacher was addressing a group of kids. "Old man Bruce, he knows it. Things out there on the street, black skies over the peak. He talks about dragons."

Ko looked away. "He says a lot of things."

"Don't act like you don't see it too. Your gangcult buddies turning into pill-poppers an' sheep? The blue everywhere you look?"

"Yeah… Sometimes. Like they want people to do it, even though that zee-three-en crap is illegal."

Fixx nodded. "That poor songbird at The Han, she's just a mouthpiece for 'em. She's a shill, hawkin' it, makin' the kids want it. A puppet." He tapped his bald pate. "Minds and hearts, slick. Hearts and minds. That poison gets in your head, holds the door open, lets other things in."

Ko gave him a sideways look. "That can't happen."

"Reckon?" replied the Op. "Your sister, when she got the bad medicine, she talked, right? 'Bout mirrors an' dragons? Snakes an' angels?"

Ko's blood ran cold. "How... How could you know that?"

Fixx ran a finger over his dark glasses. "I seen it, but just a sliver, mind. Not as much as she has."

Ko slumped against the wall. It seemed too much to take in. "You're telling me, Nikita got sick because... She tripped on zen with these corp bastards?"

"That's the meat of it, though there's more to it than that. You ever hear of Icarus?"

"Yeah. G-Mek racer, 400-series. Not as fast as the Namco Solvalu, though."

Fixx smirked. "Mean the guy wit' the wings, flew too near to the sun. I reckon that's your sis, right there. Got herself too close. Took a taste of it, got burned by Tze."

Ko's eyes unfocussed for a moment. "I gotta see how she is. If they tagged me, she could be in trouble."

Fixx reached for the Korvette's remote. "Yeah. I'm thinkin' we might wanna hear what she's got to say."

Feng stood across the courtyard by the stone guardian dogs, and he threw Ko a nod of agreement.

THE LANDSCAPE OF Tze's mind was crimson from horizon to horizon. Hills and valleys carved out of bloody wet meat, incarnadine blades of glassy grass tinkling like wind chimes in the slaughterhouse breeze. Frankie was submerged in the vision, pressed into the liquid, foetid gore. He saw streets in a city with buildings made from bone and cartilage, highways of flayed leather choked with twisted debris and vast armies of human dead. High, gelid towers climbing into a poisonous grey sky that spat screeching yellow gobbets of burning rain.

Things moved up there, appearing in eye-searing glimpses through gaps in the monstrous storm clouds; or perhaps it was just one Thing, a creation of such unfathomable size it could envelop the earth. Floating on lace wings made from sinew, a vast and primal form, engorged with wickedness and lust. Even so far away, Frankie could feel the waves of murderous animal need emanating from it, the aching want to push beyond blood and sex and pain and desire, to tear away any petty human constructs like morality and virtue and smother itself in dark pits of depravity.

Nothing lived that was not twisted in this nation of corruption. Contorted, lifeless trees poked up here and there with warped branches clawing at the bloated, ruined sky, and the span of the bay was barren and cracked. Across the hollows, a suffocated trickle moved sluggishly, dirty with corpses and stinking oil. Raptor-forms sewn together from the bodies of children, avian horrors with razor-sharp wings flitted overhead, vomiting flame where they spied prey. Malformed creatures prowled in shadows, eyes alight with preternatural fire.

But the worst spectacle was the people; multitudes of them blundering through the marshy red flows in emotionless lock-step, empty and cadaverous where all flicker of being was drawn off them. This was the Nine Hells made manifest.

Is it not magnificent? whispered Tze into his mind. *The honesty of it? The world's impiety no longer hidden but thrown to the winds, the opened flowers of blood and flesh shown to the sky... Oh, He blesses us. The King of Rapture, Danikos et Demino, hallowed is the Lord of Bliss...*

He forced the words to the front of his mind, fighting down the mad joy the other man poured into his thoughts. "You want this? How could you possibly want *this*?"

It is truth, Francis, Tze's mindspeech was a gasp of ecstasy. *Humans are creatures driven by lust. Beneath the mask of civility we want only bloodshed and fucking. Everything else is a falsehood imposed by the limited and weak, by those who believe in abstracts. Moral and immoral. Hate and love. Order... and chaos.*

"I won't help you!"

Fury boiled into him. *Stupid child! How dare you turn your face away from me! I offer you the ultimate splendour and you spit it back?*

"Get out of my head!"

So be it. The voice snaked and rasped through his skull. *Willing or unwilling, your part is cast. You will be what you were bred to be, lad. What your bloodline was made to be.* Harsh laughter boomed about him. *Lam... to the slaughter...*

"This is very irregular, Mr Chen. I'm sorry, but I have other concerns at the moment. We're swamped." Dr Yeoh's face was drawn and pale, the dull hollows beneath her eyes a sure sign that she hadn't slept in days.

Ko had seen the disorder in the hospital as he followed Fixx into the building. The sanctioned operative turned up his collar and hunched forward, as if he were walking into a rainstorm, bracing himself. Ko picked his way through the waiting room; there were dozens of people there, some of them staring into space baring wounds that were raw and self-inflicted, others babbling and weeping. There were more in the corridors on gurneys parked along the walls, and Ko had to duck to one side to avoid a big guy wearing a construction worker's overalls who blundered heedlessly past him, clawing at his arms and mewling. There had been a moment when Ko thought he saw Poon, wrapped in a stained paper smock and shouting at shadows; but then a curtain was pulled and he heard the smack-hiss of a spray-hypo.

He blinked at the woman. "Doc, please. I'm not asking you to do anything. I just need to see her."

Yeoh looked at Fixx with a wary sniff. "Visiting hours are over."

Fixx spoke without turning away from the sight of the sick and the maddened. "How long has it been this bad?"

The doctor sighed, sagging against the wall. "Day or so, I think. I'm losing track. We used to get one a week. Then it was every other day, now it's hourly."

Orderlies pushed a mumbling old woman past in a wheelchair. She appeared to have chewed off her own thumbs. "They're all like Nikita?" said Ko. "All dosed with zee-three-en?"

"Some," said Yeoh. "Maybe one in six. The others show the same symptoms but there's no root cause we can find." She sighed. "I contacted the State Medical Commission in Beijing, the United Nations Centre for Disease Control, in case... They're looking into it."

"What the hell does that mean?" Ko snapped.

She met his gaze, tired and frustrated. "Realistically? It doesn't mean shit."

"It's in the water," said Fixx quietly.

"Zee-three-en is a street narcotic. You think it's in the drinking supply?" Yeoh shot him an incredulous look. "We can't be sure that—"

"Be sure," he replied, tapping Ko on the arm. "Where's Nikita?"

The doctor did nothing to stop them as the youth led the black man away down the corridor.

THE ROLL OF yuan she had given Ko for the rent had gone to pay for Nikita's private room. Now, with the hospital filling by the moment, the expense seemed even more worthwhile. Ko closed the door behind him, shutting out the sounds of weeping. Beside him, Fixx took in a long, careful breath. He seemed uncomfortable in the armoured coat, a new and slightly worrying aspect of the otherwise unflappable operative.

"Don't like hospitals," he said, by way of explanation. "Too much hurt hereabouts."

"Yeah," agreed Ko. Even as a boy, he'd been unnerved by visits to the block clinic for checkups and N-SARS vaccinations. It was as if all the agony and the sickness of the patients who went through the building got left behind, like an invisible stain on the walls.

Fixx sniffed the air. "Brings out the jackals. They can smell it when you're weak, close to death comin'." He crossed to Nikita and tenderly stroked her face. "She's pretty."

"Yeah," Ko repeated, the word catching in his throat.

Fixx pulled back the mask and used a damp cloth to moisten the sleeping girl's lips. They were cracked and dry where she was still speaking in quiet church whispers. He listened closely to her for a few moments, nodding. "She's seen it. She knows how it's gonna play out."

Ko came closer, blinking back tears. "I don't get it. Why would that bastard Tze tell her?"

"Didn't tell her," Fixx dug in one of his pockets, "Showed her." He drew out an ornate little pillbox decorated in green and gold enamel. Ko recoiled at the sight of the blue capsules inside. "We gotta know what she does, slick. We gotta see it."

Ko stabbed an angry finger at him. "You give that shit to her and I swear I'll break your fucking neck—"

Fixx shook his head. "Not for her." He held it out to the younger man. "You an' me."

Colour drained from Ko's face. "What?"

"That's how this stuff works. Like a link-up for your mind, see. Just a quick little flick of it, little belt of the world beyond. Pop it and done." He rolled the capsules on to his palm. "Few seconds of instant telepathy, in convenient tablet form." Fixx traced a finger over Nikita's forehead. "We drop these, we can go take a look-see in there."

"You're outta your mind!"

"No," said Fixx, "your sister is. 'Less you're thinkin' you got a better solution, 'less you wanna sit here and wait for the world to end, only way to help her is to do this." He placed a caplet in Ko's hand. "C'mon. Curtain's up. Your cue."

There on Ko's palm, the indigo sphere shone like a glittering jewel.

Ropé was waiting at the helipad, the blurring rotors of the spidercopter thrumming as Mr Tze strode from the castle interior. He had changed into the garb of an ancient warlord.

"Heywood," he said pleasantly. "How is our darling diva? I understood there was an incident in the lab?"

Ropé wore a contrite expression. "Sir, yes. I have expedited the problem." He jerked a thumb at the rotorcraft. "I secured the talent in the cabin. She's been pacified."

Tze's eyebrow arched. "Not too strongly, I hope? We are on the cusp, Heywood. We can't afford any more mistakes."

His face changed to a thin smile. "No sir, we cannot. I was forced to invoke a command imprint. I believe she was attempting to determine her own origins."

"Ah. How interesting. Perhaps, if there were time, we could learn something from this for use in later models." He glanced away. "But no. When the pattern is made whole tonight, Juno's function will be at an end."

Ropé said nothing, watching the sparkle of joy in Tze's eyes.

"Miss Hi has given of herself to whet the blade. The role of absolution now falls to you, Heywood. The young one, Lam, has been prepared." Tze placed a hand on Ropé's shoulder. "I rely on you to commit the deed when the moment comes."

"For the King," Ropé gave the rote reply.

Tze smiled again and boarded the flyer. Ropé watched it vanish toward the high ridge of Victoria Peak, where spotlights danced on the low clouds. In the pocket of his coat, the metal cover of *The Path of Joseph* tore at his skin. "Such an arrogant man," he said to the air. To think Tze imagined he might cage a Dark One and become the master of the Desire-God. In Joseph's name, it would be Ropé's pleasure to show him the error he had made in trusting a secret agent of Elder Seth.

Ko sat on the chair, blinking. "I'm not feeling anything. This is looped."

Fixx ignored him. "Give it time."

The pill had disintegrated the moment he swallowed it, and now Ko was having second thoughts, his pulse racing and his hands getting sweaty. He sniffed the air and caught a whiff of something strong and redolent. "You smell that?"

"Like a steakhouse." Fixx frowned.

Ko was on his feet, making for the door. "Where's all the...? People are—" His bare feet (*bare?*) slapped on warm liquid and he glanced down. The grey tiled floor in the corridor shimmered, darkened. It became a purple-red pool, moving to fill the space before him. Tendrils of the blood-stuff inched up the walls.

"Oh. Shit. It's happening."

Fixx was following him. "Go with it. Don't fight it."

Ko panicked. "No. Damn it man, this was a jagged idea, I want out."

"Weakling," sneered another voice. Ko saw Feng, crouched at the pool's edge, looking at his dark reflection. "Your first instinct is always to run."

Fixx rubbed his chin. "Who's your friend?"

Ko swallowed. "It's, uh, a long story."

THEY FOLLOWED THE meat smell out of the decaying hospital, past huge boles of greenish fungus that were consuming the crumbling concrete. Outside, Hong Kong had transformed into a fleshy, mutant parody of the city. Pieces of perception detached and reformed; they blindsided Fixx and hammered into his thoughts, alien invaders spitting memory-seed.

He saw landscapes of wet flesh, the stench of boiled skins and torched meat. And so many screams; they pushed and pulled, rising and falling from sexual cries of pleasure to noises that chilled the blood in his veins.

Fixx did not question the new arrival, this man the thief called Feng. The aura about the swordsman was strange and complex, the shades similar to Ko's. Somewhere down the bloodline these two shared ancestry; the op wondered if either of them knew it. He toyed with the bones in his pocket. They felt spongy and indistinct.

"There she is," said Feng, pointing with his sword. Along the leathery highway, Nikita was sitting on a couch made from dead dogs. Faint whisps of face and body sat about her, giggling and laughing. She was dressed in a tattered Dior delta, streaked with mud and fluids. Fixx heard Ko gasp when she turned her face to them. Half of her skull was bared, flesh seared away. Blood ran from the torn eye socket, dripping into the wineglass in Nikita's hand. Now and then, she would laugh as if in response to some unheard joke and sip at the contents of the glass.

Feng angrily used the blade to dissipate the wraiths, and Ko stepped closer, taking the burnt twigs of bones that were Nikita's ruined right hand. "Sis?" he asked. "It's me."

"Little brother." She gave a languid nod. "You should run. He's coming."

"Who's comin'?" asked Fixx.

The flesh-world around them began to tremble. "The King," she said.

* * *

And more than anything, Ko wanted to look away, but inside his mind, there was no place to seek shelter. A frigid hurricane of blue ice ripped into them, and above–

Tze loomed, a towering god wreathed in noxious smoke and shimmering darts of painful colour...

Ko felt his ire surge at the sight of the man's grinning face. For a moment, he felt the weight of a weapon in his hand, and saw Feng's sword in his grip. But then–

Tendrils of liquid night emerged. They stabbed out and penetrated, rushing through flesh and savaging his mind...

Fixx held on to him, but it was no good. They slipped on a new surface of sheer ice and fell–

Into visions of...

Black skies filled with blinded stars.

Emerald serpent forms, congealing, forming a monstrous snake-god; a mouth of snaggle teeth, eyes blue pools of destructive sensual energy.

Jade Dragon...

Juno screaming, lit across a stage of razorblades and glass, a puppeteer's strings tied to her limbs, ranging away over her head.

Tze above, hands on the strings, directing and laughing.

In the water...

Grinning mindless salarymen in bars choking on mouthfuls of blue capsules.

Masks floating, black-clad hands pouring thick drums of azure syrup into wheeling falls of clean water.

Children across the city sharing one nightmare.

I'm the quiet mind inside, pretty voice...

Through sheaves of flashing pixels, inside flexing wave-forms.

Lies and compulsions sewn into every singing word, every rhythm and bright sparkling vision.

Legions sleeping awake at their d-screens, absorbing.

All thinking the same way...

The blue, in everything, in each breath of air, each bite and sip.

All eyes on Juno.

At the tower, Ropé bearing the wageslave's throat before a multi-bladed knife.
A rip in the sky...
Opening.
The Jade Dragon tearing through.
Slashing.
Ending the world...
Ripping.
And no one to stop it...
"Out!" Ko screamed. "Get me out!"
He felt Feng's fingers around his wrist and then...

Ko HIT THE ground and felt asphalt beneath his fingers. He barely got to his feet before he vomited explosively, bringing up thin, watery bile.

Fixx was nearby, sitting on his haunches. It took a moment for Ko to realise that they were on the roof of the hospital building. "How did we get up here?"

"Sleepwalkin'," offered the op, casting the bones and reading them. "Damn. That was heavy." He looked up. "Your buddy, Feng. Got us free of it."

Ko looked at his feet and shivered. "Is Nikita all right?"

"No change. Same for all those poor fools."

The thief found his attention drawn up to the distant shadow of the peak. "All that was true... That mad bastard is gonna summon a demon, rape the world..." Ko grabbed at Fixx. "We can't let that happen!"

But the op's attention was elsewhere, staring down at the hospital parking lot. "First things first," he said, pointing. "We got company."

A silver Mercedes Vector drew to a halt, and from inside came three distinctive figures. A man and two women in identical suits, faces hidden behind gaily-painted opera masks.

The Road to the Shining City must be marked out
  For the Dark Ones and their Servitors
Just as landing lights mark out an airfield runway

The spilled blood would guide the Dark Ones to the Earthly Plane
To the Last City

> Message embedded in Happy Carp beer commercial, origin unknown.

15. enter the dragon

BLUE SNAKE CAME into the hospital first, with her sister White Snake and Qin Hui following close behind. Blue and White had not been born as siblings, but in their service to the Cabal they had been made so, in manners far beyond the level of crude genetics. Their masks were negative images of each other. Where her visage was dominated by azure colours, honeyed filigree and pale trim, her sister's façade was white with blue and gold detail. Their masks were the faces of two mythic characters, serpent-spirits who guarded a mountain in legend. By contrast, Qin Hui's face was dominated by death-white, with facets of black and pink; his name was taken from a perfidious politician of the Song Dynasty, whose hands bore the blood of the renowned hero Yue Fei – if the stories of the playwrights were to be believed.

They advanced through people who wailed and rocked. Blue Snake felt a pang of envy for them that was quickly excised; these wretches did not yet understand the gift they had been given.

A nurse approached, her expression frayed. She had the hardened aspect of someone who had seen much trauma but still kept a kernel of humanity within, refusing to become cold to it. She wore the kevlar uniform typical of an Accident and Emergency staffer. "What do you want here?"

White Snake showed the nurse a datascreen. "Have you seen these two men? The black man's name is unknown to us, but the youth is Chen Wah Ko."

The nurse shrugged. Blue Snake saw the lie instantly, the slight dilation in her eyes and the change in her blood capillary flow. The mask fed the data to her, directly into her thoughts; it went to her sister and to Qin Hui as well.

White Snake took the nurse by the arm and spun her about, dislocating her wrist in the process. With her other hand, the Mask produced a sprayhypo loaded with Z3N doses. White Snake fired twenty ccs of the blue into the woman's neck and let her drop, stuttering, to the floor.

Mr Tze suggested that they be careful not to terminate anyone already in the early stages of the rapture, that they take every opportunity to induce more to the glory should the opportunity present itself. To this end, Qin Hui tossed a slow-release canister of aerosol Z3N into the air ducts while Blue Snake examined the hospital's computer system. Her mask extruded a wire into the reception terminal's interface socket and she sat motionless, the monitor in front of her flashing through pop-up permissions screens.

White Snake ensured that the channels on all the hospital's d-screens were tuned to the live feed from Wyldsky. They had learnt only recently that one of the clinic's doctors had been causing problems, attempting to interfere with the pattern. It was of course no accident that this same doctor had made contact with the Chen boy. This was the way of things, the play of designs laid down by the King and his brethren.

The canister began to hiss; thousands of others, some spraying mists, some dripping thick blue liquid into reservoirs, were doing the same across the city. The Masks had been planting them for months in places where they would lie undiscovered. Metro stations and schools. Shopplexes and parks. Trams and taxis. Everywhere.

But this was only the secondary objective; the primary was to locate the targets. This directive was also broken into two elements. The first was to Isolate and Apprehend. The second, the simpler of the two that would come into play if the first could not be achieved, was to Kill.

"I have them," said Blue Snake. "Eastern quadrant of the building, emergency exit stairwell number four. They are together, descending from the roof." Before her, grainy video feeds from monitor pods showed a pair of blurry figures.

"Hey!" shouted a voice, attracting White Snake's attention. A security guard with a large taser hove into view, his expression confused at the trio of incongruous porcelain masks. "Step away from the computer!"

White Snake adjusted something on the hypo, and aimed it at the guard. Reconfigured for dartgun mode, the device coughed, and one of the cartridges embedded itself in his right eye. The man screamed and clawed at his face, foam forming at the edges of his lips.

"Moving," said Qin Hui, producing a flechette pistol and pointing. He didn't need to speak; none of them did. But the public relations department felt that, at least around humans, they should converse in a normal fashion. Alienation of the client base was never good for business.

The Masks moved into the hospital corridors, laying people down as they came across them.

KO GRABBED THE op's shoulder and pulled. "Come on, man!" he cried. "What are you waiting for? We've got to run, get distance... Get Nikita out of here!"

But Fixx hesitated, thinking. "They don't want her. She's already dead in Tze's eyes. They're here for us."

"What?"

The other man rubbed his chin. *Yeah.* It was making sense to him now, the pieces of sensation and distant, weird vibes he'd been collecting over the past few months at last starting to cohere into something tangible. The waking dreams that led him to the singer in Newer Orleans, the fragments of deep fear that bled across the night from the Eastern sky. The words of the old Sifu and the steel-sharp determination in the eyes of this streetpunk. All of it reflected in the psychic aftertaste of the man who had violated Nikita's mind, the man called Tze. In The Han, they had looked at each other for a fraction of a second, and Fixx *knew*. There were other clouded souls and dark forces at work here, but this monstrous plan had Tze at its heart. He glanced at Ko, and felt a sudden understanding, a sharp and painful realisation. As much as he wanted to, as much as it seemed Maitre Carrefour had brought him here for it, Fixx at last saw the role that he was to play. The final pages of the script for this night became clear. "You have to stop Tze," he told the teenager. "He has to die by your hand."

Ko's jaw dropped open. "Me?"

"Listen," Fixx lent close to him. "World turns, she's gotta a pattern, see? Layers and levels, moves like clockwork. The whole of life works on one principle, slick. Right man, right place, right time. When one of those is off, all hell breaks loose."

The kid swallowed hard. Fixx knew he was remembering the visions, the carrion city and the horrors of the emerald serpent-demon.

He prodded Ko in the chest. "You and your boy Feng. You gotta do it. No-one else can."

"I steal cars, for Buddha's sake. I'm just a… a thief, and not a very good one at that," he said, dejected.

They were alone in the stairwell, their voices echoing. Fixx looked around. "Ask the ghost what he thinks."

Ko fell silent for a moment, looking into the middle distance. After a moment, he nodded. "What do I have to do?"

"Get up to the Peak, find that black-hearted sonuvabitch… and end him. Else, there'll be no place to run to."

"Nowhere to hide," added Ko, his voice low. "What're you gonna do? What about that Lam guy?"

Fixx smiled. "Don't you worry none, I'll give 'em somethin' to think about."

★ ★ ★

The metallic gridwork of the stairs clanged as Ko took them three at a time, vaulting over the banister to leap off to the next floor. He glimpsed Feng on every landing, nervously watching for any sign of the Tze's sinister henchmen. The running made it easier for Ko to keep his concentration in the moment, worrying about where he was going to be in the next second instead of letting the conflicted emotions inside him take over.

He was leaving Nikita alone; Fixx was standing his ground to let Ko escape; there was something awful hatching on the Peak; the man who ruined his sister was in league with monsters. Any one of these things would cripple him with fear and doubt if he let them.

Ko dropped past the ground floor and went down one more, into the basement sublevel. He was moving so fast he lost his balance and bounced off the door, practically tumbling through it into the open grey cavern of the vehicle park. He slipped on a patch of old motor oil and fell against a concrete stanchion. There were cars dotted about in some of the parking spaces. All of them were the same kind of unremarkable compacts, Kondobishi Yasumes or Toyomazda Sunrays. Nothing with any *poke*, as traditional go-ganger slang called it.

He took a breath, scanning the underground car park for Feng. On the other side of the garage, he spied the swordsman gesturing at a rank of white vans. Ambulances. Over there, the paramedics waited on alert status for calls that would send them racing out into the night; but for some reason nobody was around down here, and Ko could hear the far-off sound of a phone ringing and ringing. The meat wagons were bulkier than the compacts, but they made up with overcharged engines what they didn't have in grace. Ko jogged across the asphalt and got halfway there when Feng shouted out a wordless warning.

He turned and saw a woman in a white mask sprinting out of the stairwell toward him. She was so *fast*. Ko vaguely remembered the sight of a similar mask on the face of a driver, crossing the Tsing Ma Bridge; then she was on him, a hammer blow punch spinning him around. He turned into the impact, feeling his teeth rattle and slid away down the flank of a parked vehicle. She came at him with a kick that stove in an ambulance's fender, popping the headlight out like a glass eye.

Belatedly, Ko wished he'd asked Fixx if he could borrow his crossbow. In his pocket, his fingers traced the shape of something and on reflex he threw it at the guardian, moving and taking cover by the van's open doors.

The woman caught the missile out of the air and examined it quizzically. "Tarot card," she said, without a hint of exertion in her voice. "Knight of Wands."

Ko came at her at full tilt, dragging a heavy fire extinguisher from a snap-clip on the wall. The red cylinder swung into the masked woman's head and Ko heard something break. She staggered and fell over. He followed up by letting the thing off into her face, great gouts of white chemical foam smothering the guardian. She batted at the acidic stuff like an animal with tar on its fur.

"Mine," he grated, recovering the card. Ko tossed the extinguisher and vaulted into the ambulance's cab. He didn't even need to hotwire it; the motor was already in standby mode. The thief stamped the accelerator pedal into the floor and the hydrogen engine snarled. Automatically, a two-tone siren started wailing and the blue lamps dotted over the vehicle strobed wildly.

In the wing mirror, Ko saw the woman in the white mask getting to her feet as he launched the ambulance out on to the street. She had her head cocked, like she was talking to someone.

Ko turned on to Princess Margaret Road and headed south, watching the accelerometer needle drift up the dial. He hoped that would be the last he'd see of the Masks, but somehow, he doubted it.

FROM THE SPIDERCOPTER'S window, Tze saw the spread of Wyldsky and he was pleased with it. The sprawling mass of the concert crowd moved like wheat in a breeze, rocking as they threw themselves into the music. The noise from the towering speaker stacks was so loud that the 'copter's approach was hardly noticed. The flyer crossed behind the stage and turned to land in the statue park behind it.

Tze felt a definite spring in his step as he came down the gangway. His hands threaded together. Outwardly, he was maintaining an air of calm, but inwardly he felt almost giddy with anticipation. Tonight, the things he saw only as vivid dreams would be made flesh. Ahead, the band on stage were coming to the climax of their final number. He knew little about the group, cared even less. All that mattered was that the lead singer, the oily man who had been there that night at the tower, that he had greed and desires that the Cabal could easily turn to its advantage. Tze had seen the anti-corporate banners in the crowds, heard the flaming rhetoric in the songs. It was ample window-dressing for the main event. For Juno Qwan.

He turned, playfully tracing the face of a terracotta soldier and found her behind him, walking like she was approaching the gallows. "That won't do," he told the singer.

Juno's face was tear-stained, her eyes frightened. "Am I going... to die?"

"You're going to sing," said the executive, tapping the hilt of an ornate ceremonial sword on his belt. "And it will be perfect."

"Why are you dressed like that?"

Tze laughed. "I have a penchant for the theatrical, dear girl."

She'd been watching him all through the flight from the castle. "I know you. I've seen your face. In my head. Sometimes."

"They call that meta-engram imprinting." He nodded. "An echo, if you like, from the donor." Tze leered a little. "There's some of me in you."

"Are you my father?"

"In a way. Along with a thousand others." He sighed. "It's all terribly complicated."

Juno looked at the stage. She seemed like a child now, lost and afraid. "I don't want Heywood to hurt me any more. Please don't let him. He... There are things in his eyes."

Tze frowned. The simple honesty of the girl's statement rang a warning note within him; but he dismissed it. This was no time for distractions. "He has business elsewhere, child. Monkey King will escort you." The Mask loomed.

Juno hesitated. "I... I can't remember the words."

Tze nodded to the guardian. "Help her."

Monkey King produced the leather case with the injector device and Juno's eyes flashed with panic. "No, no! Just give me a moment..."

The Mask ignored her and shot a dose of Z3N into her jugular. She staggered and he picked her up, carrying her forward.

Tze let out a laugh and raised his hands to the sky. "Let's rock!" he told the black clouds.

THEY CAUGHT UP with him as the ambulance was crossing the Hung Hom interchange. Up ahead, past the toll booths and the spread of evening traffic, the black mouth of the Cross Harbour Tunnel yawned. Ko saw a blink of silver bonnet in the rear-view and knew it was the Vector.

Two pale masks were visible through the windscreen. The driver had the ram plate deployed from the bumper and slammed the ambulance hard, trying to force a skid. Ko took the bite out of the attack by chopping the throttle and drifting off the axis. The Mercedes sideswiped a motorcycle and the bike flew away like a fish jerked on a line.

The roar of engines turned hollow as they entered the tunnel, and the Vector came at him again. This time, one of the Masks was out of the window, crawling on to the roof, swarming over the dented hood. Ko swore as he lost a second of concentration, barely missing a snake-bus filled with clubbers. The masked man threw himself at the ambulance and caught on, clinging to the driver's side. He used clawlike fingers to advance up the outside of the vehicle.

In the wing mirror Ko saw a chilling, expressionless face in blinks of reflected blue light. He threw over the steering wheel, hard. The screaming ambulance bounced off the inside of the tunnel with a blast of sound and tearing metal. Ko did it again, seeing the Mask disappear for a second into the shower of sparks and glass. The wing mirror tore away as he pressed the ambulance into the tunnel wall and held it there. Panels sheared off, and a crimson wash streamed over the tiles.

Behind the vehicle, the distended and broken body of Qin Hui spun away, bouncing up off the bonnet of the Vector and landing behind. The robot bus rode over the guardian, grinding meat, porcelain and arcane metal implants into the road.

White Snake activated the lasers in the headlights and opened fire.

FIXX WAS NOT happy about the place he found himself in. Looking for somewhere to make a stand in a hospital was never going to be a good idea. Too much chance of collateral damage, too many civvies. For a second he smelt the toasting flesh from the ferryboat massacre, saw Cajun Pork Cathy's dead, dead eyes. Fixx blinked the thought away, and rested his hands on the edge of the nearest cot. There were ranks of bassinets in tight rows filling the ward. Each crib was cooing quietly to the sleeping babies within, monitoring them, turning them with piezoplastic paddles to keep the children content and prevent cot death. Fixx felt uncomfortable here with the SunKings in his hands, and when the door opened to admit the woman in the blue mask, it was almost a relief.

She carried a flecher, a Krupp by the looks of it, with a fat snail drum magazine. Two seconds of pressure on the trigger would murder every newborn in the room, should she wish it. The Mask nodded slightly. Fixx guessed she was listening to a comm-link.

"Mr Tze would like to extend an invitation to you, to visit the Yuk Lung tower." Her voice was a whisper, but it carried. "The choice of the state in which you arrive there is up to you." The gun muzzle never wavered.

"A moment," he said, carefully holstering the pistols. "If you please." Fixx drew the bones from his pocket and weighed them in his hand, then gently rolled them out across the top of an enclosed cot. The child inside stirred, blinking at him. Small fingers stretched at the yellow-white pieces, then sank away.

Fixx studied the lay of the bones, and as he did, he noticed the feedlines dripping clean air into all the cribs. Blue vapour twinkled in there.

The woman in the mask flicked off the safety to make her point.

He smiled thinly and gathered up the bones once more. "Never been a man to argue with fate," said Fixx, holding up his hands. "I can read the signs. I surrender."

"I'M HERE," SHE said to the world, and the world screamed back love for her. Juno stood inside a bowl of darkness, surrounded by a shifting sea of souls, crying, imploring her, begging her to complete them. The girl saw them through a hazy lens, reading the colour of their hearts. They burned with wild fires, but the shades were dull, tainted. They never even knew it, the dear poor people, but she could see it. Juno saw it very clearly now, the acrid blue that stained everything, the battery acid taste in her mind. She looked up and they did the same, joyful at the touch of the warm drizzle falling. The crowd were unaware of the invisible balloons floating up there, molecule-thin sheathes breathing out the drug into the clouds, seeding the blue rain.

They moved like a shoal of fish or the mindless uniform motion of a flock of birds in flight. The crowds were unified, drunk on the Z3N laced in the food, the water and the air. They were sharing, transforming as one. A totality that waited for one shining light to guide it. Her *voice*.

Juno's hand strayed to her throat, feeling tightness there. Her flesh and mind warred with one another; she knew she only had to release the first note to set her nightmares in motion.

Tze spoke from the wings, and despite the roaring adulation, she heard him. "Sing," he commanded, repeating the words of compulsion Ropé had used in the laboratory. "Sing for them, *infans simulare*."

"Harmony," she wept. "Come with me."

THE TWO VEHICLES exploded out of the tunnel and howled through the side streets of Causeway Bay, the sirens of the ambulance parting traffic before them like a knife. Burning jags of yellow light from the Vector lit up the flanks of the paramedic van, shattering lights and tearing at the tyres.

The Merc kept on him as he turned on to the back roads, screeching around the narrow bends up toward the Peak. The ambulance ricocheted off safety barriers and knocked chunks of old stone from the walls. Beams scorched the asphalt. The vehicle was getting sluggish. Ko knew he was on a loser.

Another shot flashed through the back of the ambulance and struck a pressurised gas cylinder. The shriek of escaping fumes brought the stink of liquid nitrogen to Ko's nostrils. The smell made him panic and he jerked the wheel hard, vaulting out of the vehicle and into a gully.

The ambulance spun out as the Vector came closer. Ko had time to bury his face in the dirt as the CryoSaviour re-sus module inside exploded. Designed to flash-freeze trauma victims, the uncontrolled detonation created a plume of super-chilled vapour that engulfed both vehicles.

Clutching at the re-opened wound on his chest, Ko staggered from his place of safety to find the masked woman frozen to the inside of her car. She appeared quite dead.

The throaty rumble of a bike engine drew his attention; a kid dressed in Road Ronin armour halted and doffed his samurai helmet. "Dang! Did you see that?"

Ko kneed the biker in the nuts and tossed him from the cycle. As an afterthought, he grabbed the youth's katana and rode on, toward the glowing summit.

THE LINES IN blood were drawn, and overhead the sickly light of ascension was forming. Ropé looked up, weighing the ghost knife in his hand, as Blue Snake arrived with the black man in custody. He searched his memory for a name.

"Joshua Fixx. You're not unknown to... To me."

Fixx studied him. "You have me at a disadvantage, sir."

"I should say so." Ropé crossed to the wooden frame where Lam was chained.

The operative had a measuring stare. "Does Tze know?" he asked suddenly. "I'm willing to bet they think you're a team player, right?" Fixx nodded. "But no. I can smell it on you, mister. More to you than just this zen thing, huh?"

"Impressive," said Ropé. "You just clapped eyes on me and you can tell all that?"

"I'm a perceptive fellah. I can smell it. I met your kind before."

"Yes, you have." Ropé had a blink of someone else's memory, of Fixx wet with blood and human carrion. "I can taste it."

"The stink from Spanish Fork carries a long, long way. What is it you all like to say? The Path of Joseph…"

"Is thorny." Ropé spun and threw the blade, burying it in Blue Snake's chest. She sputtered and perished. He looked up at Fixx and felt the burning touch of Elder Seth behind his own eyes. "Tze makes his play. Then we'll make ours."

Fixx shook his head. "Can't let that happen."

Ropé smiled, bearing more teeth than a human mouth should. "Now you're becoming interesting."

The samurai's bike took him through a roadblock at breakneck speed, but none of the guards were watching; they were crying, singing, pointing into the dark and pregnant skies.

Ko rode around the edges of the crowd, the thunder of their adulation echoing. He tasted the tingling vapour on the wind, glimpsed shapes at the corners of his vision. Sinuous things, serpents and monstrous angels, ghostly and dancing. The rapturous chorus penetrated his mind, begging him to join in.

When the lightning struck, he thought for a moment the Vector was back, but then he turned his head upwards and the sight almost stopped his heart.

In the air over the city there was a rip in the sky, and from it fell huge emerald tears. As he watched, the clouds gave birth to a thing with claws and teeth and eyes of impossible angles. It was drenched in scintillating viridian shades, scaled with jewels so magnificent they took his breath away to see them. Out of the torn maw of cloud it came, borne on vestigial wings, ephemeral but gaining solidity by the second.

Ko joined millions of people across the city of Hong Kong, watching the end of their world begin as the colossus of the Jade Dragon fell screaming to earth.

Zen, zen
I'm the quiet mind inside, pretty voice
I'm the perfect smile
Touch my thoughts and flow
There's no world we can't know
Sea of stones, sand waves
Harmony, come with me
Taste the blue
Star at dawn
Bubble in the stream

"Touch"
Vocals: Juno Qwan
© RedWhiteBlue Inc. 2026.

16. city on fire

In the corridors of the hospital, a thousand screaming babies tore at the broken minds of the adults. Dr Yeoh collapsed, plunging into hell. In her room, Nikita slept restlessly; she was already there.

KO STARED OUT over the shining pinnacles of the cityscape. Juno Qwan's voice smothered everything in a warm fog of noise. He felt her words invading him; she was crying, but he registered this in only the most distant of ways. Down in the metropolis, he could see her face everywhere, on the massive street-screens in Central, on the flickercladding of the Hotel Metropolita; her song played from radios in every apartment, every channel carried her words. The sound was worming its way into him.

He left the bike and staggered up the summit, through people screaming and crying and weeping and laughing. The freakish, sickening high he had shared with Fixx in the hospital was coming back tenfold. He could taste the Z3N in the air, the thick haze washing through his pores. It swelled his heart, made his feet light. The ecstasy of the crowd around him spilled into his mind, getting louder, becoming stronger.

Ko stumbled, his thoughts heavy and indistinct. "Why am I here?"

"For the King!" shouted a reveller, bloody and naked. "He's come for our love and pain!" A chorus of people mumbled the same words.

Ko looked away, afraid to look out over the bay where the phantom-serpent was forming, coalescing wings and fangs and lizard-skin. The gossamer thing resolved as the people gave it their attention. The Jade Dragon hooted, the sound flattening buildings, shaking the landscape. Ko could not look; his head turned. He could not help himself.

A stinging slap brought him about and falling to the marshy ground. Feng stood over him, fists balled and his scruffy face alight with fury. "Wake up!" he bellowed. "You must not gaze upon the beast! It wants your eyes, it needs your spirit!"

Ko was sluggish as he got up. "She was right… Nikita saw this coming."

Feng grabbed him, pulled him close. "Sorcery, like the black man said! It lives only through the minds of others! The Dragon is the demon man makes for himself!"

The Road Ronin's sword was heavy in his hands. "I can't fight that…"

Feng pointed toward the stage, to a place half-hidden in pools of sickly light. Ko saw Tze up there, lurking in the wings. "Then fight *him*."

SIFU BRUCE CALLED *the boys to him, had them bolt the doors to the dojo tight and close the storm shutters. They gathered sticky rice to scatter around the perimeter of the building while the old man worked with quick and deft movements, drawing wards on paper banners in sweeping strokes of his brush.*

THE JADE DRAGON arched its back and threw off rimes of frozen interstellar hydrogen. Blood spilt from hundreds of willingly slit throats came together in a wet cloud for the beast to suck in through its teeth. Clawed feet found purchase on skyscrapers; they did not yet fully exist in the plane of flesh, and so they moved ghost-like through the stone and steel, cutting out the souls of those they touched but leaving animate flesh undamaged. The mere presence of the DesireGod's aspect caused spontaneous blood orgies across a ten-kilometre radius from the demon's point of intersection. Emerald chemicals of a kind that had never existed in this dimension dripped from the tear in the clouds and burned like acid into the streets. The Dragon was slowly unfurling, shaking off the dust of eons. Newborn and yet impossibly ancient, the King of Rapture was pleased to be here once again.

THE GIRL PERFORMING *oral sex on Hung never surfaced from the shimmering water, and he tried to shift his bulk to see the source of the light flooding in through the windows of the bathhouse. One by one, the other girls turned to him, and where their pretty faces had been there were only nests of worms.*

FIXX KEPT HIS hands steady, waiting. Ropé crossed his eye-line, without apparent concern over the fact that Blue Snake had not disarmed him. The op understood. Ropé clearly didn't think that detail was of any import.

"I'm curious," said the thin-faced man conversationally. "Do we know the same people?" He recovered the ghost knife from the Mask's corpse with a sucking pop.

Fixx turned in place, watching him. "Could say that. Crossed paths with the Josephites once or twice."

"And you're not dead. That says something for your strength of character... Or perhaps that you're good at fleeing."

He shrugged. "Little from Column A, little from Column B." Fixx shifted his weight. He could get the crossbow from the stance he was in, but he doubted it would do more than just piss the guy off. "Papa Legba always said there'd be a price to pay for that. Just didn't think it would be today."

Ropé sniggered. "What sweet delusion. As if pieces of cardboard and chicken bones could augur the future!" He made a dismissive gesture. "You think your silly gutter godlings sent you here, is that it? To what end?"

"To stop Tze. I go where fate sends me. I'm the fly in the ointment. Monkey in the wrench."

"Then we want the same thing, Joshua. It has been my honour to serve the vision of Elder Seth, who sent me on my way so long ago from the Promised Lands of Deseret to this festering anthill," he bared teeth in a sneer, "here, where I lay in silence, waiting for the day that Tze would recruit me, just as Seth knew that he would. I made myself the perfect minion. We play a long game, Joshua, a very long game. I am here to disrupt the plans of Tze and his conclave of idiots." He balanced the knife in his grip. "I will stop them from binding the Jade Dragon to their will." Ropé pointed at Frankie with the blade. "This poor wretch, bred from antiquity to be a vessel for the blood that will cage the Lord of Bliss. He's the last, and when he's dead, the 'pattern' will fall apart. Tze will have nothing. He has compounded his error in trusting me with so vital a facet of his plan."

Fixx's eyes narrowed. "Missing a bit o' the tale, I reckon. You left out the part where *you* take the reins of that monster instead. Step in at the last second and leash the beast for yourself. Am I close?"

Ropé let out a bark of laughter. "Why would we ever want to put a collar on such a magnificent beast? The Cabal thought they might treat the Jade Dragon like a milk cow, feed it the odd city and in turn suckle themselves off the beast's teat. Such limited imagination. No, dear fellow, we're going to *release* it. Can you imagine what will be wrought in His wake, the world in a rapture of sex and blood?" He licked his lips. "It arouses me just to think of it."

Fixx eyed the other man. "I'm gonna kill you, you know that."

Ropé beckoned him from across the room. "I *so* want you to try."

He went for the crossbow, and in the other man's hand the ghost knife unfolded like a steel flower.

Ko KICKED DOWN the backstage door and vaulted inside, feeling Feng at his side. The sickening riot of sounds from the stage and the audience beat at him. He shook off the sensation.

"Danger—" said Feng, as part of the shadows detached and grew definition.

Monkey King appraised Ko with his expressionless mask, taking in the shabby go-ganger jacket, the Road Ronin katana. Ko thought of the white-masked woman in the parking garage, of her incredible speed; as if Monkey King had been waiting for that moment, the guardian attacked. He punched Ko down, dodging clumsy sword blows, making impact craters where his fist struck the floor.

Ko rolled away, swinging wildly. The Mask watched, measuring his movements, then came in again. Monkey King's blows were swift, efficient, designed to break and maim. The youth took a glancing hit and stumbled.

"Aim for the weak points," snapped Feng.

"Can't," Ko slurred. "Not a... swordsman."

Monkey King paused, listening to him speak, then came on, preparing to strike a killing blow.

Close to his face, Ko smelt old leather, sweat and iron. "Then let me," said Feng. The warrior's hand slipped into the youth's and faded into the skin. Ko jerked away. "No! Get out!"

"Listen to me!" said Feng. "I know you, better than you know yourself! I know what you fear, why you hate those fools who warp their minds with drugs and wine – because it was one of them that killed your father!"

"Can't ever lose control," Ko muttered. "Can't ever become like those animals!"

"And you won't," Feng was becoming smoke, melting around him. "We won't. Let me in, Ko. *Let me in.*"

A lifetime of restraint. Never once had Ko allowed himself to slip, to fall into the easy path that so many of his friends had taken. He had rejected it always, the moment of belief becoming crystal-hard when Chan had informed him, grave-faced and quiet, that his father had been murdered. The child he had been vowed never to have a waking moment where it wasn't him in charge, in control. But now he felt Feng's soul pressing into him, filling his body like water into a bottle.

Trust me!

I do, Ko replied, the answer surprising him.

The Mask grabbed a handful of the boy's jacket and dragged him off the floor. Ko's eyes snapped open and what Monkey

King saw there made him hesitate. A new and iron-hard determination, ancient and inviolate.

The katana spun in an arc and took off the guardian's hand at the wrist.

"It's been a while since I cut meat," snarled the youth, a strange dissonance in his words. "But you never forget how it's done."

The bodyguard fell back, momentarily confused, and the youth attacked with skilful, aggressive motions. Monkey King's mask broke with a bone-snap crack as the polycarbonate samurai blade sank into his skull, cutting clear across the orbit of his right eye.

OLD YEE HOBBLED *from the cracks forming in the street, his barrow falling into a void spitting with noxious smoke. The noodle seller tripped and fell. Overhead, in the low and hateful clouds, he glimpsed something huge and monstrous. A tail the size of a metro train clipped the Lippo Centre in passing, and the old man died in the rain of glass and concrete.*

THE QUARREL LODGED between the second and third of Heywood Ropé's ribs, to no ill effect. Fixx discarded the crossbow and vaulted away from the Josephite's attack, rolling and drawing the SunKings. Selecting three-round bursts, he followed Ropé across bookshelves, blowing fists of confetti from the rare and antique volumes.

"Philistine," snorted the killer. Ropé jerked his wrist and the blade of the ghost knife shot out on a wire, hissing furiously. Fixx fired at the thing, but it wove around the bullets and cut dozens of shallow nicks before retreating. He moved and went to fully automatic; a metre of yellow flame shrieked from the muzzles of the pistols as he unloaded the rest of the magazines. High-impact armour-piercing rounds punched chunks from stonework and blew out windows as the Josephite evaded. The op adjusted aim on the fly and found his target. Bullets ripped away great ragged lumps of Ropé's left arm and shoulder, drawing out a howl. The breeches on the SunKings locked open, spent and fuming. Fixx let the empty guns fall from his hands and went for his sword.

Ropé came hard as the monomolecular blade whispered free of its scabbard. Edge met edge with a glass-shattering impact, hot metal sparks stinging. They fought sword to knife, strike and feint, lunge and riposte.

Ropé made a snake hiss and Fixx glimpsed a momentary ghost-glitter of silver sunglasses, of burning hellfire behind his eyes. The op pressed the hilt of the sword forward and twisted it, baring his teeth. Fixx didn't much like holdout weapons – unsportsmanlike, really – but there was a time and a place for that sort of behaviour. Like now.

The one-shot ScumStopper Xtreme hard-jacketed slug in his sword hilt discharged into Ropé's chest with such force that it blew the man back into a hanging d-screen, bringing the flickering console down upon him. Burnt plastic and cordite gusted through the air.

Fixx limped to the young executive handcuffed to the oak lectern. "Mr Lam?"

"Fuh-Frankie," came the reply.

He tapped the cuffs with the sword. "Hold out your hands, Frankie."

"Wha–?"

The sword whistled through the air and the casehardened chain split beneath the blade, scattering links across the stone floor. Frankie swallowed hard and pulled himself away.

Fixx nodded at the room. "You know a way outta here?"

The exec's face telegraphed his terror even before he could give it voice. Fixx turned on his heel, bringing up the sword as a shape exploded from the wreckage of the screen. Ropé flew across the room, pressing the ghost knife down in his grip. The red orchard of slash-wounds across the sanctioned operative made him seconds too slow.

"Stab stab stab stab!" Ropé collided with him, burying the ritual weapon in Fixx's torso over and over, fast as lightning. He felt the sword tumble from his nerveless fingers, felt the velocity of the attack shove him across the tiles. Blood slicked the floor, and Fixx's chest and gut contracted as the auto-routines built into his armour kicked in, dosing him with shots of TraumaNix.

Ropé hazed into view. "This amusement pales, pagan. I must get back to my work." The ghost knife's blades shifted and changed, fractal edges turning like origami razors.

IN THE YIP *apartment, there was the whispering hiss of cutting flesh. The boys had made a good job of slicing out each other's vocal chords, and now they were painting a pentagram in their mother's blood. Through the heat-hazed windows, the cilia of a starborn thing followed them about the grisly work.*

THE JADE DRAGON grew, its tail looping through the streets, crossing over the bay and back. The demon embraced the waves of hate and desire on the air, tasted the foetor of the blue as it rose up in the minds of its food-thralls. Flexing its muscles for the first time in hundreds of thousands of years, it released experimental thrusts of power, warping local pockets of reality. It picked a man at random and had him explode into a horde of questing tenticular masses, probing and penetrating through the corridors of a tower block. In the dark night overhead, the King of Rapture disintegrated orbital spy satellites from a dozen different multinats; across the world, the operators jacked into them in Novograd, Seattle, Kyoto, Dublin and Sydney died instantly from serotonin overdoses. Transcontinental airliners vectored straight into the runways at SkyHarbor, swan-like fuselages turning into balls of fire and steel as the flight crews tore each other's hearts out. The Dragon's influence washed out across the water, sinking junks and sampans, forcing the simple bio-brain of the Macao hydrofoil ferry to drown itself. These things it did without really thinking about them, these small mischiefs easy like breathing for the beast.

ISE MADE IT *to the doors of the church just as Father Woo was pushing them shut. The priest held a shotgun like he knew how to use it. The go-ganger thought the padre was going to leave him out there, out on the street where the shadowy crawling things and maddened people ran riot; but then the priest beckoned him sharply. Ise threw himself through the doorway as the gun barked, killing something behind him.*

★ ★ ★

IT WAS ONLY a fragment of the Lord of Lusts, a mirror-piece of the Master of Ecstasy's monumental horror; but still the Jade Dragon boiled with inchoate power, the bubbling potency of unbridled animal hungers spilling into the world. The city reeled and went mad. Those who saw the beast in dreams over the past weeks gave it their minds, never understanding that to believe in it only made Him more real. Those who had been fortunate enough to avoid the taint spread by Tze's Cabal were fortunate no more. There was nowhere in Hong Kong where the touch of the blue did not reach. Each mind formed another link in the chain, released more caged passions and horrible secrets. Millions of people found themselves hating and loving, needing and yearning for bloodshed and lust.

WITH GREAT CARE, Alice nailed her feet to the floor and arranged it so she could seat herself on the bed. She drew the last of the cabbalistic shapes on the milk-pale flesh of her forearm with the shard from the mirror, then took the gun and rested the muzzle on her lower lip. The weapon tasted of oil and steel, and she had to fight back a gag reflex. Teasing the end of the barrel with her tongue, she squeezed the trigger and waited for heaven.

THE SONG PEALED around her mind, never-ending, looping in an infernal circle. Juno tried to stop herself from speaking the words, but they forced themselves from her mouth, the unstoppable meme washing out across the audience.

"We adore you, Juno!" came the screams. "You complete us! We love you!"

They echoed her, line for line, beat for beat, a flock of worshippers growing by the second as more minds in the city fell into the power of the Jade Dragon. The throbbing subliminals in the backbeats and the flickering hypno-commands in the screens made slaves of them, and Juno was at the core of it. Floating camera drones and emplaced lenses followed her every movement across the stage, holding her and broadcasting the image citywide.

She was the catalyst, at the heart of the expanding reaction. For every person who joined in the chorus, for each mind that willingly surrendered itself to the touch of the Z3N, the creature's manifestation became stronger. Against her will, Juno led the city into a hive mind designed and directed by the will of the beast. It was circular, a self-reinforcing metaconcert – and soon it would reach a critical mass of human thought and make the Jade Dragon fully real in the material plane.

Juno touched the very faintest corona of the demon-thing's psyche, and it sickened her beyond all words. She understood only that to pierce the veil of dimension from the Outer Darkness where it originated, the beast needed believers. It could only become tangible when men and women gave themselves over to the desires that it embodied, the blood-soaked, conflicting needs to procreate and to destroy.

As the lyrics came around again, Juno saw the flesh-city and the glass monsters of her waking dreams forming, and rejected them with all her might. "I'm the quiet muh-mind in-inside," she stammered. "Pretty… pretty…" Her chest tightened, the muscles rebelling. She tasted blood in her mouth and screamed, fighting the compulsion, forcing the words to shift and change.

"I'm the lying fiend inside!" she spat wildly, "hateful voice! I'm the bloody smile! Touch my thoughts and *die*, there's nowhere you can hide!"

Juno clutched at her skull as spikes of pain wracked her. The singer's piercing shriek was repeated by the first fifteen rows of the concert audience, each of them falling into psychic synchronicity with her.

"I won't sing!" she snarled, tearing the microphone tab from her cheek. "I won't help you any more!" The camera drones closed in, curious at her sudden change in behaviour.

Juno's angry cries died in her throat as the brilliant sodium lights of the stage were snuffed out, plunging the platform into blackness. She saw a shimmering curtain fall, cutting her off from the audience, and suddenly the screens blared out new tunes, picking up and repeating the words to "Touch" over and over. The live feeds from the cameras were abruptly severed.

From the deep shadows of the wings emerged Mr Tze, his face bright with rage. "You dare defy me?" he roared, his voice beating at her over the blare of the music. "You vat-grown, clockwork bitch. You're just a grandiose sexclone, a fuck-toy for my bidding." He brutally backhanded her. "Sing, damn you. I order you to sing. *Infans simulare! Infans simulare."*

"No more." she cried, her words strangled and sobbing. "I won't do it." Mad elation filled her, a sudden sense of lunatic freedom.

Tze spat and drew his sword. "Very well. The King is coming, it is too late to stop it now. If you will not obey him, you will bleed for him."

"Listen to me!" she screamed at the cameras, begging her fans to hear her. "The Jade Dragon will destroy you all! Don't let it in! If you ever loved me, don't—"

Tze's ceremonial blade flashed in the spilled light from the screens and opened her throat to the air. Juno staggered backwards and fell, hands at her neck, struggling to hold in a flood of rich, hot crimson.

There were bright flickers of pasts and lives that she had not experienced, the death and death and death of other Juno Qwans, an endless loop of them, lives of engineered soulnessness bereft of human warmth. Laughter. Applause. The punishing glare of fame. In the grey haze, her mind collapsed to a single point, to the touch of a man's hand on her face and the look of utter truth in his eyes. *Francis…*

Voiceless, she collapsed and died there on the stage, a blossom of red expanding about her.

"The songbird is silenced," snorted Tze. Above, the unblinking glass eyes watched and recorded.

ONLY THE GOGGLES *over Professor Tang's eyeballs had stopped him from gouging them out when the green fires fell from the air, but now he was pleased, giddy with the sight as he raped the corpse of the lab assistant he had shot in the stomach. All the secret things, all the keys to the monstrous desires in his head were free, and he had no more need of human values.*

FIXX FELT HIS breath coming in shallow, brutal gasps. There was blood all around him, making the stone tiles slippery. His vision was misty, as if everything around him was made of felt. He tasted copper. The sanctioned operative made his hands work with fierce concentration, fishing in his coat pocket for a weapon, a touchstone. His fingers found a ragged tear in the kevleather and nothing else. With effort, Fixx pushed himself off the floor, leaning up.

"Looking for something?" asked Ropé. The Josephite had the ghost knife held up high. He tipped back his head and let drops of red fall from the shifting blades on to his tongue. The killer came closer, nodding at the bones scattered on the floor. "Lost your precious things? How sad." With exaggerated care, Ropé brought his shoe down on the fetishes and ground them into powder. "All gone. Now how will you know what to do, Joshua? You'll have to make your own mind up for once."

Fixx had a dagger in his boot, but it might have well been on Mars. Agony churned in his gut as he dragged himself backwards, pressing against a jade pillar. Dimly, he was aware of a sour breeze sluicing in through the broken windows, heavy with death-scents, sirens, singing and the noises of human despair. A rough chuckle escaped his lips. "This… not goin' exactly how I planned."

"You had a plan?" sneered Ropé.

"Nah," admitted Fixx, "always been a kinda make-it-up-as-I go sorta guy."

Ropé toyed with the knife, flicking a glance at Frankie where he cowered by a console. "Perhaps there's something to your ridiculous religion, Joshua. You might be right. Perhaps your loas did bring you here for a reason – just not the one you thought it was." He bared teeth. "You're here to die, Joshua Fixx, to fail. Look." Ropé pointed at the d-screens that were still functioning. The displays were fed from cameras at the Peak. He saw the audience, the weeping black skies, the stage.

"Juno!" Frankie gasped, staggering to his feet. "Oh god, no."

The audio feed had been damaged in the firefight, and no sound was relayed; but they saw the anger ripple across the idol singer's face, her sudden surge of rebellion. Frankie's heart leapt as she flung away her microphone, freeing herself.

"I knew you could do it!" he shouted. "Run, Juno!"

Ropé rolled his eyes. "Why don't you shout a bit louder, Francis? She might even hear you…"

The live feed shifted as the stage went dark. For a second the cameras dithered, shifting to image-enhanced mode. In the corner of the display, the *Live Feed* overlay changed to *Broadcast Suspended*.

"Oh dear," mocked the Josephite. "The slave has ideas above its station. Not that it matters, too little too late."

He could not tear his eyes from the screen as Tze, resplendent in the cloak and finery of a Qin warlord, came into frame and berated the girl.

"Frankie," said Fixx, "look away. Don't…"

The ghost of Tze's blow made Frankie choke; he felt it as keenly as if it had been him that was struck. He saw the sword, and shook his head. "No, no, no, no—"

Juno looked into the camera, directly at him. He read her lips. *If you ever loved me, don't—*

"No!" Frankie's body went rigid with rage and shock. Juno fell away, life ebbing from her eyes, crashing to the stage.

Ropé made an amused noise. "Your turn now, Joshua. Take solace in knowing that your vitae will be put to good use. I'm going to paint a mural with it." The knife fell and Fixx caught it, pushing all his strength into holding the razor tip away from his throat.

Ropé licked his lips. "Don't fight it. Believe me, this is a kindness I do for you… I'm sparing you the endless agonies of living in a world where the Dragon rules."

The blade pressed into Fixx's skin; he felt his strength ebbing, and at the corner of his vision he saw movement. A flash of wet steel.

"Any last words?" said Ropé, his breath hot and pungent.

"Yeah," Fixx coughed. "Look behind you."

"Bastard!" screamed Frankie, and sank Fixx's sword into the Josephite's back. The blade punctured Ropé's heart and burst from his chest.

Fixx kicked him away and fell back, forcing himself to his feet. Frankie was gasping, tears streaking his face. Black blood covered his hands and he stared down at them, shaking.

Incredibly, Ropé was not dead. The ghost knife was forgotten as he fingered the blade, trying in vain to get a grip on the sword and pull it out.

Fixx hobbled to him and yanked on the hilt. "Mine, I think." The sword came free and oily fluids spurted from the entry and exit wounds.

"Nuh…" Ropé twittered, eyes misting. "No."

"Yeah," said the operative, and with effort Fixx gathered up the Josephite and hurled him through the broken window.

Ropé fell a hundred storeys, plunging into darkness and fire.

"Tze." The executive turned at the sound of his name to see the ragged thief crossing the statue park. He paused before the idling spidercopter. There was something different about the boy, a glint in his eye that had been absent there in the car park when he blundered in with guns blazing. A certainty, he decided. A surety of purpose.

"I'll say this for you, lad. You're a survivor." Tze eyed the bloodied katana. "My servant?"

"Dead," said Ko. "And you'll join him soon enough."

Tze drew his own blade. Juno's blood still discoloured the edge. "Be wise. Take that sword and end your own life with it, while the choice is still yours. The world you know has ended tonight. The Jade Dragon is King now, and I am his keeper." He idly ran a finger over one of the terracotta soldiers that stood nearby like a mute honour guard.

The action seemed to infuriate the teenager. "Maggot and shit-eater. You are blind and stupid. You sacrifice children to this foul creature and plot to set it lose on the world? Death a hundred times over is not reward enough." He shivered and his voice altered for a second. "I'm gonna fuck you up, asshole. You and me got unfinished business."

Tze frowned. The thief's odd behaviour was vexing; but no matter. He would die as easily as the clone had, and then Tze would take his leave to the castle and await the final manifestation of the Dragon Lord.

The katana swung at him, missed. Tze made a riposte that hummed through empty air. "You're quick," he remarked.

"Two thousand years of practice." snapped his opponent.

The swords crossed, polycarbonates and tempered steel biting. Tze snarled as he scored first blood, cutting a slash in the go-ganger's jacket; but his victory was short lived as the boy wounded him on the arm.

Tze spat and attacked again, all pretence at play forgotten. This commoner had dared to spill his blood? There would be no quarter now. He released a flurry of blows, beating the thief back into the circle of terracotta effigies. Fear spread across his opponent's face. "No cocky words now, eh?" he shouted.

"Go bugger yourself, you worthless old cashwhore."

He slashed and caught the boy's temple with a small nick, ripping away the dirty hachimaki headband in his hair. The youth stumbled against the sculpture of a swordsman.

"You are poor sport," said Tze, drawing back for a killing blow. "No match for me, little boy."

"My name," growled the thief, "is Lau Feng, soldier of his Imperial Majesty the Emperor, ghost and undead, guardian of this life..." His voice shifted again. "I am Chen Wah Ko, brother of Nikita... And you owe me blood, motherfucker."

"I don't care who you are," said Tze, and swung at his opponent's neck.

FRANKIE WAS TREMBLING, babbling. "Oh, god. Oh, god. Juno... She's dead!"

Fixx gave a slow nod. "I'm sorry." He had known it, somewhere deep inside. Fixx had understood that the girl's fate was never to be a fair one. Juno's life was a mayfly existence; bright, shining, fleeting.

"Tze killed her. He murdered her..."

"That's right," said Fixx, and he nodded at the damaged video consoles. "But it won't mean nothin' if nobody knows it."

"I don't understand."

"Show them, Frankie. Show the people the truth."

After a moment, Frankie nodded and ran his hands over the panels. "The replay is in memory. The live feed is still intact. I... I can wide-band it to every screen in Hong Kong."

"Do it," said Fixx. "Let the city hear Juno."

Broadcast Resumed.

The override from Tze's command console had worms in every public communications protocol software across Hong Kong; advertisement screens, radio and vid, digital cinema, road signs and flickercladding. The Cabal's reach extended everywhere, and Frankie used it to take revenge.

The loop of Juno Qwan's defiance and her murder spun out over the city, played and replayed endlessly into the eyes and ears of a populace who loved her.

In the thrall of the Z3N, the gestalt needed focus, and Juno was the lynchpin; but the minds of the people at the concert and throughout the metropolis were stunned into silence as they watched Tze slit her throat again and again, in hundred-metre high, tint-corrected, high-definition ultra-colour.

"The Jade Dragon will destroy you all." Her words thundered through the canyons of the city. "Don't let it in. If you ever loved me, don't–"

By the millions they watched Juno die, and with one voice they cried out for the idol they had fallen in love with. The potent blue surging through their minds came alight with grief, the flashing telepathic rush washing over the bay, a shockwave of misery that was anathema to the DesireGod.

In an instant, the Jade Dragon's psychic bridge for rapture and elation shattered, ripping the demon-serpent apart. Screaming, clawing at the world, the thing tore towers down as the sky dragged it back into the darkness.

It left only destruction and mourning in its wake, as the citizens wept.

IN THE TOWER, Frankie spoke. "Listen," he said, catching the sounds on the wind. "Hong Kong cries for her."

TZE'S BLADE BIT deep, but Ko was not there. He moved like lightning, and the killer's sword cleaved through the terracotta warrior. The statue shattered like glass, spilling broken red rock across the pathway.

Among the ancient fragments there were bones, human skeletal remains sealed inside. Fragments of flesh, metal and leather centuries old puffed into dust on contact with the air. The ashen remains were caught by wind and gusted upward. Tze coughed as the choking dust stung his face and eyes. "Aiii! I cannot see!"

Ko felt Feng there beside him, the swordsman's skill bleeding into his mind. The weak points in the corporate's armour were suddenly obvious to him, and he turned the katana into a stabbing strike, pushing the sword into a mortal wound.

Tze flailed backward and swung at dead air with his blade.

"Finish him!" Feng's voice came from somewhere distant and faraway. Ko understood that the dead man was giving him the right to take Tze's life, to assuage the failure of before. Ko smashed Tze's sword from his grip and stabbed him again, drawing a scream.

Tze stumbled, eyes focussing on the main screen atop the distant stage. On the vast display, the killing of the singer played with a chorus of anguish as accompaniment.

Ko saw the panic in Tze's dark eyes, the sudden understanding that his life's work was going to be undone within a heartbeat of succeeding.

The katana flashed in the air and Ko sliced through spine and throat. For the brief span of seconds the severed head remained aware, Tze's last experience was the hooting screech of the Jade Dragon cursing him into the darkness.

Wave-Net; with broadcast to be giving worldly factoids!

From the Tokyo Sim-Centre Virtual News Environment, this is Far-EastEye with your v-anchors Dorothea Matrix, Raymondo Trace and Webber Caste.

"Good Clockset. Our main stories tonight, a massive terrorist incident rocks the Hong Kong Free Economic Enterprise Quadrant, claiming hundreds of lives and leaving disaster in its path."

"America's President Estevez comes to blows in a White House press conference with a reporter, after allegations of financial irregularity turn ugly."

"A diplomatic storm erupts as the Nippon Space Agency steps in to rescue a crew of Chinese taikonauts after an accident in orbit."

"Residents in the city of Cologne report the apparent spontaneous formation of an insect group mind."

"And the Neo-Aum Shinrikyo group officially announce their dissolution and absorption into the growing international faith known as the Church of Joseph."

"But first, breaking news from the city-state of Hong Kong (please touch the blue dot on your d-screen for direct neural input of the raw info-feed. Infra-red and Greentooth settings are supported)."

"Today, this vibrant metropolis stands traumatized and silent after what General Jet Li of the Army of the People's Republic of China called 'an unprovoked and ruthless attack on this peaceful city'. At a press conference in Shenzhen, General Li, commander-in-chief of Hong Kong's Domestic Security Directorate and Police Battalion, described how an anti-corporate faction launched a multi-pronged assault via internet denial-of-service attacks, the detonation of several timed bombs and the release of powerful hallucinogenic compounds into Hong Kong's municipal water supply. Victims of this psychological onslaught suffered traumatic visions and mass hysteria, although the effects appear to be temporary. Mobile APRC medical squads have been deployed throughout the area to deal with the catastrophe, and crisis-management units from several major corporations are en route, although Beijing has flatly refused to allow United Nations MediForce teams to enter Hong Kong airspace. Among the key targets for the terrorists was the headquarters of Yuk Lung Heavy Industries, which was wiped off the map by a massive explosion. Yuk Lung's reclusive CEO is among the dead at this hour. While the perpetrators of this terrible act have yet to be identified, some intelligence analysts suggest that the America Alone Alliance Army may have had a hand in the incident, after their failed attack on the Cantonese idol singer Juno Qwan earlier this month. Qwan, along with several thousand of her fans, perished at the Wyldsky free concert, which was taking place on Victoria Peak at the time – yet more victims of this terrible event. Other theories lay the blame upon anti-corporate factions who may have used the concert as a cover for the attack. Reports coming out of the city are sketchy; eyewitness blogs suggest that the destruction of the Yuk Lung skyscraper occurred several hours after the terrorist strike, some even claiming that the tower was

obliterated not by an internal detonation as the APRC statement suggests, but by a missile fired from an unknown location. There are also unconfirmed rumours that elements within the Yuk Lung Corporation may have been fully aware of the attack and yet did nothing to prevent it. We will bring you more on this story as it unfolds. Over to you, Dot."

"Troubling times, indeed, Web. Now, with more on that swarm of superintelligent wasps in Cologne, here's our German correspondent, Sieben AufNeun."

bip bippa bip bip bip scree beeep bippa bip zzzzt

"We're sorry, but Sieben appears to be experiencing technical difficulties. Back to you, Ray."

17. a better tomorrow

THEY BURIED JUNO at a hillside cemetery, not far from the place where she had died. Sifu Bruce arranged a headstone, even in the traumatic aftermath of things finding a way to get this small but important matter arranged for the dead girl. The piece of granite was simple and without scrollwork or detail. It bore only her name, no date of birth, no date of passing. Lam, the wageslave — well, ex-wageslave now — had explained, in a quiet and unsteady voice, just what she really was, where she had come from. He had her files, memory cores full of DNA patterns and zygote fabrication specs. Despite all that, the man didn't seem to care any less about her.

Ko looked on and listened to Fixx as he made signs over the fresh grave and spoke about worlds beyond this one. The young man studied the turned earth over Juno's coffin and wondered about all the other Junos that had come and gone before her, or the ones that had died still trapped inside tanks of amniotic fluid as the YLHI building collapsed. They would never be set to rest. In a way, this was a funeral for all of them as well.

Fixx looked under the weather, but he hid it well, insisting that he was already on the mend. The operative spoke vaguely about somebody called Lucy living over Kowloon side, who knew about medical stuff and the business of healing. The dark-skinned man had a new companion, a cat; the animal had the feral look of a stray about it, but one of its eyes was a mechanical augmentation and it watched the proceedings with more than just feline interest.

Ko said nothing as Fixx bent down and placed a single tarot card against Juno's tombstone. He didn't need to look to know there was a priestess with a beatific face upon it, head turned to the sky and smiling.

"Ko." Lam approached him. He looked different out of the spidersilk suit, in casual clothes. Ko saw the hollowness in his eyes, the sadness and the loss, and felt a pang of sympathy for the man.

"I'm sorry," he blurted. "If I had got there quicker—"

Lam shook his head. "It's not your fault. You dealt with that bastard Tze. You have nothing to apologise about." He nodded up to where the road snaked through the graveyard. There were a string of vehicles up there, among them Fixx's black Korvette with Nikita dozing in the back seat, her head resting against the window.

They were almost alone in the cemetery. The other cars belonged to a group of shaven-headed Durdenists, chanting their death rites over a lost member of their number a few plots down the hillside. Ko let his gaze wander over the cityscape.

All across Hong Kong the streets were sparsely populated. The population stayed at home and held close to those they loved, finding solace in simple human company. There would be nightmares for a long time to come. Church congregations of all kinds would swell, as would the lines at psych clinics and Doktor-Shrink™ franchises across the city; in a few years, someone would estimate that a full eighth of Hong Kong's citizens suffered permanent psychotic breaks in the wake of the catastrophic "Wyldsky Incident".

Lam indicated the Korvette. "How is Nikita?"

"No better," admitted Ko, "but no worse either. I guess when the whole thing fell apart, the pain stopped." He tapped his head. "Up here. But she's gotta long way to go before she's better."

The other man nodded. "This might help her some." Lam produced a thick folder from a pocket in his jacket and opened it. It was a wad of share certificates from minor league multinats like Buell Tool, Inverse Smile and Titancorp. "Take these," he said. "They're as good as cash. You never did get paid for bringing me the truth about my brother."

Ko accepted the bundle. "This has gotta be, what, worth twice as much as we agreed?"

Lam shrugged. "Something like that. When I bailed out from Yuk Lung, I set some contingency plans in motion, which involved wide-banding certain corporate secrets my brother had been gathering together. Before I did that, though, I made sure I channelled a big chunk of yuan from Tze's discretionary funds into a sealed Swiss account."

Ko chuckled. "That's a fair enough revenge. Yuk Lung Heavy Industries will be history before the end of the week." He pocketed the folder and produced something from his coat. "Got something for you too. Your phone." Ko handed it back and paused, thinking. "Remember what you said, when we were on the expressway? That you used to be like me?"

"I remember."

"I think I believe you now. Only someone Street would do what you did. You might have lost your octane for a while, but you got it back, neh? It's in your blood, man, the need for speed."

"Yeah," said the other man distantly. "Listen, could you... give me a moment?" He looked at the grave.

Ko nodded and followed Fixx toward the trees. "Sure, man. Say your goodbyes."

"Thanks, Ko."

"You're welcome... Francis."

HE REACHED OUT a hand and let his fingers wander over the stone. It was cool and solid, and the action made his eyes prickle with tears. Frankie had hoped that his fingers would pass through the marker, ghost-like, that perhaps he might suddenly realise that all this was in his head. He wanted so much for it to be some horrible dream, a broken fragment left over from Tze's invasion of his thoughts.

But no. Juno was gone, the dancing, laughing sparkle in those haunted eyes snuffed out. The tragedy of her life brought to the inexorable closure that had been written into her DNA from the start.

Numbly, in the hours after he and Fixx escaped from the tower, Frankie paged through the reams of data he had drained from Tze's computers. There, bereft of the security lockouts that had blocked his path before, was the scope of Project: Juno in all her synthetic glory. Yuk Lung and RedWhiteBlue had manufactured her from raw flesh, manipulated and changed her to make the perfect idol. With callous precision, they adjusted her look and personality to touch a baseline of human attraction across the broadest spectrum. She was made so everyone who saw her, everyone who heard her voice would find something to like about Juno. Something to love.

He recalled Tze's words: *Quite something, isn't she? It's hard not fall for a woman like that.*

It wasn't enough that they had used the girl, and not just her but a whole rank of clone-sisters, treating the Junos as disposable assets just to sell records; Tze had perverted her further, making her the face of his scheme, using her to spread the use of Z3N.

Frankie took a shuddering breath. Tze was correct; Juno was created to make people fall in love with her, and Frankie had, harder and deeper than ever before. But did she love him too? Perhaps, he told himself, perhaps she was so carefully machined that he only *thought* she cared for him. It was obvious now that the Hi woman and Tze had brought the two of them together to keep Frankie distracted from what was really happening. So easy to see it now in hindsight.

His vision blurred a little, and for a second there was the ghost of her face before him, smiling up from the silk sheets, meeting his lips in a kiss.

In that moment, he knew it for sure. Frankie gave Juno the one thing she had never found in her lonely, sad existence. *Truth*, and she loved him for it.

Frankie bowed his head and wept silently.

FIXX PUT THE cat on his shoulder and the animal made a short purr in its throat. "Hush up, Pinkeye," he told it.

"Cute pet," said Ko, in a way that showed he didn't mean it.

"Just walking him for a friend." The op pulled a small metal rod from his pocket. "Here."

Ko took it and his eyes widened. "The key to the 'Vette?"

"Yeah. It's just a loaner, mind. Get you over the boundary into China, to someplace where you can use those jet tickets and not get spiked. She's pre-programmed, just let her go when you're done and she'll find her way back to me."

The youth weighed the key in his hand, studying the little chrome skull dangling off the ring. "What you gonna do without any wheels?"

"Ah, don't worry 'bout me." Fixx took a deep breath of the morning air. "I kinda like this place. They do things different 'round here. Gonna stay put for a while, rest up. See how the cards play."

After a moment, Ko said, "I've never been out of Hong Kong, not really. Trips to Bangkok, a week here or there. I don't know anything else."

"Yeah, you do," said Fixx. "You got what you need to get by, slick. Never doubt that." He tickled the cat under the chin. "Me and Pinkeye, we're gonna take a stroll. You look after your sis, now." He turned and walked away down the gentle slope.

"Hey," called Ko, "maybe I'll, uh, see you around?"

Fixx spoke without looking back. "Never can tell."

FENG SAT CROSS-LEGGED on the bonnet of the Korvette, watching the skyline. Ko found a smile unfolding on his face at the sight of the swordsman; after taking Tze's head in the statue park, it had felt like something had gone missing from his soul. He hadn't seen the warrior since.

"Hey," he began, patting his pockets, "you wanna smoke? Think I got a pack of Peacefuls here—"

"I quit," said Feng. "Filthy habit."

Ko blew out a breath. "You saved my life up there."

"Perhaps I did." The soldier jumped off the car. "Or maybe you did it. Maybe that festering turd Second Lei was right all along, that I don't exist. Perhaps, I'm all in your head."

"No," said the youth. He didn't like where the conversation was going.

Feng smiled. He looked better than usual. No stubble, clear-eyed, standing up straight, armour polished. Ko imagined this was how he would have looked on some feudal parade ground, noble and proud. "Or maybe not. It's a strange world, Ko. I have as many questions about it as you do."

"The bones in the statue... That was you."

"Indeed." Feng pointed toward the peak. "Buried up there now with all those other luckless fools. Not quite the funeral I wanted, but I've learned not to be choosy. After all this time, an end is an end."

Ko's chest felt tight. "You're leaving." It wasn't a question.

"I'm free," he said. "Free to go." Suddenly, Ko couldn't find any words. Feng nodded down the road a way. "Look there!"

Ko saw Frankie at the door of a car belonging to the Durdenists. In a moment, the man had bypassed the lock and slid inside. With deft movements, he disabled the alarm, and as the irate owners came running, Frankie gunned the engine and roared away in a snarl of smoke. The shaven-headed men spat and swore, and the car vanished over the hill, sounding its horn three times.

When Ko looked back at the Korvette there was only Nikita, sleeping fitfully in the back seat.

HE TOOK THE road over Tai Mo Shan at twice the posted speed limit, turning into corners and switchbacks until Hong Kong vanished beneath the tree line. The Korvette blazed through warning signs shouting to slow down. Ko ignored them all, a wolfish grin forming on his lips as the needle on the dashboard moved inexorably toward the redline. Skirting the fake folk villages and tourista snares, he aimed the black bullet of the car at the Shenzhen border crossing, allowing the vehicle's on-board navigator system to construct a route deeper into China. "Guangzhou," he told the drive-brain. "Plot us a speed course to the airport there. I don't want to stop for anything." He saw strobes in the rear-view as two APRC jeeps struggled to catch up with him.

"Ko?" said a sleepy voice. "Where are we going?" Nikita shifted on the edge of wakefulness.

"Just a little country drive, Niki," he told her, "Everything's fine."

She pointed out through the windscreen. "Look, Ko," she said dreamily. "I can see blue."

Above, through the clouds, he saw it too; a pale cobalt sky, drawing them towards it. "Yeah. That's where we're going."

Ko pressed the accelerator to the floor and left the jeeps choking on exhaust fumes.

COLONEL TSANG WALKED gingerly through the cavernous interior of the wrecked building; the engineers assured him the stone stub that was all that remained of the Yuk Lung tower was in no danger of collapsing. Still, he was wary. The ruined skyscraper reminded him of an ancient burial mound, heavy with dust and the scent of death. There were pieces of torn cloth everywhere, and his boots crunched on shards of plastic. He nudged something with his toe; it appeared to be part of a porcelain mask. Tsang glanced at the sergeant and his men, each bearing a rifle and a sensor wand. "Anything?"

The sergeant frowned at the scanning device in his hand. "Sir, I'm not sure."

The man came apart in a ripping shower of gore, cut in two. Tsang cried out in shock as a tattered shape like a heap of rags flashed through the other greenjackets, cutting them down. The colonel was rigid with shock, his hand an inch from his holstered pistol.

The thing slowed and approached him. It was human, after a fashion, a broken agglomeration of smashed skeleton and torn flesh. Tsang's stomach twisted as he realised that the attacker was using a blade made from the bones of its right arm. The thing replaced the makeshift sword and flexed it experimentally. With care, it knelt and tore off the sergeant's face, chewing on it.

Finally, Tsang's instincts caught up with him and he grabbed at his pistol, but there were a mouthful of teeth in his neck before the gun ever cleared leather.

For a while there was only the sound of eating and tearing. Then through damaged and torn lips, the killer spoke aloud.

"The Path of Joseph," said Heywood Ropé, "is *thorny*."

About the Author

James Swallow's novels include the Warhammer 40,000 novels *Faith and Fire*, *Deus Encarmine* and *Deus Sanguinius*; among his other works are the *Sundowners* series of "steampunk" Westerns, the *Judge Dredd* novels *Eclipse* and *Whiteout*, *Rogue Trooper: Blood Relative* and the novelization of *The Butterfly Effect*. His non-fiction features *Dark Eye: The Films of David Fincher* and books on genre television and animation; his other credits include writing for *Star Trek Voyager*, *Doctor Who*, scripts for videogames and audio dramas. He lives in London, and is currently working on his next book.

AMERICA, TOMORROW.
TOO WILD TO BE TRUE —
OR TOO CLOSE FOR COMFORT?

WELCOME TO THE DARK FUTURE

DEMON DOWNLOAD
1-84416-236-2

ROUTE 666
1-84416-327-X

WWW.BLACKFLAME.COM
READ TILL YOU BLEED